MW00893132

St. Purgatory

JOE SILVA

Read about and contact Joe Silva at www.TheJoeSilvaWebsite.com

Book cover painted by: Barbara Palana Landry
landryartist@gmail.com
www.LandryArtist.com

I dedicate this book to my children,
Charline and Tyler.

CHAPTER 1

The windshield wipers were not adequately keeping up with the furious onslaught of raindrops as Addison Ambry cautiously steered her Jeep onto Crestwood Court. It was her cut-through street when traffic backed-up due to the busy intersection ahead. Water seeped through, in-between her side-window and cloth roofing, dripping onto Addison's lap. Regretting that she didn't choose a hardtop Jeep instead, she winced her eyes in a failed attempt to see a bit more clearly through the blurred glass that somewhat protected her from the deluge of water that mercilessly pounded upon every inch and stitch of her vehicle. The flashing lights of what seemed to be at least a dozen police and emergency vehicles complicated her vision even more, as she tried to figure out what the kaleidoscope of light and color was due to. Addison gasped as she pulled to the side of the road, catching a glimpse of paramedics rolling a small covered body out of a house on a gurney.

"Oh my God," she muttered to herself. "This can't be happening. Oh my God… Angela? *Please* not Angela."

Addison taught second-grade at Hope Elementary School, and one of her star pupils, Angela Smith, lived at the house. She knew that because she had given Angela rides home from school on more than one occasion, usually because her father had drank too much during the day at the bar that he owned in town where all the cops would hang out, or he would simply forget to pick up his daughter when school ended. On that particular day, Addison had wished Angela needed a ride home, as she was concerned about the condition she arrived to school in. Angela's dress was torn, and her arm was badly bruised. It wasn't the first time that the second-grader showed evidence of bodily harm, but Addison never mentioned anything to anyone. She lived a quiet life outside of school and didn't want to complicate it by getting involved in anyone else's.

KNOCK! KNOCK! KNOCK!

Startled, Addison's head jolted away from where her eyes jumped. A water-smudged image of a large man holding up what seemed to be a shiny metal badge appeared. She caught her breath and quickly rolled the window down as he returned it to his pocket.

"Ma'am, are you familiar with this residence?" the man sternly asked.

Addison's voice quivered "Yes. Yes, I am familiar," as her gaze jumped back and forth between the man and the gurney being placed into an ambulance just a hundred or so feet behind him.

"Turn your Jeep and lights off, ma'am," he ordered before rushing back to his car in the rain.

Addison complied, looking at his older-model unmarked Crown Victoria in her side-view mirror before rolling the window up. He must be a detective, she thought, while moving the window up and down at the top inch to create a better seal. The water continued to drip nonetheless. She began to search for some napkins between her seats and console to stop the drips, even if only for a moment, when the passenger-side door opened and the man sat down next to her.

"Ma'am, place your hands where I can see them," he instructed.

Finally, her fingertips felt a wad of napkins, which must have sunken farther below her seat since she jammed them down there, one by one, after each morning's bagel-on-the-go. The problem at that moment wasn't that she never let anything go, it was that she needed to know *when* to let go. She let out a faint, but audible grunt while leaning closer toward the man to reach even deeper for a better grip.

"FREEZE!" ordered the man.

Addison froze. Her entire soul froze, too, as she noticed the man was then pointing a pistol at her.

"Ma'am, this is a murder-scene, and at this point in time I don't know who you are. You need to slowly place your hands on top of your dashboard, where I can see them," he added.

Still unsure about what was actually happening, Addison raised her hands as told, but wanted to respond that she didn't know who he was, either. The gun between her mouth and his ears suggested she kept silent. Best not to say anything. She was relieved when he lowered his gun, looked around through the rain-glazed windows, and then pulled out a pen and a small notebook that said 'Hope Police Dept.' on the cover.

"I'll need your full name, address, and phone number, ma'am," he said, with a tinge of adrenaline in his voice. He wrote without looking at his pad, but rather strained his gaze trying to make out which police officers were arriving at the scene, or exiting the house. "According to my scanner, a young girl was found unresponsive inside the house. What is your relationship to the family?"

His words confirmed her fear that the person on the gurney must've been Angela. Addison burst into tears, unconcerned that she was unable to get a grasp on the stash of napkins even as her tears competed against the rain dripping in through her window.

"Ma'am, I need a statement." He quipped.

"I'm sorry. This is all so shocking," she sobbed. "I am Angela's school teacher. Angela was with me just hours ago."

Hoping he could make his first break in a case, he re-focused his attention to Addison, and his pad. "Was there anything unusual about Angela today?"

Hesitating for a moment, she nervously answered, "Yes, she was bruised and her dress was torn when she got to school this morning. I was hoping to give her a ride home from school today to see if I could get any information out of her, but her father did show up."

"Is it normal that you would give a student a ride home?"

"That wouldn't be my norm, but Angela was different. Her mother was found dead in their home earlier in the year, and I felt that I could be a female role in her life, especially on days that her father didn't arrive to pick her up from school. This is just so terrible. Now Angela," she added. "Did the department ever figure out why her mother would have committed suicide?"

"Is Angela's last name Smith?" he asked.

"Yes."

He abruptly closed his notebook, opened the door and exited the Jeep. Leaning back in, he said, "Thank you, Ma'am. I'll get back to you with any additional questions. You'll need to leave the scene now so we may commence our investigative work." He unintentionally slammed the door and ran back to his car.

Addison started her Jeep and watched through her side-view mirror as the Crown Victorian made a lurching U-turn before speeding away in the opposite direction, just as the ambulance pulled away in the direction that Addison would eventually head in. For the moment, though, she felt paralyzed and just sat there. She was hoping that the ambulance had a reason to speed away to the hospital in effort to give young Angela a chance at continuing her life. Unfortunately, it left slowly and silently, even though its barrage of lights fleetingly alerted all that it passed of a recent tragedy.

Several blocks away, where the grid of house-lined streets gave way to industrial roads of factories, storage facilities and strip-joints, Willy Brock pulled his unmarked Crown Vic into the side parking lot of Smitty's Bar. It was a relatively small, single-story, stand-alone brick structure, nestled within the labyrinth of multi-floor factory buildings, catwalks, smokestacks, barbed wire fencing, 18-wheelers, prostitutes, and drug dealers. The river flowing through that part of town had been powering the factories from the Industrial Revolution on up until electricity took over. Even though the river had long since retired from factory work, the stench that arose from it suggested otherwise. Those that frequented that side of town didn't seem to mind the foul odors, filthiness, or shady happenings that pervaded the area. Many of those that ventured into it after working-hours seemed to bring with them their own contributions of immoral grime, and at times, crime. The number of cops that made Smitty's Bar their regular after-shift hangout was odd. It was as if their badges meant nothing once they punched their time cards out at the police station each day, and then drove past obvious hookers and druggies on their way to their usual watering hole.

Willy walked into Smitty's and noticed that the select bar stools normally taken by the veterans on the force were empty. He looked around to make sure that he wasn't taking the seat of one of his superiors. The bar was unusually quiet. It was a few hours earlier than Willy's normal time for drinking beer, challenging others to play him in a game of darts, and schmoozing with whichever police clientele happened to be drinking at Smitty's on any given night. He sat at the bar and instantly picked up the cardboard Guinness coaster in front of him, and began to nervously tap it on the top of the bar while he looked around for Smitty through the dimly lit barroom.

"Hold your horses," grunted the bartender, as he wiped a glass before placing it on an illuminated glass shelf. "You're in here early. The usual?"

Willy placed the coaster back onto the bar, and then started tapping his fingers on the surface. "Sure," he eventually responded, without looking up at the bartender. "Hey, let Smitty know I'm here. I need to talk to him."

"I wish I could. Haven't seen him since he left to pick his daughter up from school. It's been hours," the bartender replied. "He better get back here soon to relieve me 'cause I've got plans for tonight."

Marshall Smith was the sixth in a long line of Smittys. The nickname came with the ownership of the bar, which had been handed down from one Smith to the next since the early 1900's. Like the generations before him, Marshall continued the traditions that dated back before prohibition, such as allowing bookies to do business in the establishment, after-hours backroom poker games, and other shady dealings that offered kickbacks, which would financially line his pockets, along with some of the higher ranking members of Hope's finest. Smitty also inherited the family penchant for fighting, whether he was intoxicated or not, and because there never seemed to be any consequences to pay for his violent behavior, Smitty never felt a reason to control it. His temper was known in town, and fueled at times by a glorified expectation that allowed the Smitty legend to live on.

The bartender placed a pint of draught beer and a shot of Jim Beam whiskey in front of Willy. As the foam-head of the beer drooled down the side of the pint glass, soaking the coaster, Willy downed the shot and then asked for a few napkins, and Smitty's cell phone number.

"What do you need Smitty's number for?" asked the bartender.

Willy knew that the request would be considered unusual, as he wasn't as close to Smitty as he wanted to be. Actually, he was intimidated by him and was probably as close to Smitty as he cared to get, but many of the cops were friends with Smitty, and Willy wanted to fit in and be accepted as a regular cop. He figured that a relationship with Smitty might have helped him gain more credibility, and hopefully lead to a solid footing within Hope's police force.

"Smitty was talking about sponsoring the department's adult softball team, and I need to order our uniforms by tomorrow," Willy explained, wondering if the bartender could sense that his words weren't completely true. Willy had joked with Smitty in the past that he should sponsor the team and provide a keg of beer at every game, but there was never any conversation regarding Smitty actually sponsoring the team beyond that. Willy was desperate to get in touch with Smitty, and it was all he could think of as an on-the-spot excuse.

"That's weird. Smitty hates baseball," the bartender stated. "He won't even let us put ballgames on the TV's in here. Now he's gonna sponsor a softball team?"

"Probably just to support the police. I'm sure that the bar being advertised on the jerseys don't hurt, either."

"Hang on." The bartender headed toward another patron, grabbed his empty glass, and held it under the tap while looking away from Willy and up at the TV screen as the local evening newscast began.

Willy looked toward the television himself as he heard the words BREAKING NEWS. Relieved to see that the story was about the closing of another factory and not of the young girl's apparent murder, he focused his attention back on obtaining Smitty's cell phone number. "When you finish pouring that beer, I'll take another shot of Jim Beam." Knowing of the bartender's desire of whiskey, Willy added "Pour a shot for yourself, too, and add it to my tab."

The bartender pulled the glass away from the flowing beer before flicking the tap handle back. The resulting beer dripping from the side of the glass created a series of mini puddles on top of the bar leading to the already soaked coaster in front of the patron. Grabbing the tattered cloth that he kept barely tucked-in on the side of his pants, the bartender wiped the surface clean then returned the cloth to his hip. Willy wondered if he heard his request at all, while he watched the bartender walk farther down the bar away from him. As he stood in front of the cash register, he scrolled through his phone's screen then wrote some numbers onto a sticky-note. Returning to Willy, he grabbed a shot glass and the bottle of Jim Beam.

"You didn't get this number from me," the bartender said, while placing the sticky-note in front of Willy and refilling his shot glass before filling his own.

"Cheers," Willy declared while raising his shot glass toward the bartender, who ignored Willy's gesture by turning around and pouring the shot into his mouth without the glass even touching his lips. "I'll

14

probably be back later on, but I should clear my tab when you get a chance," added Willy, before returning to the more than half a pint of beer still sitting in front of him. He sipped slowly as he stared down at the sticky-note in front of him, wondering what he might say to Smitty. It was clear that nobody in the bar knew anything about the tragedy that had just taken place. For a minute, Willy wished that he was unaware, too, but decided that he knew enough that he could either help Smitty, the police department, or both. One thing he felt certain of is that he was privy to something, and he would use that to advance his chances of having a real career as a cop.

"Chief Parker!" blurted the bartender. "I never get to see you during my shift. To what do I owe the honor?"

Jolted from his trance, Willy's head looked up to see Hope's Chief of Police at the opposite end of the bar. He turned his body so as to not be detected in the dark barroom, crumpled Smitty's number into a pocket, then fumbled for his wallet so he could leave a twenty on the bar and sneak out through the back door. His heart began to race as he realized that he hadn't stopped at the bank like he planned on, up until his home-scanner alerted him of that day's tragedy. He looked over at the ATM, which was along the sidewall next to the jukebox. It was the most brightly lit structure in the bar after the wide-screen TV, and coupled with the digital display of the jukebox, it would have been hard to extract money from it without being noticed.

"I wish I could say I was here to order a drink from you," answered the chief. "God knows that I could use one, but I'm here to talk to Smitty."

"Join the club!" the bartender half-joked.

Willy felt a rush of uneasiness take over his body. He wondered if the bartender was going to expose him, sitting at the end of the bar drinking, and also waiting to talk to Smitty. It wouldn't be good if

Chief saw him drinking that early, and it would have been awkward and considered somewhat disrespectful if Willy hadn't already walked to the end of the bar to say hello to Chief Parker by then. In his mind, Chief was his ultimate boss, even though his full-time job had nothing to do with police work. Willy was determined to be a full-time police officer, no matter what it took. He decided to hide in the men's bathroom, which was only steps away from Willy's barstool, rather than be discovered by Chief Parker.

"Any idea where he might be?" Chief inquired.

"I wish I did. He's been gone for hours." The bartender replied, while grabbing the TV remote and flipping through channels. "He's never usually gone for more than an hour or so," he added, while settling on a fishing show.

"Well, maybe I'll give it a minute or two to see if he shows up. You can jot down his cell number for me," instructed Chief, as his gaze shifted up toward the TV screen. "Maybe I'd take up fishing if we could eat the fish that swim in the Black Bank River. How do they survive in that toxic cesspool? You can even smell it inside here today. Thank the Mayor for that."

Chief Parker was right. The river smelled bad at all times, but when it rained as hard as it was raining that day it was almost too pungent to breathe within a quarter-mile of its banks. Nobody in town could ever answer as to if it was due to the past century-worth of factory toxins being churned up from the river's bed, or if it was from sewage run-off from Hope's antiquated septic design and its ongoing decay. Once, a town councilman suggested that Hope do a study of the river in effort to understand all of the variables that continued to lead to its demise, but it was shot-down in a unanimous decision at a monthly Town Hall meeting. The mayor presided over each and every meeting, and if she didn't like a proposal, or the person making a proposal, it would go no further. The mayor knew that nobody else's budget could get cut without serious consequences to her re-electability, and anything that a study on the river could have revealed would have surely resulted in a majorly expensive undertaking. Someone else could deal with it once her mayoral reign ended.

"Here, Chief." The bartender handed Chief Parker a sticky-note with Smitty's cell phone number written on it. "I stay out of politics, if I can help it."

"I wish *I* could," admitted Chief, "but the mayor is my boss so I can't avoid politics, OR her. I think I'll hit the head before heading out. Did you guys fix the urinal that Smitty threw that punk against last weekend?

"No. It was from the nineteen-sixties so he had to special-order it. Probably be another week, but I'd bet it'll be installed before that jerk gets out of the hospital, though," answered the bartender.

"Ha-Ha! True. I heard the crack in the guy's head was bigger than the one in the urinal. Hey, if Smitty happens to walk in, don't let him leave," instructed Chief.

"Sure thing, Chief. The other urinal works, and the stall may or may not be in working order today. It's a crap-shoot!" the bartender chuckled.

All of the patrons sitting at the bar nodded as Chief Parker walked by them on his way to the men's room. The chief had a very commanding demeanor about him. Even his walk had a certain authoritative gate to it, which seemed to be amplified by his uniform, which he never wore into Smitty's Bar. The only time he'd wear his uniform inside Smitty's Bar was when he covered someone's late-night shift and stopped by to drink after-hours with the owner.

Inside the men's room, Willy paced back and forth within the small space between the urinals and single stall while wondering how much time he should wait it out in there. He looked at himself in the mirror and found the image of his stressed and worried face looking back at him. He thought about how he had just pulled his gun on the woman outside Smitty's house, and his stomach began to churn. He had previously held his gun to his own head, but never pointed it at another person before. Feeling instantly nauseous, he stepped into the stall and slid the mini-bolt to secure the flimsy plywood privacy partition. Just as he squatted down to sit on the toilet, the men's room door opened. At that point, Willy just wanted to calm his nerves and settle his stomach. He didn't have much time to ponder who may have walked in, as the few heavy footsteps stopped in front of the stall and a large hand reached for the top of the partition. Checking to learn if the stall was out-of-order, or not, a quick tug at it proved it was unavailable. Willy was just about to say that he'd be out in a minute when he heard the unmistakable timbered tone of the chief's voice as he mumbled something under his breath. Willy held his words, and his breath, while looking down at his own feet in an effort to feel as invisible as he could. He felt his heart beating out of his chest by the time Chief flushed the urinal.

Without washing his hands first, the chief dialed the numbers that the bartender had provided him with, and then leaned against the sink with his back to the mirror. While he waited through several rings, he looked at the broken urinal that was covered with a few black garbage bags and some duct-tape, and then shook his head. The chief waited for a beep and then left a voicemail, "Hey Smitty, it's Fred. We need to talk as soon as you get this message. Call me back at this number." Clipping his phone onto his belt, not far from his gun, Chief Parker turned around and quickly washed his hands while studying the

18

deepening wrinkles on his face in the mirror. Retirement would be soon, and very much welcomed. He turned off the faucet and reached for the paper towel dispenser, only to find that it was empty. "Son of a bitch," he grumbled, while tugging one last time on the stall partition as if something might have changed, which would have allowed him to dry his hands on a wad of toilet paper. Paying no attention to the rain water still dripping from his uniform, he began shaking his hands dry while nudging open the door with his feet as he exited the men's room.

"Oh crap!" Willy said to himself. Although relieved that The Chief didn't find him in the stall, he felt like some of the wind was taken out of his sail. What kind of info would the chief be sharing with Smitty? Surely he hadn't spoken with Angela's teacher. Not yet, anyway. Willy felt like he needed to call Smitty right away, so he decided to not return to his unfinished pint of beer, and tab, but rather exit from the barroom's back door near the men's room. He could explain later that he got sick in the bathroom, and would just pay his bill at that time.

The rain remained unrelenting as Willy hurried to his car. He noticed the chief's taillights heading toward the exit of the parking lot just as Willy remotely unlocked his car, causing his headlights to flash. The entire lot seemed to illuminate red as the chief's brake lights went on. Red turned to white when Chief's reverse lights lit up. Willy quickly jumped into his car and fumbled to turn off his car's interior light switch overhead. His anxiety rose while his thoughts scrambled for an excuse to give to Chief Parker for being at Smitty's Bar so early in the evening, if in-fact it was true that The Chief was backing up to learn who was trying to get his attention by flashing his car lights. He didn't want to blow his chances of getting into the next police academy class, yet within the past hour, he lied about the police softball team, evaded the Chief of Police, and pulled a gun on a woman. He reached for his gun that he kept between his seat and console, knowing he should hide it under his seat in case the chief came up to his window.

"OH NO!" Willy said to himself as he began to panic. "I must've left the damn gun inside that woman's Jeep!"

While Willy leaned over his seat in a desperate attempt to search the back of his car's interior, he noticed red and blue flashing lights reflecting off his back window. Turning around, he watched through his rain-blurred windshield as Chief Parker's car peeled-out of the parking lot and sped down the street. He sat for a minute to collect his thoughts and allow his heart to settle back down inside his chest. After a minute passed, he took out his phone and garnered up the courage to dial the numbers that the bartender wrote on the sticky-note. Smitty's phone went straight to voicemail. Willy waited for the beep and then nervously left a message.

"Oh, um, hey Smitty," Willy began, noticing of himself that his voice seemed to be a few keys higher in tone than normal. "It's Willy from the department. Hey, I'm not sure what happened at your house today, but you might want to be aware that your daughter's school teacher said something about her showing up at school this morning with bruises on her body and rips in her clothes. I sent the lady on her way before anyone higher-up on the force was able to grill her on anything." Willy paused for a second. "Anyway, you can probably see my number on your phone now, so feel free to give me a call. I have her address and phone number in case you want it," he added, while trying to think of how he should end the message. "I'm sure that you'll be cleared from any wrongdoing, and I'm wishing the best for both you and Angela."

Willy cringed as he hung-up, realizing that he knew close to nothing about the crime scene at Smitty's house and probably stepped way out of line, and yet he had just left a recording on Smitty's phone as documented proof of his inappropriate behavior. He turned the ignition key and pulled his car away without allowing the engine to warm up.

Pacing throughout her house, Addison Ambry was having difficulty accepting that her young student may have been killed inside her own home. She clasped in her right hand a few drawings that Angela had recently given to her. On her fridge hung a few of Angela's A+ quizzes. Angela would often receive her corrected papers from Miss Ambry, and after reviewing them, hand them back to her. In the wake of her mother's death, Angela gravitated to the love that she felt from her teacher, and Addison couldn't help but offer her affection and pride. She was never married, nor had children of her own, so the adoration she felt for Angela was one of the only things that she ever gave away.

Her house was crammed with boxes and books from floor to ceiling in every room, with just a single pathway to move about. Various storage bins on all sides encased even her bed, with only enough open access to barely squeeze through and onto her mattress. Though her hoarding would have been considered extreme, Addison's overabundance was at least well documented, with each box and container sorted by category and date-range. One of her closets was dedicated to her teaching career, with one box of important or meaningful papers and artwork from each of her school years filling most of the space. There was only enough area left for one more box, and she was in the process of filling up two boxes for that school year, with one of them devoted to Angela Smith only.

Addison would stress endlessly over which box should make it into the closet at the end of the school year, and which would begin a new pile. To compound her worries, she was running out of space in every room of her house, and throwing anything at all away to make room for more hoarding wasn't an option for Addison. She had already submitted paperwork at Hope's Town Hall for a building permit so she could have an addition built onto her house, which would be utilized for the sole purpose of storing more items that Addison refused to part with.

Outside, Willy Brock turned off the lights on his Crown Vic before rolling to a stop. A hundred or so feet away was the end of Addison's long, forest-lined dirt driveway. He could barely see her small house through the foliage that Addison considered her privacy fortress. Aside from an occasional delivery person that may have missed the sign at the edge of her property that read 'Please leave packages in shed', nobody ever ventured up to her house. The shed was set back several steps from her mailbox. It looked more like a decorative outhouse with a crescent moon shape cut into the weathered plywood door, which hung crooked as a result of rotted wood where the top hinge dangled insecurely.

Willy was relieved to learn that Addison's surroundings would provide some natural cover for his covert operation of retrieving his gun from her Jeep. Walking slowly so as not to alert any dogs in the neighborhood, Willy felt the suction of mud trying to imprison his shoes with each step he took down the long, dark, and weather-drenched driveway. As he got closer to her house, he couldn't tell if Addison's interior house lights were on. Water cascaded over his military-style haircut, dripping endlessly over his eyes and off the end of his nose and chin. Willy was happy that no exterior lights were on because he would need to pass in front of it to get to her Jeep. He decided to try walking just inside the lining of the woods to avoid detection. A branch cracked loudly under his foot and he stopped in his tracks. He looked up at the house and could see a crack of light escaping between a few boxes that walled the inside of a window. The light seemed to blink for a split-second and Willy guessed that it was most likely Addison walking within that room of the house. After waiting a brief moment, he stepped from the edge of the trees and back onto the muddy trail that led to the Jeep. Eventually, he reached for the passenger-side door handle and found it locked. He could just about make out the shape of his gun on the floor of the Jeep. Frustrated to see that the driver-side door was also locked, he started back down the driveway without the gun.

Inside the house, Addison sat at an antique wooden table. Boxes lined three sides of it, pinning the other chairs against the table and rendering them useless. She never had a need for them, as she never invited anyone to dinner. Addison preferred to eat, and live, alone. It had been years since Addison went on a date. It wasn't that she was never asked out. Most every single male teacher at Hope Elementary had asked her out, along with some of the married ones. She was an attractive woman who simply kept to herself. Unfortunately, she kept everything to herself, including her heart. The top of her table was surprisingly clean and devoid of clutter. It wasn't only used for Addison's meals, but also used as her desk, a laundry folding station, and an easel when she felt the need to paint. She placed Angela's papers that she was carrying off to the side of the table and took out her school planner for the next day. Opening it to the current week, she soon realized that it was trash night. She considered holding off on bringing the trash bag to the street until the following week in an avoidance of going back out into the rain, but sighed when she remembered forgetting trash night the week earlier, too. There was an additional trash bag under her steps that would've become quite ripe and maggot-filled if she left it there another week longer. Begrudgingly, she rifled through the closet near her front door in search for some rain gear.

Back inside his car, Willy didn't care that the registration papers he was emptying from the Crown Victoria's oversized glove compartment were getting soaked. He didn't stop his search until he unearthed the box cutter that he had mistakenly taken after helping his friend in the shipping department of his day-job. He closed his door quietly before quickly making his way back toward Addison's driveway. His shoes seemed to sink a bit deeper into the mud this time around, slowing him down as he passed the outhouse-style shed. His steps abruptly stopped when he realized the house exterior light had been turned on. The sound of the rain and wind seemed to escalate as a growing shadow of Addison carrying a bag in each hand entered his frame of vision. Panicking, Willy made a dash toward the small shed. The mud claimed his left shoe as he felt his sock absorb the cold dirt-and-rain mix with the next step. There wasn't a second to spare without getting noticed by Addison, so he abandoned the shoe, hoping she wouldn't see it, and slipped into the shed. Instantly, the scent of the old wood brought him back to a tree-fort that he and his friends would hang out at as kids. How he wished he could return to those worry-free days of youth as he crouched down below the crescent cutout in the plywood door. The only items in the shed were a few seasonal decorations that Addison would have adorned her mailbox with at various times throughout the year, and an empty plastic trash barrel.

"Shoot!" Willy whispered to himself when he realized that Addison would most likely try to utilize the barrel for her trash bags. He quickly burrowed his fingers through the dirt and mud under the

24

plywood and grasped it with his fingertips, and then waited. He could hear the mucky footprints of Addison getting louder and he held his breath. A finger entered through the crescent cutout and tugged at the plywood door, jarring the upper hinge. A couple more fingers grasped at the door through the moon-shaped cutout and tugged more firmly. Willy almost lost his grip of the door's bottom when a screw fell out of the upper hinge, bouncing off Addison's left hand that was still holding one of the bags of trash. She assumed that there must have been a build-up of mud and dirt around the base of the door, due to the storm, and abandoned her effort so as to not cause any additional damage to the shed. After propping the bags on either side of the mailbox-post along the edge of the road, Addison Ambry started back toward her house.

Leaning back against the plastic barrel, Willy waited over a half-hour until the outside house light went off. His knees cracked as he stood up and gently opened the plywood door, making sure that it didn't fall completely off of its hinges. Estimating where in the driveway he was when his shoe came off, he spent several minutes searching for it before giving up. He hurried along the muddy driveway in the pouring rain while wearing only one shoe. Without even a glance toward the house, Willy Brock took out the box cutter from his pocket, extended the blade, and then sliced the Jeep's canvas top as close as he could get to the passenger's inside door handle. Within a few minutes, he was back inside his Crown Vic. He took off his wet and muddied sock, started his car while cranking up the heat, and wedged his gun along the side of his driver's seat. Willy waited until he got well past Addison's driveway before turning on his car's headlights as he drove into the night.

Early the next morning, Addison cleaned her paintbrushes and returned to her artwork. She had spent most of the night painting, and realized that the less than two hours remaining for her to sleep wouldn't do her much good, so she decided to make some coffee and then get ready to go into school early. It wasn't unusual for Addison to paint throughout the night. Each watercolor brush stroke was like therapy to her. She had developed quite an artistic talent, having painted hundreds of paintings over the years. Each of her paintings reflected something or someone that made an impact on her life, a place or landscape that she wished she could escape to, or an image of what she imagined her prince charming would have looked like. Sadly, nobody ever saw her artwork. She would look at them for a while herself, and then stack the paintings in a dedicated room over the years. Miss Ambry didn't need to paint the image of a gun being pointed at her face to remember the experience, as she knew it would never leave her mind, but she did. She inhaled the rush of steam rising up from her freshly poured cup of coffee, then leaned over her new creation to gently blow on the fresh paint still drying at end of the gun's barrel. As disturbing as the painting was to Addison, it allowed her to feel a sense of being in control of the situation, albeit an illusion.

The sun was beginning to rise as Miss Ambry made her way to her Jeep. Evidence of the torrential day before remained as pockets of puddles and mud, forcing her to think about each and every step she took. She would normally walk around to the passenger-side of her Jeep to place her workbag on the seat, but considering the muddy conditions of her driveway, she leaned over through the driver-side to place her bag on the passenger-seat. Addison noticed some water seep up from the seat as her workbag sunk into it.

"Ugh! I'm trading this Jeep in," Miss Ambry proclaimed, believing that some rain must have seeped in through a faulty seam in the vehicle's canvas roof. Moving her bag to the Jeep's floor, she noticed the large slice in the canvas. "What the heck is going on?"

Addison walked to the passenger-side of the Jeep and saw a few sets of foreign footprints in the mud. Some had markings of a shoe's sole, and some were simply in the shape of a foot. A left foot, to be exact. She knew right then that the cut in the canvas was intentional. A chill raced through her spine as she looked around in all directions in case the culprit was still lurking about.

A quick assessment of her glove compartment and back seat suggested that nothing was stolen from the vehicle. As she drove down her driveway toward the street, she noticed something sticking out of the mud. "Is that a shoe?" She quickly grabbed it and jumped back into her Jeep, not caring that some mud got onto her pants as she placed the dirty shoe on the floor next to her bag.

Willy Brock had not slept overnight, either. He walked into the Hope Police Station, hoping that his check would be ready to be picked up. After working a few traffic details the week prior, Willy would normally stop in at the station after his shift at the factory to collect his check, but he wanted to learn of any developments pertaining to Angela's death. Surprised to see Chief Parker in his office already, he could tell through the glass wall that he was in a heated discussion with the State Police Commissioner. He walked past his office and into the small lunchroom down the hall.

"Hey, it's Willy Wonka," one of the police officers joked as he walked in.

Another officer chimed in by singing "Who can stop the traffic – Tell 'em when to go – He wears his little uniform like he is in a show – The Traffic Man – Willy Traffic Man can!" The two cops laughed, and then returned to their coffee and newspapers.

"Ha, ha," Willy responded under his breath. Willy Brock hated being teased at the station. He desperately wanted to be accepted into the academy, and by his perceived peers, but he had failed the personality test and interview the past two years in a row. "Any word on what happened at Smitty's house?"

"We'll let you know as soon as us real cops finish the investigation," responded one of the officers.

Willy walked over to the mailboxes labeled 'Auxiliary & Cadets'. His check wasn't in his box as of yet. He tried to think of something clever to say on his way out of the lunchroom, but opted to take one of the last two donuts left on the table without saying a word.

"Hey, we haven't eaten yet!" said the first cop from behind his newspaper. "It's supposed to rain again this weekend, so don't forget to wear your galoshes while you're standing in the intersection of Main Street and Nowhere Avenue."

Willy turned around and stopped. As he felt his ears getting red, he wanted to punch the cop right in the face but knew that doing so would end his chances of advancing into the police academy. Instead, he walked back over to the table and grabbed the last donut also, just as the police officer lowered the paper from his face. "I get hungry out in that intersection," uttered Willy.

"Screw you, Brock!"

When he got outside, Willy Brock threw one of the donuts at the cop's personal car in the Hope Police Station's lot. He was sick and tired of getting pushed around and made a fool of, especially by that particular officer. He watched the custard of the Boston-cream donut explode all over the black metallic paint-job on the muscle-car's rear fender... "Or was it called 'Midnight Blue'?" Willy sarcastically asked himself. Either way, Willy felt satisfied because that cop wouldn't shut up about his "ride". Whenever he could, he'd go on and on about how the color changed depending on day or night, sunny or rainy, and how not just anyone could get that car in that color. "Ya gotta know people," the cop would brag, and Willy was tired of his demeaning comments and cocky attitude.

It was still too early in the morning for him to punch the clock at his day-job, so Willy sat in his car to eat the other donut that he still held in his hand, all the while watching to see how far down the side of the cop's black or blue ride the yellow custard would ooze. Taking a bite, some jelly broke through the bottom of the donut, plopping a sticky deposit of staining raspberry on Willy's work khakis. He reached hastily for a napkin near his seat and felt the handle of his gun. It gave him a sense of security. A feeling of power. He was a master at the shooting range, which was at least what the owner of the range would tell him at the end of every month when it was time to pay his dues. Willy felt like he'd be the best cop on the force if he were given the chance. Heck, he KNEW he'd be the best. It wasn't fair in Willy Brock's mind. He WAS the best, and deserved the opportunity to show them! He caught himself gritting his teeth, wincing his eyes, and clinching his fists as he let his mind run away in thought. More jelly fell onto his lap and he let out a loud grunt of frustration. All of a sudden, Willy's body quickly teetered down, with his face pressed against his passenger seat. He held it there for several seconds then slowly lifted his head to watch Addison Ambry pull her Jeep alongside the handicap parking spot near the station's front door. Willy Brock felt his body enter a stage of shock when Addison walked up to the front door of the Hope Police Station, carrying a muddy shoe. He hadn't slept in over a day, yet Willy felt trapped in a nightmare. He just wanted that nightmare to end, one way or another.

Two hours later, Addison was placing coloring sheets of an angel on the top of each student's desk in her 2nd grade class at Hope

Elementary School. She embraced the warmth of the freshly copied papers as she cradled the stack against her body like she was holding a child. She lived a memory of Angela and herself with each paper that she floated onto the desks. She felt herself wading in a sea of disbelief, with what seemed like several minutes passing in-between each student as she handed out the... *the students*! Addison hadn't even noticed that they had arrived, and somehow all took their seats without any issues, all by themselves. She usually did everything for them during their morning routine. From hanging up their jackets, to placing their backpacks in their cubbies, to helping with making their school-lunch choices for the day by placing their name-cards in the correct pouches on the classroom lunch chart. The students needed Miss Ambry for assistance, daily. At least that's what Addison believed to be true, up until that moment. She let an angel coloring sheet sail down toward the desk where Angela sat, which just barely skimmed the edge of it as it swayed away, floating atop the air then back again, landing at Addison's feet.

"Miss Ambry!" a few students shouted, while pointing past her toward the classroom door. Instantly, most of the other students added their own screams. "MISS AMBRY!"

BANG!!   BANG!!

With a ringing in her ears, Addison felt dizzy and eased her way onto the floor, grasping the coloring sheet on the ground as she sensed gravity grabbing a firmer hold of her for a few last moments.

"Miss Addison?"

"What is going on?" she asked, while feeling someone grabbing an arm to help her stand back up.

"My name is Mother Madre," replied a soothing, yet authoritative voice. "I am the principal here at Saint Perpetua Academy. You just had a fainting spell so you may not recall being transferred to our school. The children are at recess now, so maybe you should take a few moments for yourself to relax in your new classroom," Mother Madre said, just as someone passed by in the hall. She took a step out of the room and asked for that person to come to her.

"I don't remember transferring here," she asked.

"Ambry, this is Saint Perpetua's Resource Officer, Brock Williams," Mother Madre said while ignoring Miss Addison's confusion.

"It's very nice to meet you Miss Addison," Brock said while extending his hand to her.

Ambry Addison felt a bit of uneasy familiarity as she shook Brock Williams' hand. She kept trying to reel in any recent memory that she may have had, but none were biting. Ambry was bewildered.

"Officer Williams, please show Miss Addison to her classroom," instructed Mother Madre.

Ambry looked at the coloring sheet of an angel that she was still holding, then back at the woman who started to walk away. "I'm sorry," she said, while shaking her head slowly in confusion. "Your name again? Madre?"

"Mother Madre."

CHAPTER 2

Mayor Murphy paced about her office, awaiting word from Hope's Town Planner, who was in the Town Hall's public meeting room for the monthly town council session. The mayor's lawyer was making the case for Marjorie Murphy's proposal to turn a few of the abandoned mills that lined the Black Bank River into a few hundred low-income housing units. It was a controversial subject in town, with not much support from the town's citizens, the entire school board, and personnel from safety departments that included fire and police. Everything that Mayor Murphy did or said was pre-calculated, and that was evident whenever she needed to go off-script and lie in an unencrypted manner, as she would stutter uncontrollably. There was no way that she, herself, would face the squad of disapproving people that were ready to fire away at her fairly long reign as mayor. She wouldn't be able to answer most questions honestly if she expected her low-income housing development plan to pass the council vote.

Hope's Fire Marshall stood at the doorway of the meeting room, clicking away on the numerical counter he held in his hand with every person that entered the room.

"What are we looking like?" Chief Parker asked, as he arrived at the meeting room's door.

The Fire Marshall looked at his counter and answered, "We're at twelve over capacity as it is, with folks still strolling in here. If some people don't leave soon to counter the counter, I'll need to close this meeting down."

"Let's just pretend your counter stopped working," suggested The Chief, who in his own prepared way had tucked some large currency in his palm before shaking hands with the Fire Marshall.

"Understood, Chief."

Finally, there was a chance that Mayor Murphy could be defeated in the next election, and Chief Parker wanted to make sure that the citizens' voices were heard so loudly that the negative polling numbers on the mayor would grow exponentially. In addition to the many disagreements that he had with the mayor over time, the fact that he and his police department had not received a pay raise over the prior three years bankrupted any support that he may have had left for Marjorie, whatsoever, along with some other issues. He gave the Fire Marshall a pat on the shoulder as he personally escorted two reporters from competing local media outlets into the room, asking The Fire Marshall to retrieve a few additional folding chairs to be set-up for them up near the front.

An idolatrous murmuring quickly grew among those in the hallway who were still waiting to get into the meeting room as Dyson Devlifar walked past. Known to the rest of the world as D.D. Divine,

Dyson was the biggest thing ever to come out of Hope. It had been over twenty years since he had a hit record, but D.D. continued to perform concert tours throughout the world. Sightings of Dyson in and around town were becoming more frequent, though he hadn't performed any local shows since the huge concert he performed on the grounds of Rolling Hills Park a few years earlier at Mayor Murphy's request, just prior to her last election win. The aging rocker walked past the meeting room entrance and straight to the mayor's young secretary, who he watched take a bite of a ham & cheese sub and unprofessionally start chewing and talking at the same time.

"Can I helph oo?" she said, with a full mouth of food, while quickly looking back down at some shredded lettuce that dropped from her sandwich onto the paper deli wrapping that covered her desk.

"What? No, I'll let you chew your food," D.D. answered with a disgusted tone before walking past her. Giving two quick knocks on the mayor's door before opening it, he walked in.

Mayor Murphy hung up her phone and turned away from the window she was staring out through. The Town Hall parking lot, which sat two floors below her office, was completely full, with several cars still circulating the area and jockeying for any open spaces they could find on the street. The ongoing honking of automobile horns that wafted up to her ears were a nerve-wracking reminder that her constituents had grown weary of her as a leader, and her housing proposal, along with her reign as Mayor of Hope, might have been facing its end. Placing a business card facedown on her desk, she acted surprised to see D.D. Divine walk into her office. "Dyson!"

The unkempt secretary rushed in behind D.D., still holding her sandwich. "I'm sorry, Mayor," she said. "He just walked right in."

"We'll talk later, Miss Tousle," Mayor Murphy responded. "Mr. Devlifar and I know each other. Please close the door behind you, and no more disturbances."

Reaching for the doorknob with the same hand she held her sandwich in, lettuce fell onto the Mayor's Office rug, punctuated by a tomato chunk.

"Lock it!" sneered the mayor through her teeth.

D.D. waited for the door to click closed. "Well, I can see that you're running a tight ship these days, Marjorie."

"She's new, and please, it's Mayor."

"That's right. I'm in your office, so I should call you Mayor. Sorry to disrespect the office," D.D. said, in a not-so apologetic tone.

"It is me you are disrespecting. It's Mayor whether in OR out of this office," added Marjorie before trying to change the manner of the conversation. "So, Dyson, it's g-g-g-good to see you," she stuttered. "This is a big s-s-surprise. Aren't you supposed to be out on a tour?"

Well, it can't be that much of a surprise to you," D.D. said, squelching the pleasantries right off the bat. "You were looking down at my car when I pulled-up. When I found out about your little development plan, I postponed a few shows so I could fly here and confront you, face-to-lying-face."

"Oh, is that *your* sports car parked on the street? At least it's getting a good wash with all of this rain."

"Yeah, that's about all us tax-paying citizens can expect from this office. A free car wash in the rain," jabbed D.D. "Quit the small talk, Mayor, You know exactly why I am here."

"You, and everyone else in town that don't know what's b-b-b-best for them," The Mayor arrogantly replied.

"What's best for them are the arts-related businesses that I proposed opening in those empty factories when my touring ends next year. It was all such a great idea to you when you wanted me to organize and perform at the town's music festival last election cycle. You even said yourself that it was the biggest event the town ever had, and that I had your full support of utilizing those buildings to bring more of the arts to town and elevate the quality of life here. Your promises are as empty as those buildings are right now, and if the residents of this town are smart, they will convince the Town Council to shoot down your plans tonight and then all show up at the polls to vote you out of office in November." D.D. said with anger in his voice.

"Dyson, the town n-n-needs a shot in the arm now, not when your tours end."

"A shot in the arm? Are you kidding me? Your proposal is more like a shot in the head for the town of Hope," D.D. warned. "Do you really think that hundreds more people drawing on Hope's limited resources are a good idea? Low income equals no money being pumped into our town. Dozens upon dozens more children will be overcrowding our classrooms, receiving free lunches, and draining our school budget."

"Dyson, you d-d-don't know what you're-"

"It's Mr. Devlifar, and I'm not done talking," stated D.D., raising his voice while pointing his finger at Marjorie. "Every time I come home from being on the road, I am shocked by the amount of cars on the road. It's like there's a non-stop traffic jam from one end of town to the other, no matter what time of day it is. Do we really need to add a few hundred more cars to the streets of Hope? And what do I see while sitting in traffic? Kids hanging out on street corners with nothing to do, which, as you know, don't always lead to the best activities. My businesses would have provided positive music and arts programs for all ages, raised the quality of life for many citizens of

Hope, and given back to Hope's band and chorus programs that the School Department keeps cutting back on because of its ongoing money woes."

"Listen, we have a major financial deficit in this town. Our budget is nowhere near where it needs to be, and I n-n-need to take advantage of federal funding available to Hope if we add a certain amount of low-income housing units," explained Marjorie.

"So, instead of raising the competency in Town Hall to manage taxpayers' money better, you add a permanent detriment to Hope for a one-time budget fix?" asked D.D.

Mayor Murphy walked around her desk, sat down, and took some anti-acid tablets from a drawer. Popping them into her mouth, she began chewing them in-between her words. "Where do you come-off calling Town Hall incompetent?"

"Are you kidding me?" questioned D.D. "It was on full display during the weekly meetings that we had in this office when I was putting the music festival together for your election benefit. There wasn't a single person on your team that did what they were assigned to, or volunteered to do, from week to week." Dyson walked over to a photo of Marjorie's cabinet that hung on a wall in the mayor's office. "For example, your Town Planner, Kylee Tarry, is completely useless, yet you keep her appointed. Taxpayers paying for absolutely nothing."

"She's an in-in-intelligent lawyer," mentioned Marjorie.

"She's a joke that couldn't handle the workload of the law-firm that she worked for, which is why she is now here. I'm not sure what your definition of "intelligence" is, but the one I subscribe to is 'The global aggregate to think clearly, act purposefully, and deal effectively in one's environment', which makes Kylee the *least* intelligent of all the people that ever held her position," stated D.D., as he continued

37

along the border of the office, studying the framed photos and plaques that adorned The Mayor's walls. "

"I thought you were friends with Kylee."

"We were acquaintances up until we worked on that music festival together, or rather, the one *I* worked on, *alone*. No one in town would know that, though, because she loved to steal unearned credit by jumping into every newspaper photo-op that she could. I can't stand her, actually," he added. "I just don't do fake."

Mayor Murphy popped another antacid pill into her mouth while D.D. was talking, then finally said "This conversation is getting off-track, Dyson."

"You will address me as Mr. Devlifar."

"Whatever!" Marjorie discounted. "I suggest that we continue this conversation some other day, once you've garnered some respect for this office, which includes me."

"Do you think I'm completely stupid? You want me to come back *after* your ridiculous low-income housing project gets voted on? Are you kidding me?" D.D. walked over to a photo of Mayor Murphy holding an oversized pair of scissors in front of a business that already closed down in Hope. "If my business aspirations for that side of town die tonight, maybe it is time for me to run for mayor, myself. I'll need something to keep me busy once my touring ends."

"Don't be ridiculous, this job is w-w-way over your head," laughed-off the mayor.

"I'm pretty sure that I can cut ribbons and shake hands just as good as you," said D.D. as he walked toward Marjorie's desk. Placing his hands on the desktop, he leaned over and added in a vocal tone just above a whisper, "And I'll guarantee that I'm a LOT more popular in this town than you are."

Marjorie rose from her chair and faced Dyson squarely in the eyes. "You will n-n-NOT sit behind this desk," she said defiantly. "I know all about your little charity scam, and would have no problem exposing it to all of your little aging fans, especially those that vote here in the town of Hope."

"What the hell are you talking about?"

"You know damned well what I'm talking about, and so would anyone smart enough to research your non-profit's annual numbers." The mayor paused a moment, expecting rebuttal from Dyson, who only winced his eyes. "What a joke. One of your songs becomes a hit in an animal movie and all of a sudden you are the savior of animals, worldwide? 'The D.D. Foundation for Animals' is nothing more than a barely-legal mechanism that funds your touring expenses, lavish lifestyle, and keeps your bank account filled while your record sales decline. You may have fooled thousands of adoring fans, but you haven't fooled me one bit."

"My foundation has given thousands to the cause of helping animals!"

"And millions to helping you, personally!" charged Mayor Murphy, adding "Vehicle expense of over $100k? More than $200k in annual flight & hotel expenses to performing for built-in audiences around the world at zoos, where you sell your own merchandise and convince parents to contribute to your foundation while their children, and the surrounding zoo animals, tug at their heartstrings? Brilliant. Brilliant, yet deceitful, MISTER Devlifar."

"That doesn't take away from the attention that my notoriety brings to the well-being and adoption of animals."

"What you mean to say, if being truthful, is that animals are allowing you to remain somewhat relevant, giving you the means to stay in the public's eye while "on tour" as you get more wealthy than your actual music career itself provided. If people did their homework only to learn that 2.5 cents from every dollar they donate actually goes to the animals, I doubt you'd be eating caviar and driving sports cars." Marjorie paused while she walked toward the window. D.D. remained silent, as he knew that she was correct. "As a mater of fact, I will be holding a campaign rally in the high school gymnasium next week, and you will be my special guest entertainer."

"Have you lost your mind? D.D. Divine does NOT perform in small venues like high school gymnasiums."

"D.D. Devine will play for ONE person if I tell you to, unless you want to be exposed."

"Over my dead body!" D.D. replied, angrily. There was a knock at the mayor's door. D.D. unlocked and opened it without checking with Marjorie first.

Hope's Town Planner, Kylee Tarry, darted straight at The Mayor with words spewing out of her mouth uncontrollably. "Oh my God, I wish you saw the look on Chief Parker's face. The meeting wasn't going in our favor, so I made the Fire Marshall shut it down until next month's meeting, just like you said to-"

"Kylee-" The Mayor said, trying to stop her blabbering in front of D.D.

"It felt so good. He said his counter broke, so I showed him the count on the counter that *I* was clicking away on, and then The Chief came over-"

"KYLEE!" Mayor Murphy pointed past Kylee and she turned around to see D.D. standing near the doorway.

"Wow! Dyson! You're in town? I didn't realize anyone was standing there," Kylee said, but too incompetent to realize that she may have said too much in front of him.

"I guess you assumed that Marjorie Mayor Murphy had an automatic door installed?" D.D. replied.

"What do you mean?" Kylee answered.

"Really?" D.D. asked, while tilting his head to the side while curiously looking at Kylee. "Never mind." Dyson let the door-handle sail out of his hand, causing it to shut loudly with hopes that she might get the hint.

"We should get together for a drink while you are here," Kylee suggested, hoping for yet another crack at her high school crush.

"It sounds like you may already have started," D.D. suggested. "Are you're slurring?"

Flashing yellow lights reflected off The Mayor's face as she peeked through the window down at the street. "Kylee, please give Dyson Mister Devlifar a ride. It'll give you two a chance to catch up," she said nonchalantly.

D.D. walked over to the window to see his car being towed away. "Are you serious?" he sternly asked.

"I *do* keep a tight ship," confirmed Marjorie.

Kylee wasted no time, as she bid goodnight to The Mayor and walked out of her office with her pocketbook and the travel mug that she seemed to carry at with her at all times. Dyson gave one last glance of death toward Marjorie, and then slammed her door behind him as he followed Kylee out of Town Hall.

D.D. stood in the rain, waiting for Kylee to unlock the passenger-side door of her car so he could get in. He noticed her license plate had her initials, 'KT-1'. "Typical," he said, as he finally heard the click of the door unlocking. He remembered how self-centered Kylee was all throughout high school. Even though she had earned her law degree, Kylee hung her Hope High graduation tassel from her rear view mirror. Looking up at it, he remembered her 'na,-na-na-na,-na' childish personality. Kylee was a person that could never admit when she was wrong, or the cause of a failing end result. The sad thing was that she actually believed her own delusions. It was probably why she never got married, not that she never tried. It was quietly known between her small circle of friends how desperately she would cling to whoever gave her the time of day. They felt bad for her, or at least odd for her, but wouldn't dare engage in any conversation with her that she may perceive as confrontational in any way. They knew it would end up in frustration, like trying to reason with a drunk, so they often bit their tongues in effort to continue their friendships that started in elementary school. Kylee's adult-made friendships never seemed to last, as her high school mentality remained.

"So, to which dungeon did Her Majesty condemn my chariot?" D.D. asked.

"You've always been so clever with words", Kylee began, while giving a quick pat on D.D.'s leg and pulling out of the parking lot. "I'll always remember how cute you were in Mrs. Jones' English class when you would-"

"Kylee, where is my car?"

"Relax. It's not like you can retrieve it tonight anyway. The car-pound opens at 8am. The earlier you can get there the better because there is usually a line."

"You make it sound like quite the business."

"You aren't kidding. The town makes a ton of money from the tickets, and The Mayor gets a huge campaign donation from the tow company. It's a win-win!" Kylee said, with inappropriate excitement in her voice.

"It's a lose-lose for Hope's citizens," D.D. responded. "And those citizens are losing Hope, literally."

"Well, I'm doing ok."

"Well, good for you, but if you aren't taking me to my car you are going the wrong way. You know where I live."

"You heard Mayor Murphy. We should catch up with each other," Kylee said suggestively, while placing a hand on Dyson's thigh. "I live this way, and could drop you off at the car-pound in the morning. It'll be fun, like the old days."

"WHAT old days?"

"You know, the good ole' days of hanging out in high school."

"You and I never really hung out, though."

"Better late than never."

"Haven't you been dating Willy Brock, like, forever?"

"He spends all his time kissing-up to cops at Smitty's Bar these days. I could go for a little on-the-side kissing, myself," Kylee continued, slipping her hand higher up D.D.'s thigh as she sped her car up a bit.

"Are you drunk?" D.D. inquired, again, while stopping Kylee's hand.

"That reminds me!" answered Kylee, as she abruptly swung into a liquor store parking lot without giving any turn-signal as a warning to the car traveling behind her. "You're a silly boy, but awful cute. I'll be right back."

Kylee zigzagged her way into the store, as if she was trying to evade the unavoidable assault of raindrops. D.D. waited for her to get inside, then he took her travel mug from the console and removed the lid. Just as he had expected, it held an ounce or two of pure vodka. Who knows how much Kylee's 20oz mug held at the beginning of the Town Council meeting, or at the beginning of the day? He grabbed the keys from the ignition and then sighed as he listened to the rain as it pounded on the hood of Kylee's car. "She can call the mayor for a ride," D.D. thought to himself as he got a running head start away

43

from the liquor store, and more specifically, Kylee Tarry, before he stuck his thumb out to hitch-hike back toward the direction of his home.

Back in Mayor Murphy's office, a shouting match erupted between Marjorie and Chief Parker.

"You sneaky witch! How dare you send your little assistant into the meeting just to cancel it!" Chief's face was beet-red as he followed the mayor around her office while she paced in search of an excuse or an escape hatch. "You look at me!"

"The woman you called my little assistant just so happens to be Hope's Town Planner, Chief," she responded.

"Neither she, nor you, Mayor, have any right to abruptly end a town council meeting that so many of our citizens took time to attend in effort to make their voices heard!"

"The room was over-packed! Kylee had her own counter!"

"Kylee is an incompetent fool who obviously didn't know how to subtract when people left the room! BUT, worse than being incompetent, she was being deceitful upon YOUR orders. You may be one of Hope's longest sitting mayors, but you are also the most evil!"

"Show some respect, Chief. Remember, I'm YOUR boss, too."

"I think it's time for you to show a little respect to the citizens of this town and step down as mayor."

"On what grounds, exactly?"

"Where do I begin? Let's start with the fact that ninety-percent of the town's building contracts go to your brother's construction firm, which I'm sure is your ultimate plan for this ridiculous low-income housing scam that you are trying to ram down everyone's throats!"

"That is n-n-n-not true!" Mayor Murphy stuttered. "We publicly post all of those jobs before awarding contracts to any company."

"It IS true! You post available jobs in newspapers five towns over that nobody reads. You've become nothing but a scam-artist to keep this office and your family's pockets lined!" the chief added, "On top of that, you threaten to take the property of Smitty's Bar that has been there for over a hundred years, just to put in a new traffic rotary? Thankfully, the editor of The Beacon will be posting my editorial this week, which exposes everything about you. Not only will the residents of Hope learn about the fraud that you are, but also everyone that lives in the Black Bank Valley!"

Marjorie took a few staggering steps toward her desk, and then appeared to clench her fists toward the top of her blouse before falling to the ground.

The chief shouted, "Mayor Murphy! – MAYOR MURPHY!"

CHAPTER 3

Mother Madre lightly hummed a hymn to herself as she made her way down the main corridor of St. Perpetua Academy. Her footsteps often became the cadence of her hymns as she moved about the school. They were louder than earlier strolls that she made down the halls because of the unusual number of empty classrooms, and the echoing effect that it had on each of the principal's steps. She purposely wore shoes with loud soles because it kept her staff on their toes. "Those rooms will be filled-up soon enough," she thought, passing Miss Addison, who smiled and nodded to her as she strolled by her class. Mother Madre responded by humming slightly louder for a few notes before turning down the next hall. At the end of that hall was the Resource Officer desk. Sitting behind the desk was Officer Williams. Mother Madre paused and took off her shoes. She could see that Brock's head was leaning back against the wall with his eyes closed. Allowing the officer to sleep, her socks helped her glide silently toward his desk. Knowing that dreaming was important at St. Perpetua Academy, she smiled down at Brock Williams in what could have been perceived as a lovingly manner, and placed on top of the desk the satchel that she often carried with her. Taking a seat in the heavy wooden chair in front of Mr. Williams' desk, she pulled five extra-long pencils from her bag and began snapping them into several smaller ones for all of the students attending the academy to write with.

Sticks snapped under Willy Brock's feet as he made his way along the path in the woods on his way to the bus stop. The early morning dew that gathered on the forest's floor of leaves and brush began to soak through the top of his sneakers. In the cool, damp air, lingered a slight residual scent that gave evidence of what might have been a standoff between a skunk and it's opponent. Mixed with the essence of fern, moss, and decaying tree bark, Willy didn't mind as he inhaled the morning with an invigoration he hadn't felt in a long time. He stepped on a branch that had made its way across the path within the past day, angling several inches up and resting atop one of the many stone walls that were built a few centuries before the forest even existed there. It made a loud crack and Willy heard someone call out "Hello?" Startled, he stopped and heard the snapping of branches up ahead.

"Willy?" Dyson Devlifar said while stepping back on the path from behind a large rock about fifty-feet ahead. "What are you doing out here so early?"

"D-Boy? I could ask the same about you," answered a relieved Willy, who resumed his stride.

"This is the time I always head to school," answered Dyson.

Both boys attended Hope High School. Willy was almost two years older than Dyson, but he had stayed back once or twice so they eventually ended up in the same grade. Willy Brock was a weightlifter, and much bigger and stronger than everyone else at school, where he was somewhat a bully, but Dyson didn't fear him like most other kids at Hope High did. Dyson was popular because his rock band already had a song playing on the local radio stations and Willy used his acquaintance with Dyson as an advantage whenever he could, especially when he wanted to be introduced to girls or get into a nightclub. Being a child prodigy, Dyson had already been performing regularly in concert clubs before his freshman year of high school. It would've been another six years before he'd be of legal age to gain entrance to the nightclub world, but all of the clubs opened their doors to Dyson, knowing that his band would bring many thirsty paying concertgoers to their establishments. Willy would often tag-along as a roadie to gain early access to that world of grown-ups. He believed that it gave him power over most of his peers, which is something that he spent most of his time and energy working toward.

"I'm always out here this early," Dyson replied, while holding up the pillowcase that he had just recovered from behind the big rock. The off-white cloth sack held in it a bottle of shampoo, a hairbrush, and a towel. "As soon as the grocery store opens, I go into the employee bathroom and wash my hair before heading to school."

"Are you kidding me?"

"Nope. My stepfather doesn't let me shower in the morning because our bathroom is close to his bedroom and it wakes him up, so I shower when I get home from rehearsals at night and wash my hair in the store so I don't have bed-head at school."

"He is such a jerk!"

Willy didn't like Dyson's stepfather at all. Not since he arrived home from work years earlier and found Willy wearing his Navy uniform while laying in the backyard mud during a game of war with Dyson, who got grounded for a month. His stepfather was a prejudiced man who grew up on a tobacco farm in the south before joining the service. He didn't accept anyone who wasn't just like him, and Dyson was an all-out rocker with long hair and an earring. If there were any ways that he could make Dyson's life difficult, his stepfather would find them. He called his stepson D-Boy instead of his actual name, even though Dyson had requested that he call him by his real name. Willy started calling Dyson D-Boy, too, when he first heard his stepfather call him that. At first, Willy said it to pick on Dyson before he started to get locally famous, but the nickname eventually stuck for years. Dyson didn't mind when Willy called him D-Boy, but he loathed it whenever it came out of his stepfather's bigoted mouth. "How long have you been getting ready for school in the supermarket?" inquired Willy in disbelief.

"I don't know. I think maybe it's been two years now," admitted Dyson.

"Two years? Just let me know when you want me to take him out, D-Boy." Willy had offered to "take him out" several times before, but Dyson never knew if Willy was serious or not, or what it even meant. What he did know was that the few times Willy visited Dyson at home, he would stare his stepfather down. It made Dyson very uncomfortable, not knowing how his stepfather would retaliate against him once Willy left, but Willy always wanted to be the one with the most power in the room regardless of the consequences that somebody else might need to endure.

"Don't worry about it, I'm used to it," Dyson explained, while both boys got to the end of the path that spilled into the grocery store's parking lot. "Plus, it builds character. Not everything is easy in life."

"You're an interesting guy, D-Boy," Willy added. "So, don't you want to know why I am getting such an early jump to get to the bus-stop?"

"Actually, it was this first thing that I asked you."

"Police Cadet sign-ups are this morning before homeroom," Willy proudly stated. "There are only a few openings this year, so I want to make sure that I'm sitting at the front of the bus so I can be the first one off when we get to school."

"You'd make a great cadet. Good luck, man."

"Thanks. I'm definitely going to be a cop someday."

"Follow your dreams. That's what I always say."

"Wait! How do you even get to school? You are never on the bus."

"By the time I wash my hair the bus has already come and gone, so I hitchhike to school every day," explained Dyson, while looking at the far end of the parking lot near the street where the bus stops to pick up the students of his neighborhood. "I almost made it once, but felt stupid running across the parking lot while everyone on the bus watched, so I stopped and signaled to the driver to leave without me."

"You're not afraid to get picked up by some murderer?"

"Nah. As a matter of fact, the Chief of Police even picks me up sometimes and gives me a ride right to the school's front door."

"Chief Parker? He's going to be my boss someday! Maybe I should thumb to school, too, so he can get to know me."

"I'm not sure that hitchhiking would make the best first-impression on the chief, if you are hoping to work for him, but you're welcome to hitchhike with me if you're willing to wait for my hair appointment to be done," Dyson said while laughing.

"No way, D-boy. I'm the first one on and off that bus this morning."

"Go get 'em, Willy!"

"You, too, D-Boy! You're giving a school concert today, right?"

"I am! It's a benefit for the Hope Food Bank. Did you bring in any canned goods?"

"Shoot, I forgot."

"Don't worry, after I wash my hair I'll pick up a can of string beans for you to donate."

Willy Brock continued to the bus stop as Dyson disappeared into the supermarket. He didn't mind that it would be several minutes before any of the other students from the neighborhood would arrive. He took out a copy of the Hope Police Department Handbook, and began to study.

When he finally arrived at school, Willy darted straight to the school's foyer where there were already several of his classmates standing in front of the police cadet recruiter's desk. He started to dissuade the hopefuls that were standing immediately ahead of him from signing-up by making up fictitious scenarios, like saying there would be an intense basic training that includes a muddy obstacle course after having sand thrown into their eyes, a full background check that will expose every single time they ever cheated on a test in school or lied to a teacher, and the public humiliation of when they would need to stand in front of their entire police cadet class wearing nothing but underwear during a physical inspection. Once a few of those students left the line, he turned around to tell those who were just arriving from a late bus that they already had too many sign-ups, and that everyone after him should report directly to homeroom.

When Willy got to the front of the line, he recited the Hope Police Code of Conduct to the officer that was sitting behind the desk. His over zealous approach was a red flag to the officer, but Willy stood there proudly, feeling sure of himself over all the other students that remained in line.

"And what is your name, young man?" the recruiter asked.

"Actually, I'm not as young as the others, sir," Willy replied.

"You never answered my question. Name?"

"Yes, sir. Sorry, sir. Willy Brock reporting for duty, sir."

"Um, at-ease," the recruiter advised, while placing a form and a pen in front of Willy. "Fill out your name, age, and address, Willy."

"I'm hoping to soon be called Cadet Brock, sir."

"Cadet school begins in two week, and is every Saturday from 9am to 5pm until June. Is that a schedule that you can keep, Willy?"

"It sure is, even though I already know everything in the police department's handbook, sir," said Willy, overconfidently.

"Well, it is nice to know that you did some prep-work, but there is much more to learn than what is written in books."

"Whatever it takes, sir," Willy replied, while saluting him.

"Um, I am looking for a few volunteers to work security outside the school's auditorium doors at this afternoon's concert. Would you be interested in helping?"

"Yes, Your Honor, um, I mean I'll be honored to serve, sir. What time should I report for duty?"

"I believe the assembly begins at 1:15pm, so 1pm should be fine."

"Affirmative. I will report at 1300 hours, sir," Willy replied before walking away, convinced that he made a great impression on the recruiter.

Minutes felt like hours to Willy, as he filled up his class-time by boasting about his new status, even though he wasn't quite a cadet yet. Some of his classmates were hoping that it would make him less of a bully, while most feared that he would bully everyone even more. Either way, everyone thought that it was going straight to his head.

At 1pm, Willy stood outside the auditorium alongside the other students that signed up for cadet school while the recruiter gave instructions. All of them took a natural stance while being coached on their assignment. All but Willy. He stood at attention, glancing back and forth at the casual demeanor of his peers, knowing in his mind that he was already the best cadet. He envisioned how he would look in his uniform. His thoughts raced to hypothetical situations that he might find himself in while being a cadet, like helping to direct guests as they arrived at the town's annual picnic for police, collecting donations for the F.O.P. outside the supermarket and at Little League baseball games, or tackling another student in the hall if they were caught skipping a class. Willy let out a loud audible grunt while he imagined taking that student to the floor. The Recruiter stopped talking, and each of the other students looked over at Willy, who snapped out of his trance at that moment. He faked a cough so that they would think that his grunt might have just been a cough.

"Ok, so you have your assignments," stated The Recruiter. "Consider this your first detail, and have fun."

Willy began to panic inside, as he hadn't really heard what the recruiter instructed them to do. All he heard were the words 'backpack', 'one at a time', and 'no food'. The Recruiter handed each of them a t-shirt that read 'FUTURE CADET' in big letters across the front. Willy got even more distressed, as he told everyone that he was already a cadet.

"Do we *need* to wear these shirts?" Willy asked.

"Do you have a problem with wearing uniforms, son?" inquired the recruiter.

"No, sir."

"Then slip it on. Why would anybody follow your direction if they don't know that you are authorized to give it?"

"Understood, sir."

Two cadets-in-training were assigned to each of the main auditorium doors, and one near the food-drive box. Inside the auditorium, Dyson finished his sound-check and the theater teacher opened the doors for the students that were beginning to arrive for the concert assembly. Willy wasn't getting the adoring attention that he expected while the students began to file into the large assembly hall. The prettiest girl in school was gushing over how cute and talented Dyson was as she brushed by Willie without giving him a second look. Eventually, a student entered the auditorium with their backpack instead of adding it to the pile of them that was amassing in the foyer just outside the doors. Willy caught a glimpse of it from the other door that he was assigned to and ran toward that kid, pushing several students out of the way as he rushed to the culprit. When he caught up to him, he forced the student against a wall to detain him before stripping him of his backpack. That student, and others, began screaming for a teacher to intervene, believing that Willy was beating the kid up for no reason. While Willy's large and muscular body leaned against the skinny student, he began to search his backpack.

"What is this?" Willy shouted at the student while revealing a small machine that looked like it could possibly be a bomb to him.

"It's a nebulizer for my asthma," the student replied in agony.

"What is a nebu-"

"It helps me breath!" the student shouted, as the recruiter pulled Willy away from the student.

As he was being escorted out of the auditorium, Willy could hear several of the students jeering him, with comments like 'Who's the tough guy now?', 'What a jerk', 'Oooh big Cadet'. Willy felt like he was in a bad dream as the recruiter escorted him to a far corner of the foyer. He could tell that he was being scolded, but the recruiter's words were being interrupted by the opening drumbeat to Dyson's concert. RAT-A-TAT-TAT... RAT-A-TAT-TAT

Rat-a-tat-tat... Rat-a-tat-tat... Mother Madre tapped away on the top of Officer Williams' desk with two of the many pencils that she made from the original five pencils that she pulled out of her satchel. The pile of pencils made a mound larger than Mother Madre's bag, but she was somehow able to pack them all inside of it while Brock Williams abruptly woke up from his nap.

"Oh, Mother Madre," Officer Williams said, while gathering his consciousness. "I'm sorry. I must have dozed off."

"That's alright, Brock. We do encourage napping at St. Perpetua from time to time, even though time isn't relevant here."

Brock wasn't quite sure what Mother Madre meant by that, but he was relieved that she wasn't upset by his slumber.

"It's a bit slow in the halls so this may be a good time for us to catch up with a quick review," Mother Madre suggested. "Please follow me to the Hall of Truths."

Officer Williams lagged a few steps behind the principal as they made their way to the opposite end of the building. He couldn't seem to shake the dream he just had from his mind. It had felt so real.

Mother Madre opened the door to the Hall of Truths and took her place at the end of a very long table. Brock's footsteps echoed loudly as he entered the cavernous room, which measured 450-feet long, 75-feet wide, with several 45-foot-tall stained-glass windows built into one of the walls along the side. Aside from the stained glass, the entire shell of the chamber was built out of granite, including the stage that was inset at the other end of the room from where Mother Madre sat. He pulled out the heavy chair closest to where she was sitting and he took a seat while thinking how odd it was that the fairly loud sound that the chair made didn't create an echo like his shoes did.

"So, are you enjoying your time at Saint Perpetua Academy, Officer Williams?" asked Mother Madre, while unfolding a transparent screen that she pulled from her satchel.

"Yes, I am(aaam)," replied Brock, while amazed at the echo of his voice.

"As our Resource Officer, do you have any suggestions that would possibly make St. Perpetua a safer environment?"

"I think that if I had a real badge, everyone would have more respect for me. They'd be able to see that I have the power(errr)."

"The power to do what, exactly, Officer Williams?"

Brock looked around the chamber for a second, hoping that a good answer would come to him. "Well-"

"Officer Williams," interrupted Mother Madre, "please tell me about the dream that you just had."

"My dream, Mother Madre?"

"Yes, as you honestly remember it," she replied, while adjusting the transparent screen in front of her. It began to turn colors and form images as Officer Williams started to speak.

"It all seemed so real(aal)," Brock began. "It started out in a forest, where I met someone that was sort-of a friend in the dream. I'm trying to remember his name. Dylan? Devon? I must have been a high school student because I remember being excited that police cadet sign-ups were that day."

"And did you sign up, Brock?"

"Of course(ourse)!"

"And how did that go?"

"It went good(aaad)," Brock replied, while looking around in confusion because his echo didn't seem to match his words.

Mother Madre touched the screen in front of her and the colors changed its form. "Do you believe that memorizing the Police handbook and reciting the department's Code of Conduct is what set you above the other students that were hoping to become a cadet, too?"

Brock became even more confused because he hadn't told her about that part of the dream yet. "Yes, I imagined that it would(ood)."

"But, do you truly believe that, Officer Williams?"

"Yes(ooh)," Again, Brock looked around because his echo sounded as if he said no.

Touching the screen in front of her again, Mother Madre asked, "What happened next?"

"Well, that kid that I met in the woods was giving a concert at the school. I was assigned to make sure that nobody entered the auditorium with a backpack."

"Were you sure that was the instruction given for your assignment?"

"Yes(ooh)."

"And were you successful in fulfilling your assignment?" Mother Madre continued while sweeping her fingers across the screen.

"Yes(ooh)."

Mother Madre stared at the screen and began to speak without taking her eyes off of it. "Officer Williams, book knowledge is one thing, but how we apply that knowledge is quite another. Written words are often composed as general information for the masses. A framework, if you will, on a particular subject matter. As you know, there are many, many souls, and every soul is different, and will have a different approach from the next as to how information should be absorbed, and when deemed appropriate, dispensed onto others. One of the keys to success is u-u-understanding the s-s-s-souls that you are interacting with, whether being a general knowledge or and in-depth one, depending on the subject matter and situation. How they perceive things, their sensitivities, their personal culture, and previous experiences will all play into how they may or may not react with another's approach. One may have all the knowledge that they can garner from books, claiming themselves an expert, but when they fail at delivering that information in a way that the receiver will welcome it, that person with the book-smarts is reduced to having zero power over that soul and situation. Furthermore, h-h-h-honesty will always be a factor in one's success. If a soul cannot achieve what they are working toward without lying, then they never will reach that goal, and if it appears that they did, it will not be everlasting."

"I read about-"

"AND, Officer Williams, it is very important to l-l-l-listen to what others have to s-s-say. One may discern if another's words were accurate, useful, or justified *after* they had a chance to speak, but to block out any other soul before giving them their opportunity to express can be a gravely mistake. Do these values, which we teach here at St. Perpetua, make sense to you?"

"Yes(ess)."

"Very good. You are free to return to your post."

Brock stood up while Mother Madre folded her screen.

"Thank you, Mother Madre."

Just as Brock was about to exit the Hall of Truths, Mother Madre added, "Oh, and Brock, bullying will always send you to the back of the class."

CHAPTER 4

Connor Dander entered the conference room as the nervous chatter of his sales-force fell silent. As National Sales Manager for the Noah Zu Corporation, Mr. Dander was not known to be patient with his team, and the company had just finished its worse fiscal year ever. With Noah Zu's dog food sales declining more than ten percent over the previous year, Connor forced all of his salespeople to fly-in from around the country so they could report on their specific regions as to why the sharp decline. It was late afternoon. Most of the team had flown in that morning, or the night before, and had some time to catch up with each other before the initial meeting. Connor spent that time in his office with the shades drawn, collecting and reassembling the pre-meeting presentations that he ordered his crew to provide him with. He spoke not a word to those gathered around the large conference table as he took his position at the head of it, opening his leather-bound notebook and pointing a remote control at the large video screen at the far end of the conference room.

"Larry, get the lights," began Connor. A Pareto chart appeared on the screen, showing several bars at various heights with dollar numbers along the left side, and annual dates along the bottom of it. "Folks, as you can see here, Noah Zu's numbers aren't looking very healthy and I need answers as to why. Clearly, the growth that we experienced over the past several years has been stripped away over the past twelve months, and I'm not a happy puppy." He stood up and slowly walked around the conference room, examining the demeanor of each member on his team. Once he determined who appeared to be the most nervous, he sat back down and re-pointed the remote toward the screen, choosing a presentation to appear. "Bradley, what am I looking at here?"

"This slide shows the month-by-month numbers for-"

"I can see what it shows," interrupted Connor.

"But, you asked-"

"Explain to me WHY your numbers are down!"

"Well, the dog food market for mom-&-pop pet stores in the Midwest is down, generally, Mr. Dander. It seems that-"

"It SEEMS? Seriously? It SEEMS? That's not good enough! I need facts, Bradley. Do you have ANY facts to share with me and the rest of the team here today?" Connor stood up and began to walk around the table again as each member of his sales-team squirmed uncomfortably in their seats.

Bradley tried to find words that wouldn't heighten Mr. Dander's anger. "Sir, big-box pet stores have been popping-up in seemingly every town in my region, and they are selling dog food at retail pricing less than what I'm selling wholesale to the mom-&-pop stores. It is getting hard to-"

"Hard to WHAT, Bradley? Hard for you to sell a superior product? Hard for you to sell the value? Hard for you to communicate the benefits of our products over our competition's rubbish? We sell a premium product, NOT the garbage that the box-stores sell."

"I understand, Mr. Dander, but when the general public-"

"The general public is NOT your job. Your job is to convince pet storeowners to buy Noah Zu premium dog food. Period! I am now trying to understand how you plan on pulling your territory out of a pile of dog crap!"

"With all due respect, Mr. Dander, I have on several occasions, requested a conference call with you so I could explain Noah Zu's past market-share versus what it is today, and the ideas that I have that may help to get Noah Zu dog food back on track in the Midwest. You never got back to me."

The conference room got eerily quiet, and the air became vacuum-like as Connor made his way back to his seat at the head of the conference table. He switched the screen to a different team-member's presentation. Looking down at his notebook, he said in an unusually calm voice, "Bradley, you are dismissed. Hand-in your laptop with Human Resources before you leave the building."

"Are you seriously firing-"

"NOW!"

Knowing that the other salespeople would most likely have similar facts, or lack thereof in his opinion, he turned the video screen off. He also knew that he didn't properly prep his team with detailed instruction prior to the sales meeting, so he shifted his approach. He couldn't afford to lose another member of his sales-staff, and had already felt immediate remorse for firing Bradley on the spot. The episode would either have implications of motivating his team to work harder, or eroding more of their already crumbling morale. But, he did fire him and he wasn't going to reverse his decision. He hardly ever did, even when he knew that he was initially wrong. From his seat, Connor looked at each of those still seated at the table. Nobody looked more or less comfortable than the next. Each of them was equally nervous, and that reflected in every set of eyes.

"Before we continue, I'd like each of you to open your laptop and put together a brief S.W.O.T. analysis for your region, with just a few bullet-points for each." Most of the gathered salespeople opened their computers and began to type, but Connor could see that the salesperson who covered the southern territory was hesitant and looking over at her neighbor's computer. "Do you even know what a S.W.O.T. analysis is, Donna?"

"I believe so, Mr. Dander. I just want to get a little peek of how Larry is setting his up."

"Can you tell me what S.W.O.T. stands for?"

"Isn't it Strengths, Weaknesses, Opportunities, and Taxes?"

Connor let out a long and loud breath before speaking, "Larry, can you please explain to Donna what the 'T' stands for?"

Not happy that he was placed in the position of correcting his colleague, but relieved that Connor placed some confidence in him, Larry answered, "Threats. Anything that could be a potential threat to our company and products, which *could* theoretically include taxes."

"Does that make sense to you, Donna, or do I need to enroll you back into a Sales 101 class?" Connor asked in a derogatory manner.

Donna didn't lift her head, but simply shook her head no as a tear landed on top of her keyboard.

"Speaking of weakness," Connor uttered under his breath, just as the conference room intercom buzzed. He walked over to a speaker on the wall and pressed a button next to it. "Yes?"

"Mr. Dander, could I see you in my office?"

"Yes, Mr. Steward. Right after my meeting, Sir?"

"Right now."

Connor knew that his being summoned to Mr. Steward's office was probably not a good thing. Mr. Steward was a fair, yet stern boss. He had started the Noah Zu Corporation more than a decade earlier, and he only missed one day of work in all that time, which was the day that his dog died. Mr. Steward cared about people, but he cared about dogs even more. He felt like his purpose in life was to provide a healthy alternative dog food to a market saturated with over-processed and undernourished cans and bags of canine cuisine. The more than ten percent drop in sales concerned him as much as it concerned Connor, but not for the same reasons. Connor was driven by financial growth, yet Mr. Steward worried that most consumers were also being driven by money and opting for the lower-cost, less-quality dog food options that were squeezing Noah Zu dog food products off the shelves, therefore resulting in a less healthy population of dogs. One thing was clear, both Mr. Steward and Connor needed to see sales increase.

The Noah Zu Corporation's sales-force breathed a sigh of relief as their dictator-like leader exited the conference room, after instructing them to continue to work on their S.W.O.T. analysis during his absence. Connor's walk to Mr. Steward's corner office brought him along the floor-to-ceiling glass wall that normally allowed the outside light to filter through to the village of office cubicles inside, but the only thing seeping in as he walked by was the ominous sound of rain as it traveled sideways to batter the panes, almost as if some sort of warning aimed at Connor. He sure didn't want to face Mr. Steward, based on the tone of the company owner's voice when he demanded that Connor report to his office, but he felt that it was better than being outside in the storm. He looked at his reflection in the glass and adjusted his tie before taking the last few steps to Mr. Steward's office door.

Connor's less than confident voice announced his arrival as Mr. Steward sat at his desk while looking over a document. "You wanted to see me, Sir?"

"Yes, come in Connor. Please close the door behind you."

Taking a seat in front of Mr. Steward's desk, Connor sat still in the awkward silence while his boss continued to review the paperwork on his desk in front of him. The moment seemed to last for several minutes. Connor didn't move or mentally prepare for whatever conversation awaited him. He just sat there without a single thought running through his mind. On the outside he appeared to be a stern business manager, but on the inside he was growing wary and insecure of his work. It had been a long time since he earned his college degree, and he had been working at the Noah Zu Corporation since the day after his graduation. He knew that several members of his sales-team were more proficient with the latest technologies, along with trendy sales and marketing tools. If he asked anyone to show him new tricks, he felt that it would expose his inferiority to those that reported to him. Instead, he grew more and more demanding that his team provide him with reports and specific information that he could massage and reassemble into his own reporting to Mr. Steward. Connor did his best to keep the sharp minds of his sales-force hidden from his boss. Finally, Mr. Steward cleared his throat while placing the documents in front of him into a manila envelope. Opening his laptop, he faced it toward Connor and pulled-up a multi-media presentation titled 'Noah Zu Corporation – Yesterday, Today & Tomorrow'.

"Have you seen this presentation, Connor?" Mr. Steward asked.

"I don't believe that I have, Mr. Steward," replied Connor, knowing that he was lying. Bradley, the salesperson that he had fired earlier, had emailed it to him on several occasions as an attachment, along with his many requests for a conference call so that they could discuss his ideas.

"Connor, this is Bradley's presentation, and it is excellent. There are a lot of fresh ideas here that could really help to turn things around for Noah Zu's dog food line. He informed me that he tried to send it to you several times, but that his requests for a conference with you went unanswered."

Connor knew that Mr. Steward was correct. He tried to think of the best words to explain his inaction, but continued to sit in front of him in silence as his word search came up empty.

"You were my first salesperson, Connor. Sometimes I consider you like a son, but lately my confidence in you as Noah Zu's sales manager has been eroding. This company is my child, and my first priority is to see it get healthy again. I have rehired Bradley, who has agreed to relocate here and take over as sales manager."

"You are firing me, Mr. Steward?"

"I am re-assigning you, Connor, which could mean a big opportunity for you if you put your all into it. I have decided to add a non-food product to Noah Zu."

"What kind of product, sir?"

"Medical. I believe that I found a product that we could sell over-the-counter and through veterinarians. It is a medication that relieves the symptoms of arthritis, and in many studies, actually prevents it. Originally, its target was for human use, but accelerated lab results revealed that it might cause cancer in humans over prolonged usage. I have invested in a study that shows the drug is actually very effective on dogs, and any onset of cancer as a result of the medication wouldn't happen within any given dog-breed's life expectancy."

"Wow. Potentially eliminating arthritis in dogs? That sounds exciting, Mr. Steward."

"I thought so, which is why I purchased the patent, along with the company that manufactures it," Mr. Steward pushed the pile of documents that sat before him toward Connor. "Take these and study them, then do some research on that segment of the industry and present to me a S.W.O.T. analysis."

Connor picked up a brochure from the pile while asking, "Where are they located?"

"If you did about ten seconds of research by looking at the address on the back of that brochure in your hand you would have saved a few syllables during those seconds and then asked a more intelligent question built upon a known fact. That is what I need from you in this role," Mr. Steward said, speaking in a most serious tone.

"I understand. Are you looking to relocate this new division here?" Connor replied while reading the back of the brochure.

"That is my intent, if I can find the right building, and workforce, which is something else you may add into your report for me. Do yourself a favor and tap Bradley's brain for ideas while on the ride."

"On the ride?"

"Yes. You will give Bradley a ride back to the airport."

"You're not serious."

"I'm not?" Mr. Steward began to inch the documents back toward himself across the desk.

"The airport is all the way on the other side of Hope. I had plans for-"

"That will give you some time to learn something from Bradley."

Connor pulled his car under the awning and popped his trunk open without getting out. Bradley walked out of the Noah Zu Corporation's front door carrying his briefcase and overnight bag. He wondered if Connor hadn't pulled his car completely under the shelter on purpose, as the rain cascaded off the edge of the awning and onto his head and luggage. He paused for a moment from the cold and wet shock of it, and then hurried to close the trunk's lid.

"Thanks for offering to bring me to the airport," said Bradley, as he shut the door. "This is some weather."

"I didn't offer."

Connor gunned his car away from the building and swung onto the street wildly without checking for any oncoming traffic before Bradley had a chance to reach for his seatbelt.

"Listen, I really didn't-" Bradley tried.

Connor turned up the radio to a level that left no room for any additional sound waves. He didn't know who to be mad at. Bradley? Mr. Steward? Himself? All he knew was that all he knew, or all he thought he knew, had been stripped away from him. Deep down inside, he didn't feel that he had the skillset to be successful in the new role that Mr. Steward had assigned him to.

Bradley looked out the window and through the pouring rain at the passing scenery that would soon be his home, and began to nod his head to the ridiculously loud music.

Connor became even more annoyed. As he pulled onto the freeway, he began to panic internally, believing that his days at Noah Zu were numbered. He needed help, but there was no way he was going to ask Bradley for his. Connor had too much pride for that. He felt like he needed a miracle.

Bradley began to sing along to the song that was blasting through his speakers, so Connor hit the scan button on his radio. It switched to an evangelist in mid-sermon. Connor left it there at full volume.

"You're a Christian, too? My family and I have a deep faith in The Lord," stated Bradley, fitting his words in-between those of the preacher on the radio.

Connor stared straight ahead, not acknowledging anything that Bradley had to offer.

"I never had any intent of taking your job, Mr. Dander," Bradley finally proclaimed.

"Well, you sure did a good job at crucifying my career," replied Connor, just before switching the station back to the loud music.

Once they arrived at the airport, Connor pulled up to the curbside and remotely popped the trunk open. Bradley attempted to shake Connor's hand, but Connor chose to look out his window instead. Bradley slipped a Christian flier along the side of Connor's seat before he got out of the car, and as soon as Bradley closed the trunk, Connor sped away into the wet evening.

Connor felt relieved to finally be alone with his thoughts, albeit thoughts riddled with worry. He turned off the radio and tried to think of any friends or acquaintances that might work for a pharmaceutical company or a doctor's office. He knew close to nothing about the medical industry, yet his welfare hinged on quickly becoming an expert in it. His worry lingered and his thoughts drifted until the Low Fuel light started blinking and dinging. Passing a freeway sign that read 'Hope – Exit 5 Miles', Connor joked to himself that he *hoped* his car would make it another five miles, running on fumes.

The metal canopy that sprawled over the top of the cars and the gasoline pumps did very little to protect anyone from the rain.

Connor kept his head down as he held the hose to his car while the windswept deluge assaulted him unapologetically from the side. Just as he thought that he was probably having a worst day than anyone in his path or vision up to that point, he heard a loud swoosh-sound and looked up just as a hitchhiker was given an impromptu shower by a passing pick-up truck. The man let out a scream of frustration as he stood there, looking up at the sky with his arms held up in defeat. Connor hung the gas hose back onto the pump and rushed back inside of his car. He sat for a minute, watching while the man collected his will and continued to make his way along the road, one step at a time. He wasn't one to pick up hitchhikers, and he couldn't remember the last time he even saw one, but he felt a sense of connection to this other soul that was experiencing a day that must have been as bad as his. Another swoosh sent a wall of water hitting the side of Connor's window as he waited to exit the gas station. He finally felt that it was safe enough to pull out onto the road and he headed in the direction of the hitchhiker, who was a hundred or so feet away.

"Man, I can't thank you enough," the man said, while getting into Connor's car.

"This isn't a night to be thumbing. Let me guess. Car broke down?"

"Nope. Even better. I parked it in a no parking zone and it got towed from right under my nose. What pisses me off is that they won't let me pay the fine and get it back until tomorrow morning."

"They'll get you coming or going," Connor said, while pulling up to a red light. "My name's Connor."

"Nice to meet you, Man. I'm D.D."

Connor gave a longer look at the man's face. "Wait! You're D.D. Divine!"

"Last time I checked, anyway."

"You're kidding me! I am a huge fan of yours!" Connor sat there staring at D.D., "I can't believe that you are in my car!"

"Um, the light turned green."

"Oh. Right."

Connor started driving. Instantly, he began to believe that picking up D.D. Divine was a sort-of miracle. An idea quickly came together in his head that would surely save his existence at Noah Zu.

"So, where are you from?" D.D. asked.

"I actually lived in Hope when I was a kid, but the last few decades had me living just a few towns over. I work for Noah Zu."

"The dog food company?"

"Yes, and we are adding an arthritis medication for dogs to our brand," explained Connor, "and I think that you'd be the perfect spokesperson for the product, considering your notoriety and animal charity work."

"I'm not sure that I want to get involved with a drug company, even if it is for animals."

"Why is that?"

"I imagine that it would take me a bit too far away from the music industry to make sense. With my charity, I am able to keep live performances in the mix."

"All the articles that I have read about the music industry suggest that it is in peril, with less and less people buying music these days. I'm guessing that a big fat check presented to you for your appearance in a few ads would earn your interest?"

"I'm listening."

"Dinner?"

"Sure. Take a right at the next set of lights if you like Italian food."

A mile or so back, Kylee Tarry walked out of the liquor store with a brown bag that held two large bottles of booze. She appeared confused as she stumbled about the parking lot in the hard-driving rain. It wasn't a large lot, but she somehow managed to make her way to a car and open the back door to place her bottles down.

"Can I help you?" a voice asked from the front seat.

Kylee looked up and realized that she was placing her bottles of booze in the wrong car. Without saying a word, she reclaimed the bag, closed the door, and staggered toward her actual automobile. By then, the paper bag that held the bottles were soaking wet, and as she opened her door one of the bottles fell through the drenched bag and smashed on the cement near her feet. She tossed the other bottle over to the passenger seat and then sat down behind the wheel. It appeared that she forgot about D.D. for a few minutes while she searched around the inside of her car. "Where the heck did I leave my keys?" she thought to herself before extracting the extra set that she kept in her pocketbook. "Wait a minute. Where the (hic) heck did Dyson go?" she slurred out loud to herself while starting the car. A few passing blaring horns sounded as she swerved too close to the centerline in the road. Eventually, Kylee found herself camped-out in her car near the gated entrance to D.D.'s driveway. She took a long swig from her bottle, and then put her head back and waited.

Connor and D.D. walked out of the restaurant, but then quickly ran to the car. The rain had not let up at all. If anything, it got heavier. Evidence of the wind getting stronger, also, appeared like a ghost whisking by in the form of a sheet of water as it ran under a streetlight. Both men paused as they watched it eventually hit the windshield, and then continued to secure their seatbelts before Connor backed out of the parking space.

"Man, I'm glad the restaurant sold sweatshirts. I have no problem advertising food to get out of that soaked shirt after my cold shower on the side of the road," D.D. mentioned.

"Well, at least the food was good. I think that was the best Italian dinner I ever had," professed Connor. "Lucky for the restaurant, it doesn't have to pay close to half a million to have D.D. Divine promote it like Noah Zu will be paying."

"You really think that you'll get the owner to sign off on that amount?"

"Look, I'm in charge of this division. It's what I say and he signs the check."

"Cool. Hey, take a left out of the parking lot. I'll show you the buildings I was telling you about. It's worth seeing while you are here, and I can almost guarantee that the mayor's plans for them will get voted down."

"Awesome. And if you open up your arts-related businesses there, too, Noah Zu and D.D. Divine will be neighbors!"

The two engaged in small talk as Connor drove through the rain toward the Black Bank River. As the road sloped down toward the river's valley the air got more pungent.

"What's that smell?" asked Connor.

"Oh, that's just the river. It's only because it is raining this hard. When the Black Bank rushes, the sediment on the bottom churns-up. When you get to the bottom, take a right."

"I love these old brick buildings. They just don't make-em like this anymore."

"Take a look at that one on the left. It's where I plan on building my music studios. Nice tall windows and ceilings, so I can manipulate the acoustics inside however I need to."

"It would be a shame if the mayor does get her way regarding housing development here."

"Stop worrying. She won't. Check out the second building up ahead. It might be perfect for Noah Zu."

"It looks like a bar," replied Connor.

"Ha! Not that one. The one on the left side of the road."

"That *would* be perfect. It's unoccupied?"

"Most of these are, aside from the Hope Metal Badge & Button Company, which has been here for over a hundred years."

"Wow. A hundred years?"

"Dude, these buildings are a few hundred years old. Lots of history here. Pull into the bar. I'll but you a beer."

It had been over a year since Dyson had stepped foot inside Smitty's Bar. He knew that the patrons inside would be worshiping him as he walked in. That would solidify Connor's desire to crown him as Noah Zu's celebrity spokesperson, justifying the large financial payout that he promised him earlier in the night. His hometown admirers didn't disappoint him as Dyson and Connor entered Smitty's. Hollers came from each corner of the bar – D.D.'s back! World-traveler Dyson! Hey, Divine!

Dyson got Connor situated at the one pub-style table that was available, then headed up to the bar so he could order two beers. He knew that he wouldn't have to pay for them. He hadn't had to pay for a drink at Smitty's for the past two decades, or however long it had been since his first song hit the radio stations. He squeezed in-between Hal Perkins, the town's local barber, and Patrolman Dickens, as he stood at the bar.

"Chief Parker?" Dyson said out loud to himself when he saw Hope's chief of police pouring drinks behind the bar.

"That's what *I* said," mentioned Hal. "Smitty is nowhere to be found, and the bartender is in the back room, passed-out drunk."

"Two drafts, Chief!" ordered D.D., once he got the chief's attention.

"Dyson! Good to see you, lad," Chief Parker said, while working the taps.

"So, did Smitty finally sign over the deed to the business, Chief?" blurted out Patrolman Dickens.

The chief looked over at his patrolman with a scowled look on his face and said, "Not now, Dickens!"

Dyson returned to Connor with the two beers and took a seat across from him. Several people came over to their table to say hello, including someone he never saw before that asked him to sign his napkin. Eventually, the mini-mob cleared and Dyson picked up his mug and clinked it against Connor's.

"Cheers!" Connor said before lifting the mug to his lips. "Here's to the union of D.D. Divine and Noah Zu!"

Meanwhile, Kylee Tarry snored so loudly that she woke herself up. For a split-second, she didn't know where she was. The gated driveway and the bottle of booze between her legs quickly reminded her that she was hitting on Dyson earlier in the night. She began to get nervous. What if Willy was looking for her? What if Dyson decided to call Willy to explain her behavior? She needed to come up with a story as to where she was all night. She decided to come up with something on her way to Smitty's. Willy hated it when she showed up at the bar unannounced, but she needed to know where she stood with him and was pretty certain that she would find him there. The two had an argument about Willy's future a few days earlier and they hadn't spoken to each other since then. She didn't want to mess things up further via any reports of her hitting on Dyson, and figured that a little late-night intimacy might make everything right again. Noticing that the bottle was open, she took another swig before twisting the cap back onto it and placing it on the passenger seat before driving away from Dyson's gated driveway.

Connor and D.D. finished their beer at the same time. The thirsty patrons that gathered around the bar were two people deep by then, as Chief Parker struggled to keep up with their drink orders.

"Another round, on me?" offered Connor.

"I need to head home. My house is on the other side of town so I'll just call for a taxi, but feel free to stick around and get to know the locals. You never know, some of these cats may be working for you at Noah Zu someday."

"Don't be silly. I'll give you a ride home."

"Honestly, it's getting late and you have a bit of a drive ahead of you already. I'll be fine."

"Are you sure? I don't know if you smoke or not, but I've got some killer bud that I'll be lighting up when I get out of here," said Connor, enticingly.

Dyson stood up. "Twist my arm. I'll race you to the car." He walked straight for the door without looking at anyone, knowing that if anyone started talking to him it could mean another hour or so inside the bar. Connor followed closely behind, feeling proud that he was hanging out with a rock star.

"What a fun and productive night this has been," Connor said, while pulling a joint from a compartment built into his dashboard and lighting it. "This is the real McCoy," he added, while holding his breath and the hit of smoke inside before a series of coughs evacuated his lungs. "Be careful," he added, while passing the joint to Dyson.

"Don't worry, I'm a veteran when it comes to weed," D.D. responded.

Connor started his car and drove to the parking lot exit. "Which way?" he asked.

"So, take a left and head up that hill," Dyson replied, before drawing on the joint. He held his breath as long as he could and eventually let out a cloud of smoke. "That's good stuff."

The car started to make a dinging sound. Connor looked at the dashboard where a seatbelt sign was illuminated. His car started to climb the hill as his right hand reached and brought the seatbelt across his chest. There was something blocking the buckle from clasping along the side of his seat. "What the heck is this?" he said, while pulling out a flyer with the same hand that was still holding the seatbelt buckle. His knees took over steering wheel duty as his left hand reached for the interior light, which allowed him to begin reading the paper, "Everyone who belongs to Christ will be given new life – 1st Corinthians"

"LOOK OUT!"

Connor looked up to see a car's headlights and license plate, 'KT-1', just as his car collided head-on with it. After an initial loud crash, each car's horn blared endlessly as the night sky continued to cry without mercy onto the saturated valley of factories just below the accident.

CHAPTER 5

The sound of the horns faded before falling silent, first one, and then the next, as both of the young trumpet players ran out of breath at almost the same time. St. Perpetua's music teacher, Mr. Dyson, clicked his stopwatch before walking over to his two red-faced students as they each gasped for air.

"Not bad," he said, "but you'll both need to do better if you are to play the piece of music that I'm thinking about for the graduation ceremony. Please, do yourselves a favor and make sure that you spend enough time practicing the breathing techniques that I showed you. It's just as important as the notes themselves."

As the students left the music room, Devin Dyson walked back to his desk and picked up the day's class schedule that was freshly printed. He looked back up at the golden harp that he passed as he walked down the diminuendo of platforms that made up the floor of his music room. "I don't remember that being here," he thought to himself, while surveying the rest of the room more suspiciously. None of it felt all that familiar to him, but he was the music teacher at St. Perpetua. The framed music education certificate that hung on the wall behind his desk proved it because it included Devin's name in writing, but he was confused. Looking down at the schedule in his hand he realized that he had a 'prep' period next, so he could enjoy some student-free time. He sat in his swivel-style chair and tilted his head back. Feeling an instant coldness against his neck, he turned around to notice a sweatshirt hanging on the back of his chair. "How did this get wet?" he wondered. Feeling strange, he folded his arms on his desk and put his head down.

D.D. Divine wasn't sure what to expect when he arrived at the film and music conference, but he knew that his career needed a jumpstart, and one sure way to do that was to land the soundtrack for a movie. Dressed in a leather blazer and his signature black cowboy boots with one bootstrap of a cross, Dyson stepped-up to the convention center's lobby bar after picking-up his conference badge.

"I'll take a tall one from whichever tap is running the coldest," requested Dyson.

Before the bartender moved, the person sitting next to him offered, "May I suggest the Devil's Door Autumn Ale? It may not be the coldest, but it'll give you a more interesting buzz."

"What he said," Dyson responded before looking over at the person. "Man, you look really familiar," he added, while looking at his long white mane and mustache.

"As do you," the man said as he waved his finger up and down at Dyson. "I've got it! You're D.D. Divine. I met you two months ago on the other side of the country while you were standing outside, waiting for your producer. It was in the city, and I read your numbers for you. I'm a numerologist, and if I recall correctly, you are to do big things in life. Remember?"

"Wow! I do! How weird that we'd meet here."

"What's even stranger than that is I was listening to the CD you had given me that day on the way over here today."

"Really?"

"This is amazing. The woman I was driving here really liked it. She produces films."

"Can I meet her?"

"Better yet, grab your beer and come sit at our table."

D.D. followed the man into a large ballroom that was decorated with moons, inverted stars, old vinyl records and vintage movie reels. Cauldrons with artificial dancing flames created centerpieces on large round tables. Spilling beer onto the carpet while trying to take in the scene while keeping up, Dyson turned a few heads before arriving at his offered seat.

"D.D., this is Maura Pheme. Maura, D.D. Divine," the man introduced.

Standing up and extending her hand, backside up, Maura said, "Divine indeed! Enchanted."

D.D. took her extended hand with his and inhaled her scent of patchouli before giving it a kiss. "The pleasure is all mine."

The white-haired man, who reminded Dyson of a wizard, walked around to the other side of the table without taking an eye off the two as they became acquainted. A distinguished looking man walked up to a podium and began to speak.

"Thank you all for being here, and thank you, Universe, for allowing us to gather here today," the speaker began.

"Follow me to the lobby so we can talk," Maura whispered alluringly into his ear.

Pausing for a moment so he could take a sip of his beer to minimize the spilling on his way back out of the ballroom, Dyson felt an exciting chill rush through his spine as he followed the attractive filmmaker back into the lobby.

"Finish your beer then we can head outside," Maura suggested.

Considering that she didn't have a drink, Dyson took a quick sip and placed the almost full beer on top of a stand next to an exit door. "I'm all set, Miss Pheme," he said, while opening the door to the blinding light outside. "After you."

Dyson squinted as the sunlight reflected off the white cement walkway that that darted in and around the tropical gardens of the convention center grounds like a labyrinth. Maura placed a diamond-encrusted pair of sunglasses over her eyes and maintained a moderate pace as D.D. followed her away from the main building.

"I heard some of your music. It's good," Maura finally said.

"Well, I'm glad that you like it."

"Are you open to changing lyrics around here or there?"

D.D. hesitantly replied, "Maybe?"

"Look, I know that songs are like babies to a songwriter, but maybe it's time for a few of them to grow up. I have a new movie in the works and am hoping to lock-in someone for the soundtrack soon. Any interest?"

"Absolutely."

Maura began digging through her pocketbook without slowing her pace, as she entered the convention center's vast parking lot. She turned right, then left at the second row of cars, eventually stopping

80

and placing her bag on the trunk of a car and digging deeper into it. "Ah, here it is," she said, while extending a business card to Dyson. "Meet me at this address at six tomorrow evening."

"How did you know that this was my car?"

"Oh, is this your car?" Maura answered in a detached manner. "Shouldn't we go back in?"

"Why should you go back inside on such a beautiful day when I can give you everything that you came here for? I'll see you tomorrow, D.D. Divine."

Dyson watched her walk away while thinking of the serendipitous nature of the day, so far. He decided that it would be rude for him to go back inside in effort to find a different opportunity, especially if Miss Pheme were to see him schmoozing with others right after offering him a private meeting. He was amazed by the surreal way the first twenty minutes went for him and he didn't want to mess anything up. Satisfied that meeting Maura Pheme was meant to be, he got into his car and drove away.

The next day, he found himself driving up a canyon road until his car was hugging curves along the top peaks of what the locals would call hills, but that he called mountains. His grip on the steering wheel was firmer than normal as he navigated his rental car around hairpin turns on his way to meet Maura. He wasn't a fan of heights to begin with, but the fact that there were no guardrails along the edge of the jet-view road made it all that much more harrowing to him. Stopping at the edge of a driveway with a large open gate, he double-checked the address on his card before pulling in, as he gazed in awe of the Spanish style mansion in front of him.

"Welcome to my humble abode," Maura said, standing in her driveway once Dyson parked and got out of his car. He walked around the large circular fountain that sat in the center of the drive, admiring the life-sized statue, which the erupting water surrounded. "That is the Greek goddess Apate," she added, as she noticed his wonderment. When he didn't ask of Apate's Greek story, Maura Pheme thought to herself that her work would either be very easy, or very hard. She would soon find out.

"What a beautiful place. This is where you live?"

"This is my slice of Heaven, if you will." She swung open one of the two high mahogany arched double doors, exposing an expansive foyer made from exotic tiles and marble. "I think you'll like the acoustics in here," she said, while walking over to a grand piano.

"Gorgeous. Do you play?"

"I don't, but feel free to tickle the keys. It's a Steinway. It's in tune."

"I'm ok, but thanks for the invite to play it."

"Perhaps with a little inspiration?" Maura walked over and took hold of the pulley-system on the side of the ceiling-to-floor curtains that covered an entire large wall. As the curtains parted, an amazing landscape of hilltops and valleys formed beyond a gigantic pane of glass.

"How breathtaking," D.D. gasped, while walking toward the capacious window and fathoming the sprawling estate grounds that spread out in front of him from his vantage point inside the mansion. "How can you ever leave here with a view of God's country like this?"

"Aha!" she erupted, jubilantly, "The yin and yang, above as below, freedom or prison, good or bad, right from wrong," she said, very chant-like, "the sun or the moon," as she allowed her feet to glide across the marble floor to a decorative brass pedestal stand holding what looked to be a burnt Bible, fused together with a melted candle... "truth or bullshit." Maura turned to D.D. and smiled a smirked. "Or is it the other way around? The moon or the sun, wrong from right, bad or good, below as above, prison or freedom? Which came first, D.D.?

"Um-"

"Did what *you* call *god* create that which stands before us, or was this made by other forces that also gave us the means to build within that beauty?"

"I think-"

"I think that you have an imaginary friend, Mr. Divine. Imaginary friends don't go anywhere in this industry. Understood?"

Dyson looked out the window, and then glanced over at the burnt Bible for a second before looking back at Maura. "Understood."

"Good. Then once you understand, what's the price? Is this the climax of all that most may ever desire? Without a prince, it just one's prison. Contained inside Heaven alone."

"Please excuse my candor, but were you speaking of yourself, Maura?"

She walked around the grand room, lighting candles and incense, and then to a wine rack. "You may not know this about me, but I'm actually married, still. Been four years since we separated. We figured that it would be best for our two girls if we maintained a loose and amicable relationship. They spend most of their time at their father's house, which is twice the size of this one, of course, but he's the one in front of the cameras, so he's the cool and famous parent. I just help to make everyone famous."

"Is he dating anyone?"

"Dating? Miss Twenty-something has been living in his house for over a year now."

"Then why don't *you* date?"

"It's not like I'm trying not to. I'm just not attracted to most men I meet. I'm lonely, but I don't want to settle."

Returning with two glasses of red wine, Maura sat on the long black leather sofa that ran perpendicular to the glass wall, facing a large fireplace. Dyson took a few steps toward the piano but was quickly beckoned back by Maura.

"Come sit here next to me and have a drink to relax. Don't worry. I won't bite. Not at first, anyway."

D.D. sat down before accepting the drink. "Cheers!"

"To much success with this new film, your music, and us."

"So tell me what the film is about," begged Dyson, while sitting along the edge of the sofa before he took a sip from his wine glass.

"In a nutshell, the story follows the life of seven animals, with each one of them teaching humans a different lesson. The premise is that animals, collectively, are god. No need to look any further than our furry, feathered, skinned or scaled friends."

"That sounds like an interesting thought-provoking tale."

"Tale? It sounds more like truth, and YOU will provide the sound of the main song for the film."

"Sounds like a fun project! Can you provide me with a script? I can write a song around it."

"I already have the song picked out."

"You want me to record a cover of someone else's song?"

"No, D.D., I want you to re-record one of your songs, but with some changes. 'Animals and People under God Above' will now be titled 'Animals and Humans are the Light and Love'. I have already drafted up the lyric changes within the song to reflect the belief that humans invented god while animals were in peaceful control the entire time."

"I'm not sure that I can agree to that. I could write an entirely new song for the film in no time," Dyson asserted.

"Is that your imaginary friend speaking for you? As a matter of fact, wherever you use the word God, Christ, or Jesus, you will substitute those with Love and Light"

"It's just that-"

"It's just that this contract expires at midnight, and if it remains unsigned I will need to move on to the next songwriter," Maura explained, before reaching into her black cloak and pulling out a scroll. Handing it to D.D., she said, "Look this over, and then sign it with the raven feather, freshly dipped into the inkwell on the book pedestal."

"Where The Bible is?"

"Where the burnt fairytale ends, sweetie," she said in a condescending tone, just as she rose and walked over to the stand. Opening the lid on the ink well, she looked-in at the scarlet mixture inside then bent over to sniff it. "Mmmm," she purred, stirring the reddish-brown clots that congealed along the side of the vintage bottle with the tip of the feather. Maura licked the tip clean, then held it out with two fingers for D.D. to take.

"I really should read over this contract well before signing it," Dyson pronounced, as his mind raced.

Maura closed the lid and placed the feather on top of the burnt Bible. "Fair enough," she sighed. "Do you like seafood?"

"I LOVE seafood."

"Good. You fly, I'll buy," she said, as she gulped the last of her wine and grabbed her pocketbook that hung from the peak of a marble pyramid near the mansion's front entrance.

Dyson pulled his rental car into a seaside parking lot that sat in front of a restaurant built on pilings, hovering several feel above the ocean water that flowed freely beneath it. He followed Maura up several stairs to the fancy eatery's entrance. The Maître D' catered to her as soon as she walked in.

"Maura Pheme! Looking devilishly ravishing as always," she gushed. "Follow me. You are just in time for sunset!"

Maura and D.D. followed the Maître D', passing a woman striking a golden harp on their way to a window table that faced west, overlooking the ocean. The Maître D' sliced a fresh lemon as they sat down, and then poured two waters before handing them each a leather-bound menu, embossed with the Greek god of the sea, Poseidon.

"The woman playing the harp reminds me of the statue in your driveway. They are almost identically dressed," Dyson mentioned. "What did you say her name was?"

"D.D., the sun is setting, and you only have until midnight. Why are you so hell-bent about keeping your imaginary friend in the picture?

"It's just that Christ has been a big part of my life, throughout it all. I feel that I should remain faithful and keep him in it."

"God is in ALL of it. Your life, your thoughts, your heart, blah-blah-blah, your rental car, your fork, plate and napkin, all of the grains of sand out there on the beach, AND the pile of dog poop that was deposited on top of it, until the waves, also containing god, wash it all away."

Dyson looked out at the approaching tide, "But I do believe that God-"

"What you should believe in is the contract being offered to you, which will revive your career and bring you riches that you can't even imagine yet."

"I know, I know, I will," he assured, so as to not lose Maura's interest in him. "I just need to work through my thoughts and vindicate my conscience first. God knows I could use the money."

"Who knows?"

"My imaginary friend?"

"Good!" Maura said enthusiastically. "You're almost there."

Suddenly there was a flash of green and the sun dipped below the sea's horizon.

An hour later, D.D. and Maura were driving north on the freeway that ran along the coast. There were less and less lights dotting the landscape with each mile they drove. Maura eventually instructed D.D. to pull-off onto a hilly and isolated dirt road.

"I'm pretty sure that this rental isn't rated for four-wheeling," Dyson joked, as he navigated the sedan around road erosion and boulders. "How far in is this party, anyway?"

"Just around the next bend," she replied, just as a huge bonfire became visible. "There!"

Dyson parked the car in a clearing, alongside a Bentley and a Maserati. As they walked, he could see that a few dozen people were embraced in a hand-held circle around the blazing fire, many dressed in fancy suits, while others appeared to be wearing burlap rags. As they got closer, D.D. couldn't quite make out the words of what sounded like a chant. The circle of arms reached up to the full moon overhead before the celebrants dispersed to various areas of the isolated, yet sprawling moonlit land. Maura led the way to a Tiki-bar that was surrounded by torches.

"Maura Pheme!" said the bartender, announcing the popular filmmaker's arrival. "A Devil's Door Autumn Ale?"

"Make that two, Zagan!" Maura ordered. "Hey, meet our new friend, D.D. Divine."

Zagan reached out and shook D.D.'s hand. "Nice to make your acquaintance."

"Likewise," replied Dyson. "Wow, that's quite the ring on your hand."

"The all-seeing eye. Thirteen diamonds, with a bloodstone for the pupil. There are only two like it in the, well, in this world anyway."

"It's very striking."

"If jewelry is your thing, I'm sure you'll be able to afford plenty of your own custom pieces to serve the master, now that you're one of us."

"Soon," Maura chimed in.

The fire grew ever higher, forcing the revelers to retract from it. Several people gathered in front of a large stage and a group of musicians appeared and began to perform.

"Wow, they sound great!" D.D. exclaimed, while watching in awe.

"I'm glad that you like them, because they may very well be your touring band members soon. This is where all of the musicians at the top of the food chain get their practice in, every full moon."

"So, all of these people come here to play and listen every full moon?"

"That's not the main reason, but yes, there are always musicians offering up their talents on the altar of the stage."

"Mmmm, I smell barbeque," Dyson observed, while surveying the grounds. "Where are the grills?"

"Oh, here comes the host," said Maura, ignoring his question. "He doesn't like to give his name to newbies, so don't feel bad if the introduction is lacking or awkward."

At that point, D.D. expected to meet a sorcerer-looking character. As he was looking beyond and trying to guess whom the host would be, an unassuming character stepped into the forefront of his vision.

"Welcome," the host said, simply. "Are you enjoying your time here so far?"

The host had an ordinary appearance, like he could have been any middle-aged person that Dyson might pass by in a supermarket or in a park, without giving that person a second thought or look.

"Oh, hi," Dyson replied. "I'm D.D. Divine. Thanks for having me, man. What a great party!"

"I know who you are, and I know your producer. It's a small world, and now that you are here, you can make a much bigger mark on it." The host turned around at the sound of a gong. Women in long black flowing dresses carrying several goblets on trays came from behind a huge tapestry that was tied between two trees. A flickering orange glow came from behind it. "Maura, make sure that D.D. gets a goblet."

"Not just yet," she responded.

"Oh?" the host responded, tilting his head and tapping his watch while raising one eyebrow in Maura's direction.

"We're almost there, sir," she said, taking D.D.'s hand and walking away.

"What was that all about?" Dyson inquired. "I feel rude to the host just walking away like that."

"And I'm feeling aroused, all of a sudden. Let's head back to my place."

Navigating his rental car back up the winding roads that lead to Maura Pheme's mansion, Dyson appreciated that he had made the challenging drive once in the daylight, so he knew where some of the more harrowing curves were located. He felt Maura's hand land on the top of his leg and migrate up to his crotch. Where he could, he sped the car up in anticipation until he reached Maura's mansion. Surprised that the gate was already open, he quickly parked the car and followed her as she dashed to the front door, opening it for D.D., and leaving it that way once he walked in. Passing him in the foyer area, he followed her down a long hall until Maura stopped in the doorway of her bedroom. She pulled him up against herself, giving him a kiss on his neck before stroking her hand once down his back, and then feeling around to his crotch again.

In a breathy voice, she asked, "Where is the contract?"

"Right here," he proudly said, pulling it out from his inside pocket. "I already signed it, when you went to the ladies room at the restaurant."

"No, you need to sign it with the bl-, um, ink and feather that are in my foyer." Maura looked over at a pendulum clock in the corner of her bedroom. Three minutes until midnight. "HURRY UP!"

Dyson watched for a second as Maura began to unbutton her shirt. He quickly darted back down the hall toward the foyer. Maura walked over to a window, flew it open, then sent her shirt sailing into the midnight breeze. Topless, she turned around and saw Dyson holding up the contract. A drip of red fell from his signature onto the metal cross on his bootstrap.

"Bring the contract to me," she ordered, while laying a frame atop her bed. Her bedroom walls were over-populated with framed contracts, but Dyson didn't notice. He couldn't take his eyes off of her breasts as he handed it over to her. "Now, leave one of your boots here by the bed, and leave the one with the bootstrap outside the bedroom."

Dyson hurried to get his boots off, unbalanced and stumbling a little as he followed Maura's instructions. He placed the one boot outside the doorway then returned to her. Somehow, she had already framed the contract and was holding two crystal goblets, each containing a sip or two of what looked like the ink that he just signed

90

it with. Excited to get on with the intimacy, Dyson held his glass out to clink it against Maura's. A strong breeze blew into the room, slamming the door shut. Maura smashed her crystal goblet into D.D. Divine's.

SLAM! CRASH!

Mr. Dyson woke up, startled by the music room door slamming closed and his framed Music Teacher Certificate falling off the wall, with its glass shattering all over the floor behind his chair. He looked at the certificate among the glass shards near his feet. The document was ripped from the broken frame. He hadn't previously realized that his name was printed on it twice. Recalling his dream, he slowly lifted his head and was quickly spooked by finding Mother Madre standing in front of him, holding out a crystal goblet of water for him to accept.

"Wet your whistle with this, instead, Mr. Dyson."

"Wait, how-"

"This is p-p-pure, Mr. Dyson," she insured, while nodding once and extending her reach with the goblet another inch. "MUCH b-b-better for your soul."

"But, I-"

"Your certificate. We won't worry about fixing and rehanging it. I believe that it is time for you to work toward a tenure certificate."

"Tenure? The contract that never ends? What an amazing opportunity!"

"It will take lots of effort on your part," she began to explain, while pulling a parchment paper scroll out from her satchel. "Fairly often, I will hand to you a scroll like I am now. Each will have either a future conversation or a concept printed onto it."

"Future conversation?"

"What you will need to do is compose a song to reflect the printed sentiment, and write the lyrics of your song on the opposite side of the scroll, with a pure white dove feather dipped in majestic blue ink."

"Where would one find a pure white dove feather, Motherrrr-"

"Madre. Mother Madre. Oh, of course," as she pulled from her satchel the largest dove feather Mr. Dyson had ever seen, before walking toward a book pedestal in the corner of the room. "The ink is here, near The Bible."

"I hadn't even realized that there was a Bi-"

"There is a Bible in every classroom at St. Perpetua Academy, Mr. Dyson. It is the f-f-f-f-foundation of all learning, regardless of the subject, including music. *Especially* music!" Mother Madre continued, "Each song must catch the essence of its scroll's sentimentality, with a high focus on empathy. If you don't feel it while you write and sing it, I mean *really* feel it, I won't accept it."

"Well, that's the only way to write, right? To really feel and believe in it!"

"Hmmm," she responded, tapping her chin with her pointer finger. "It seems to me that a certain writer might have gone against their beliefs somewhere along the page."

Mr. Dyson stared blankly.

"I'll need this first one rather quickly," she instructed, "and will alert you just before you are to perform it."

"Perform it? Where?

"On the Hall of Truths stage."

"That's a huge hall. It will take an awful lot of marketing to fill it up."

"Mr. Dyson, this isn't about how many souls you can squeeze into a room. What matters is the quality of the service you deliver, even if to one person.

"Well, it's not like I'll be performing any concert just for one person."

"One person can experience the right message and carry that on to so many more souls than a thousand Hall of Truths could ever fit."

"But, I'm not actually going to-"

"You will earn your tenure certificate by performing for whoever is in front of you. And, Mr. Dyson, make sure that your lyrics reflect YOUR b-b-beliefs."

Mr. Dyson unrolled the scroll as Mother Madre had an unnoticed glide to the top of the music room's crescendo-designed platforms. She looked back at the music teacher, waving her hand like an orchestra conductor before opening the door. "Don't worry about the broken glass behind your desk. I'll have Mr. Karcin take care of it," she nonchalantly said, before floating down the hallway, humming along the way.

CHAPTER 6

"Miss Kylee! Welcome!"

Tarry Kylee turned around, disheveled, focusing-in on Mother Madre.

"It's great to have you onboard as our PTO President, Tarry. How is the planning going for the next meeting?"

"Oh, yes, all is well."

"I haven't seen the meeting flyer in my mailbox yet. Have I missed it?"

"No. No, I just wanted to make sure they were perfect. They look really good, so they'll be distributed soon."

"Fantastic. May I take a peek at one?" Mother Madre asked while pausing at Miss Kylee's PTO office door.

Tarry sat behind her desk and then opened a file drawer, but closed it a second later. "Well, they aren't actually printed just yet. I have the final design in my head."

"Then, what were you just looking for if you knew there was nothing tangible for me to see?"

"C'mon, I-"

"Miss Kylee, deception is not tolerated here at St. Perpetua. Nor is laziness. Nobody likes a sloth, do you understand?"

"Yes, Mmmm-"

"Mother Madre"

"Yes, Mother Madre. Is there something that you'd like me to do right away?"

"Yes, Tarry. In your head, near the flyer design for the next PTO meeting, is the most recent dream that you had. Can you remember?"

Tarry Kylee made a sudden face of shock. "Oh my! Yes."

Mother Madre turned around and locked Tarry's door. She then took two steps toward her, paused for a moment pondering, then finally said "Look, Tarry, I'm going to give it to you straight. Only truth passes on from here."

"Passes on? I'm a little bit confu-"

"Tell me what you remember from your dream, as you honestly recall," Mother Madre instructed, while unfolding the screen that she pulled from her satchel.

"I remember sitting in my car at the end of someone's driveway, waiting for him to return."

"From?"

"Just somewhere."

"You don't know?"

"Not really, just from wherever."

Mother Madre shifted her fingers across her screen. The glow reflecting off of her face changed color. "In your dream, what were you drinking?"

"How would you even-"

"Not only what you were drinking while sitting in the driveway, but even before that. This is THAT serious now."

"So, in my dream, I had vodka in my water bottle. I thought that was weird myself."

The glow on Mother Madre's face changed again. "No. You didn't," she sternly stated. "Even in your dream, that felt like the norm to you."

"Honestly, Mother Ma-"

"Do we need to have this conversation in the Hall of Truths?"

Miss Kylee just remained there in silence.

"You know yourself, even in a dream, that drinking like that and driving could result in a very bad accident, and in your dream, it did."

"But, the other car crossed the center line and crashed into *me*," Tarry pleaded.

"That doesn't erase the fact that you were in the wrong, and that had you done the right thing, you wouldn't have been on the road at all, and that accident would not have happened. You need to learn how to take r-r-r-responsibility"

"It seemed so real."

"What seemed so real?" Mother Madre asked.

Miss Kylee paused for several seconds. "I'm sorry," she said, furling her brow. "What were we just talking about?"

"The PTO meeting. I look forward to it."

Tarry politely smiled and pretended to reach for her schedule planner when she nudged her open bottle onto a shelf, spilling into an open container of glue powder before both items landed together and splattered all over her office floor.

"And, Miss Kylee, that was unnecessary. All lies become flushed, and all fluids become pure here."

Tarry walked over to the paper towel dispenser.

"Please. Work on f-f-fixing you, Miss Kylee. I'll get Mr. Karcin to clean up the mess."

Mother Madre unlocked and opened Miss Kylee's office door. Shouting could be heard from one of the classrooms. Tucking her satchel under an arm, Mother Madre made her way toward the screaming.

Dan Connor stood in the front of his class, red-faced. The business teacher didn't realize that Mother Madre was standing in his doorway as he lectured and scolded his students. Pacing between student desks like a tyrant, Mr. Connor was merciless. "You call this a business plan?" he bellowed, while ripping a report from a student's hand. "No S.W.O.T. analysis? No financial forecast? Know what this is?" Mr. Connor tore the report into several shreds of paper and threw it at the student. "This is GARBAGE!"

"Mr. Connor?" Mother Madre tried.

"You are FIRED from this class."

"Fired?" the young student questioned.

"Just GET OUT!"

The student just sat there for a few seconds, baffled.

"NOW!" yelled Mr. Connor.

Mother Madre entered the room, which changed Dan Connor's demeanor instantly.

"Oh, hello, um-"

"Mother Madre"

"We were doing a mock heated boardroom meeting," Mr. Connor said.

"No we weren't," one of the students toward the back could be heard saying.

"Your face is beet-red, Mr. Connor. I suggest that you come with me to the nurses office."

"I'll be alright, Mother Ma-"

"I insist," said Mother Madre, sternly, before doing an about-face then a quick march, forcing Mr. Connor to accelerate his movement in effort to catch up with her down the long hallway.

"Hey! No running up and down the halls!" Officer Williams shouted from behind his desk.

"Chill out," responded Mr. Connor, dryly.

Mother Madre gave a displeased glance directed at each of them, individually, just as she arrived at the nurse's office door. She faced Mr. Connor as he walked the last seven or so feet toward the nurse's room, making him most uncomfortable and self-conscience. "Just like a well-written business plan, you should be displaying a sense of n-n-knowledge and confidence right now, shouldn't you, Mr. Connor? Isn't that what you expect and demand from your young students?"

Dan Connor walked past her without making eye contact, as he entered the room. St. Perpetua's school nurse was standing behind a table that had on it a dozen white eggs in an egg crate, and a large empty bowl.

"The eggs are chilled to the perfect temperature, just as you instructed, Mother Madre. Are you sure that he won't need a few pills, too? His face looks awful red," the nurse asked.

"JUST the eggs, Miss Nostrum," Mother Madre responded with frustration in her voice. "Thank you. Go ahead and take your break

98

now. Oh, and please bring an egg to Dr. Nihil in the science lab so he can try to explain how the big bang formed it perfectly."

Mother Madres waited for the nurse to leave the room before taking her place behind the table. She began talking while inspecting each egg individually by holding them up to the light as she spoke.

"Please take a seat Mr. Connor."

"Honestly, I feel-"

"Any effective teacher, leader, parent-"

"But, I-"

"BUSINESS Manager," Mother Madres waited a beat to make sure that Dan wouldn't again interrupt before continuing, "needs to have a great deal of p-p-patience and understanding in order to be effective." She set the last inspected egg back into the egg crate carefully and then set her satchel on top of the table. She moved her hands around, inside of it, haphazardly, then pulled out a long and sharp needle that seemed to glisten even in the lowly lit nurse's room. "This little exercise is geared to help build that level of patience, Mr. Connor. What you are to do is pierce each end of the egg once, without breaking it, then stick the pin back into this pincushion."

"Oh, I can do that," Dan confidently said, as he began to reach for the crate of eggs.

"NOT so fast, Mr. Connor," she scolded, while landing her hand in front of the eggs just as his hand was getting there, resulting in Mr. Connor hitting her arm accidentally.

"I'm sorry-"

"I'm done here, unless you are willing to l-l-listen to all instructions so you may actually u-u-understand, and THEN execute, just like you expect your students to," she stated clearly.

"Yes, ma'am."

"Good." Mother Madre continued, "You will then take an egg and hold your mouth on one end, blowing through it so that the yolk and cytoplasm gets pushed out the other end into the bowl, again without the egg breaking. This will represent you evacuating the rage from yourself and replacing it with patience before you, yourself, crack, Mr. Connor."

Dan Connor sat without moving.

"You can begin now," she instructed.

Mr. Connor took an egg and stood over the bowl, blowing into one end of the egg. His face got even redder, and then he eventually stopped to catch his breath, turning the egg around to find that only a tiny balloon of material had begun to come out of the egg. "Wow, is there a trick to this?" he asked, in-between breaths.

"Yes, Mr. Connor," Mother Madre said assertively. "Patience. And from that patience will come the knowledge of technique, making each sequential egg easier than the one before it. Just be careful regarding complacency as you work your way deeper into the crate of eggs, so to speak."

He got to work, leaving unbroken empty shell after another until he got to the eighth egg. He stuck the gleaming pin back into the pincushion and looked up at Mother Madre, who was displaying much patience of her own. "I'm sorry, but I'll need to rest before continuing, Mother Madre."

"That's quite alright, Mr. Connor. Go ahead and put your head down on the desk for a while."

Connor Dander stood in the kitchen, eating the last piece of his four-year-old younger sister's birthday cake while he watched her ride her new tricycle around the driveway through the window. He knew that she'd most-likely want the piece of cake, but considering she got all sorts of new toys at her party a few days earlier, and he didn't, Connor felt justified in his unethical appetite. Well, that was up until he heard his mother close a door and walk toward the kitchen. He reached up and released the plate inside the sink. Although he was pretty sure that the crunching sound he heard upon impact probably wasn't a good thing, he swung open the kitchen's screen door and joined his sister in the driveway.

"Let me try your tricycle. I'll show you how to do a figure-eight."

"No."

"Come on, I'll give it right back," seven-year-old Connor insisted.

"No."

Connor grabbed one handlebar as his sister tried to ride past him, which caused a sudden tipping of the tricycle. She fell off of it and sat on the pavement crying while Connor stood on the back step of the small bike, pushing off with his feet while balancing himself and steering with the handlebars. A mailman walked up the driveway to place some envelopes in the box near the screen door.

"Why are you crying little girl?" the mailman asked.

"Her name isn't little girl, her name is Lisa, you stupid jerk!" Connor wisecracked.

"Well, that wasn't very nice," the mailman responded, while Connor's sister ran inside to tell her mother what happened.

A few minutes later, Connor was sitting at his kitchen table, scared and crying because the police were on their way to pick him up for what he had done. Well, that's what his mother had him believe when she fake-dialed the phone to call the Hope Police Station.

"I promise to be good," Connor pleaded. "I promise! Lisa can have my Easter basket on Sunday."

"That's if you even *get* an Easter basket," Connor's older sister said as she walked into the kitchen. "You know that he can see everything, right?"

"How can he see everything?" Connor asked.

"Come with me," she replied, taking Connor's hand and leading him to the large window in the living room. "See that small house in the woods at the end of the street? That is where the Easter Bunny lives. He just saw everything."

"How do you know?"

"Mom, doesn't the Easter Bunny live at the end of the street?" she shouted.

"If you say so," came the faint answer from the kitchen.

"Wow," Conner said in amazement, as his tears started up again.

"Connor, get back in here," his mother shouted.

Returning to the kitchen, Connor listened as his mother fake-dialed back to the police department, explaining that she would give the young seven-year-old another chance. Relieved, Connor grabbed a napkin from the table and wiped his eyes.

"Hey! I was using that to dry the eggs," his younger sister exclaimed.

"Enough, you two!" exclaimed Mom, as she brought some dye to the table to dip the eggs into.

The next afternoon, Connor's mother dressed him in a bunny costume. "This doesn't fit your sister Janice anymore so it looks like you'll be passing out the eggs to the neighbors this year." It was a family tradition that went back as far as Connor's grandmother.

"I don't *want* to give out eggs. Why can't we just keep them?"

"Do you want me to call the police again?"

Connor felt a little embarrassed as he left the house with his mother. He wished his younger sister fit the suit, but she was inside taking a nap while his older sister babysat her. When he got to the edge of his driveway, he looked over toward the small house in the woods. "What if the Easter Bunny sees me taking his job?" he thought. His main goal was to give out all the eggs before he got to Kylee Tarry's house at the opposite end of the street. He had a crush on her and there was no way that he was going to let her see him wearing a rabbit costume.

The first house was Mr. Lucian's, and Connor was comfortable knocking on the door because he often helped the elderly man water his garden. When Mr. Lucian opened the door, he pretended that he didn't know who was in the bunny costume. Connor carefully reached into his basket and took out one of the fragile eggs, wishing the man a Happy Easter as he handed a blue one to him. Mr. Lucian asked Connor to wait a moment while he went to grab his wallet from his jacket. Connor looked back at his mother who was waiting on the street at the end of his driveway and raised his pointer finger, letting her know it will be another minute. When Mr. Lucian returned to the doorway, he handed young Connor a dollar bill, wishing him a Happy Easter back. Excited about the unexpected tip, he slipped the dollar into the rabbit costume's pocket and began to run to the next house.

"Don't run! You might break the eggs," his mother warned, as she strolled along the street to the next driveway.

Connor rang the doorbell, and then chose a pink egg for the middle-aged woman that came to the door. "Happy Easter," he said gleefully, while holding out the egg.

"Well, what a nice Easter surprise, Connor," the woman said, while taking the egg and waving to his mother at the end of the driveway. "Thank you."

Connor paused a moment after the woman closed the door, but she never came back with a tip. He eventually moved on to the next house. When that neighbor came to the door, Connor said, "Happy Easter. I have Easter Eggs, and they are a dollar apiece."

"Oh, ok, give me a moment to find my purse," she said.

Connor waved to his mother while he waited for the woman to return.

"I'll take two," she said, while giving Connor two dollars.

He slipped the money into the pocket that already had the dollar from Mr. Lucian, and then walked down the driveway to get around the hedges and to the next house. Dismayed that the boy didn't say thank you, the woman nodded toward Connor's mother before closing the door.

"How do they like your eggs, sweetie?" Connor's mother asked him.

"Good! Maybe we can make more when these are gone."

"I only have a few left in the refrigerator, and those are for your sister's lunch when she gets up from her nap."

When Connor got to the next house, he told the man who came to the door that he was selling Easter eggs, three for two dollars. The man informed him that he didn't have any cash on him so Connor walked away.

"Why didn't you give Mr. Owens an egg?" his mother asked.

"Maybe he's allergic."

"To eggs?

"I dunno."

A few houses later, Connor ran out of eggs. As his mother relieved his older sister of her babysitting duties and tended to his younger sister, Connor decided to go behind his mother's back and color the eggs that were in the fridge with a magic marker before convincing his older sister to accompany him to the houses that he hadn't visited on his first round as the Easter Bunny. The money that he would possibly make meant more to him than any consequences he might have faced from taking the last of the eggs. Plus, he thought, she didn't follow-through with the last punishment that she threatened him with. At age seven, Connor felt that he found his purpose in life – making money.

The next morning, Connor's aunt came by the house to pick up his mother to take her shopping at the local department store. It was an annual tradition that Connor's mother enjoyed with her sister every year on her birthday.

"Can you pick up a new sandbox truck for me?" Connor asked, while his mother and aunt sipped on tea in the kitchen.

"Whose birthday is it?" asked his aunt.

"Mom's, but can you, Mom?"

"You have enough toys that you don't even play with, Connor," his mother stated. "Plus, the Easter Bunny is coming this Sunday and I'm sure that he'll be bringing something fun for you."

"But-"

"The answer is no. Now go get dressed before the babysitter gets here," ordered his mother.

"Maybe you can draw a birthday card for your mother while we are out," his aunt suggested.

"I don't draw good."

"You're a great drawer, Connor!" his mother said, adding, "and a card from you would be my favorite birthday gift."

"Can you make a jug of lemonade before you leave?"

"We'll see. Go get dressed!"

Early that afternoon, the babysitter was trying to get Connor's little sister to take a nap. Connor convinced the sitter to allow him to take a TV-tray outside and set-up a lemonade stand at the end of the driveway, saying that it would be quieter in the house if he were outside. He had passed a lemonade stand a week or two earlier that some older kids had and thought that he could cash-in on the concept, too. He decided that he could make even more money by offering peanut butter sandwiches, too. Searching high and low in the cupboards, Connor found no peanut butter, but he did find peanuts and figured he would make his own to sell. In a bowl, he mashed two sticks of butter together with the peanuts. It looked gross to him, but he wasn't the one that had to eat it. He just had to convince others to do so. Pre-making the sandwiches would hide the makeshift filling, but he figured he wasn't lying. It truly was peanut butter, and he planned on making a buck or two by convincing others that it was the best in town. He took the lemonade that his mother had made earlier, some paper cups and plates, and he was in business.

An hour or so passed before any car made its way down the street, let alone stop. The only customer that he had was a walk-up by a kid that lived down the street who bought Connor's combo special – a lemonade and peanut butter sandwich for a buck. Twenty minutes later, the kid returned to complain about the worst sandwich he ever ate, demanding his money back. When Connor refused, the kid threw one of the magic-marker colored eggs that he sold to his mother the day before at him. It broke on Connor's chest and oozed down the front of his shirt. He never smelled anything so bad before in his life. He began to cry just as Mr. Steward pulled his car over to the side of the street.

"What's the matter, young fellow?" Mr. Steward asked, while reaching for his wallet. "Oh, I see," he added, while noticing the smelly egg matter all over his shirt. "Business isn't all that great today? Maybe I can help. Show me what you are selling."

Connor just continued to weep and wipe his eyes.

"Alright, so it looks like you are selling lemonade. You don't have any signs on your stand, so anyone driving by has to guess that you are selling it. There is no pricing listed either, so people may not stop because they don't understand how much money it will cost them if they do, so the first thing I would suggest is a sign that lists what, and how much. Does that make sense?"

Connor nodded his head.

"You also need to make sure that you have a product that people will want to buy. Here is a dollar. Can I try your lemonade?

Connor nodded again.

"I'm not sure how long it has been sitting out here in the sun, but the lemonade is warm. Most people will want cold lemonade."

"You paid a dollar, so you get a sandwich, too."

Mr. Steward picked up one of the two sandwiches that sat unprotected on top of the TV-tray and looked inside. "What kind of sandwich is this?"

"Peanut butter."

Chuckling, Mr. Steward replied, "I guess it is. The problem is that this peanut butter isn't in the usual form that most people would expect peanut butter to be in." He reached back into his wallet and handed Connor a twenty-dollar bill. "Here, consider this your first business loan. Next time that you go to the supermarket with your mother, pick up a large container of peanut butter, some bread, and sandwich bags to keep the sandwiches fresh, along with more lemonade mix and a large thermos to keep the lemonade cold."

"Wow! Thank you, mister!"

"Sure thing, young man. And one more thing - Pay attention to forecasting."

"Forecasting?"

"Trying to know how many people will have the chance to see your product, and how many of those people would be most apt to buy what you are selling."

A short time later, after Connor changed his shirt and made a lemonade sign with the cardboard that he was going to use for his mother's birthday card, he began to bring the items from his failed lemonade stand back inside the house. His neighborhood crush came walking down the street.

"Whatcha doin?" Kylee Tarry inquired.

"Just putting my lemonade stand away."

"A lemonade stand? I'm having a backyard carnival next week. Do you want to set it up there? My Dad made postcards that I'll be handing out in school. There will be lots of kids there!"

"Sure!"

The next time his mother went to the supermarket, Connor went, too, buying lemonade and peanut butter supplies for Kylee's backyard carnival with the twenty dollars that Mr. Steward gave to him. On the day of the carnival, Connor set his stand up in Kylee's backyard. He had made a more permanent sign for it, and even had a cooler to keep the sandwiches and extra container of lemonade inside of. At the same time, Kylee's mother was setting up a few games around the yard, along with helium balloons that she tied to the fence, while Kylee sat on the back porch and watched.

"What time does the carnival begin?" Connor asked after standing near his stand for a few hours.

"I forget," Kylee answered. "Let me go inside and check the postcards."

"How many of them did you end up handing out to kids at school?"

"I was busy doing other things, but I told a few people about it."

"Told a few? Like, how many?"

"I don't know. My friend Stacey said she'd come."

"One friend? I bought enough lemonade and made enough peanut butter sandwiched for like twenty-five people! Every time I asked you in school you said that lots of people were coming!"

"It's not MY fault. I got busy!"

"Busy doing WHAT?"

Kylee's mother shouted to Kylee from the kitchen window, "Stacey's Mom just called. She isn't feeling good so she won't be coming today."

"Stacey is a jerk!" Kylee exclaimed before ripping a balloon from the fence and popping it on a rose bush.

"At least she's not a lazy liar!"

Connor's crush on Kylee Tarry ended then and there. Using his wagon, he disappointingly spent the next hour bringing all of his supplies back to his house. It was the Town of Hope's spring-cleaning weekend, which meant that an extra garbage truck would be going through town that following Monday to take any large items that were placed at the curb. A year earlier, Connor found a cage in a neighbor's pile and convinced his mother to buy him a guinea pig from the pet store. Two years earlier, he found an old bicycle that served him well for that summer, until he bent the bike's handlebars on the day that he set up a ramp to jump his sandbox trucks. Not only did he ruin the bike, but ended up with five stitches in his chin. Connor made his way down the street with his wagon full of unsold lemonade and peanut butter sandwiches, but nothing that anyone kicked to the curb interested him. When he reached his house, he noticed a small television within the pile at the end of the dirt driveway that led to the Easter Bunny's house in the woods. He found it odd that the famous rabbit would have a pile at the end of his driveway that included a TV set. Once he unloaded his unsold goods from his wagon, he made his way diagonally across the street. In addition to snagging the small television, Connor also took a canvas painting of a boy that looked like someone in his school.

That night, his older sister was complaining that her mother always got control of the television, and how she never watched the shows that the kids of the house wanted to watch. Connor got an idea. He set the TV on his desk and turned it on. Frustrated that only static came onto the screen, he went from channel to channel until he finally found a station that offered reception on the small screen. He grabbed the television guide from the living room so he could find out which movies were going to be broadcast over that station during the next week.

The next day, he handed his older sister a "movie guide" of films being shown on his television every night at eight-o'clock. If she wished to watch a film, it would cost her a quarter, or she could purchase a five-night admission pin for a dollar.

"These are pretty good movies. I'll take the five night special, but I'll need to pay you tonight."

"Just pin this to your pajamas and be at the door of my room at least five minutes before the movie begins," instructed Connor.

At 7:53, Connor started to walk up and down the small hallway of the house, announcing that it was almost movie time. His younger sister Lisa came out of her room and said that she wanted to see the movie, too.

"You don't have any money to get in," Connor explained.

"I'll ask Mom."

Standing outside of his closed bedroom doorway, Connor welcomed his older sister, who handed him a dollar. "Where's your pin?" he asked.

"I forgot to wear it."

"Hurry up and get it or you don't get in."

"What if I can't find it?"

"You'd need to buy another one."

"Give me a break. I'm sure it's in my room."

As she walked away to get it, Lisa returned. "Mom would only give me ten cents."

"Nope. Twenty-Five," Connor insisted, maintaining his post in front of his door while his young sister returned to her mother and back again.

"She said no."

"Then you can't get in."

"Mom, Connor won't let-"

"SHHH!" Making sure that there was no reaction from his mother, Connor urged his four-year-old sister to sneak into the kitchen and quietly take a dollar from her pocketbook. "You'll be able to get in to see the movie all week. Do it quietly."

Returning with her pin, his older sister took a seat on Connor's bed and took a bag of cookies out of her pocket while the television warmed up.

"No way," Connor said, grabbing the bag of cookies out of her hand. "No eating in here."

"That's stupid, Connor. Give me my cookies."

"No. It's a rule."

"Then give me my money back."

"No. That's another rule. No refunds."

"You're a jerk!" she yelled, while almost running into Mom on the way out of Connor's room.

"I just sent your sister Lisa to bed for stealing," his angry mother said in a calmer-than-expected manner while ripping the television's plug from the wall forcefully and cradling the TV under an arm while pointing at Connor with the other one. "And YOU are going to bed RIGHT now with NO television for a WEEK!"

She turned off Connor's bedroom light and closed the door. In pitch-black, he felt around for the edge of his bed. He sat on it and reached for his pillow. The movie pin that his sister left on his bed pierced his hand.

"OWWWW!"

"OWWWW!" shouted Dan Conner. The bowl of egg matter flew across his shirt and all over the floor when Mr. Connor jerked his hand back after placing it on the glistening pin while he slept. "Whoa, now *that'll* wake ya up!" he said, while watching the egg yolk migrate down the front of his shirt.

"That must have been some dream," Mother Madre said while handing him a paper towel. "Don't worry about the mess on the floor," she added, while touching the transparent screen that was already set up in front of her. "Tell me about your dream, Mr. Connor."

"It was interesting," he began. "I was just a child, and in the dream I had a few sisters and a mother. It must have been Easter time because I was wearing an Easter Bunny costume and handing out-"

"You mean selling? Eggs?"

"Well, I-"

"As an adult, what do you *now* think about selling the eggs?"

"Pretty funny. What a little entrepreneur," Mr. Connor said with an added chuckle. "Bound for beautiful beaches and pretty ladies!"

"It's not your fault that the elders in your dream turned the resurrection of Jesus Christ into a pagan holiday, but I do consider how quickly your young mind was lured by money to be very disturbing."

"How do you-"

"How do you think your mother would have felt if she found out that you were selling eggs to your neighbors while she stood at the end of each driveway, believing that you were giving them away as a nice gesture?"

"She would've-"

"With several jobs to keep a roof over the heads of you and your sisters, your hard-working mother would have been embarrassed to know that those neighbors must have thought that she was having her son peddle eggs for money. Reputations are very important, Mr. Connor, and it is very easy for a person to ruin another's."

"But, it was only a dollar or two."

"You were willing to taint your mother's reputation for a dollar or two? What about the health of your baby sister?"

"What do you mean?"

"You knew that your mother was going to feed her with the eggs that remained in the refrigerator, yet you couldn't fight off the temptation of making a few more dollars at the expense of your sister's meal. Not only did you cheat your sister and mother, but also your so-called customers that ended up buying a much lower-quality product due to your instant greed and deception."

113

"Lower quality?"

"Did you empty the contents of the eggs? Did you take time to dye them properly?"

"I colored them."

"Properly?"

"Yes."

"Do we need to have this discussion in the Hall of Truths?"

"No, ma'am."

"At what point does a relationship mean more to you than money, Mr. Connor?"

"Relationships mean more."

"Yet, you would not only steal from your own mother, but corrupt your younger sister to adopt your ways?"

"But it was only a dollar."

"You just made my point, Mr. Connor. Money, like a few other things, is at the r-r-r-root of all evil. All it takes to damage a weak soul is a single dollar, if desperate enough, or worse, greedy enough."

"I understand, Mother Madre."

Mother Madre glanced a finger across the screen in front of her, and the hue of her face changed. An announcement came over the school speakers, "Mr. Dyson, please report to The Hall of Truths for a performance."

"Come with me, Mr. Connor."

Mother Madre entered The Hall of Truths first, walking the many steps to the end of the long table that was closest to the stage. Mr. Connor hadn't actually been inside The Hall of Truths before, and in amazement, stared around the room with his mouth agape. He couldn't imagine that such a large hall would actually fit inside the walls of St. Perpetua, although, for some reason, he couldn't remember what the academy looked like from the outside to begin with. Strange.

"Sit here, Mr. Connor," Mother Madre ordered, while turning the end chair such that it faced the stage. "I'll be right back."

The stage curtain opened as Dan Connor took his assigned seat. Music teacher, Mr. Dyson, was onstage with a single spotlight on him. Dan looked back around the cavernous space and wondered what was happening. Mr. Dyson seemed to wonder the same.

"Is this a joke?" Dyson asked out loud from the stage.

Mother Madre's voice came from the dark far corner of the hall, "Only if achieving t-t-tenure is a joke to you."

Dyson looked down at Mr. Connor from the stage, then back over to the scroll on his music stand before he began to perform:

CORRUPTION

MONEY
WILL MAKE YOU SELFISH
IT WILL CORRUPT YOU
WHEN YOU GET RICH
YOU MIGHT DO COCAINE
OR DRIVE A SPORTS CAR
YOU'RE NEVER HAPPY
SO DID YOU GO FAR?
TROPIC PLACES AND PRETTY FACES
PLASTIC POINTS OF VIEW
ALL YOUR THOUGHTS ARE MATERIAL
AND THINGS YOU'LL NEVER – THINGS YOU'LL NEVER DO
IT'S SUCH A FOOLISH GAME
BECAUSE NOTHING STAYS THE SAME
A FORTUNE MADE IN VAIN

UNTIL DUST BECOMES YOUR NAME
POWER
WILL MAKE YOU GREEDY
EVERYONE WANTS SOME
IT'S NEVER EASY
THEN YOU'RE GREEDY
WITH YOUR POWER
DESTROY YOUR FAMILY
WITHIN AN HOUR
TROPIC PLACES AND PRETTY FACES
PLASTIC POINTS OF VIEW
ALL YOUR THOUGHTS ARE MATERIAL
AND THINGS YOU'LL NEVER – THINGS YOU'LL NEVER DO
IT'S SUCH A FOOLISH GAME
BECAUSE NOTHING STAYS THE SAME
THE RISE AND FALL OF FAME
UNTIL DUST BECOMES YOUR NAME

"That was quite a performance, Mr. Dyson," Dan said, after offering a couple of handclaps. "A little judgmental."

"What do you mean? It's not like the song's about you."

"You could've fooled me."

"Look, I was given a scroll with a conversation written on it, and my assignment was to write a song about it."

"Seems to me that you were listening in on my conversation with"

"I wasn't listening in on any-"

"Gentlemen!" interrupted Mother Madre, as she walked toward them. "I think that song reflects a little of each or us, doesn't it? Nice job, Mr. Dyson."

"Mother Madre, I can't perform again to only one-"

"You will," she responded. "And as for you, Mr. Connor, please follow me."

The two walked down the hall, back toward the nurse's office. Connor opened the scroll and re-read the words that Mr. Dyson had just sang to him. "I'm really confused about what is happening, Mother Madre."

"Things will become more clear as we go along, Mr. Connor. Let's go back to your dream. Do you recall a man pulling up to your lemonade stand and teaching you some basics about how to market and run your new business?"

"Yes. Yes, I do remember that."

"Did he yell at you?"

"No, I don't believe that he did."

"And did you hear his advice?"

"I did."

"That's because he wasn't yelling or scolding. You were more receptive to his words than you would have been had he been screaming at you. Did you do as the man said?"

"I did, but little good it did. I lost everything when nobody went to the backyard carnival."

"So, you didn't do what the man said, then. You didn't forecast how many potential buyers would have been there."

"But the girl told me lots of kids were to be there."

"How many is *lots*? 10? 5? 50?"

"I don't know, I just guessed."

117

"Did you ask around at school to get an idea who was going, if anyone?"

"No."

"You just trusted some young lazy girl?"

"Well, I didn't know that she was lazy. I was young in the dream, too. Why are you getting down on me like this?"

"To prove a point, Mr. Connor. All of your students here at St. Perpetua Academy are young to the subject matter that you are teaching them. All that I hear coming from your classroom is lots of yelling by you. Do you see where I am going with this?"

"Yes, Mother Madre."

She led Mr. Connor back into the nurse's office. "You may take the eggs that you haven't emptied yet and finish them in your classroom. Try to get them done before you face your next students."

Feeling one of his feet lose traction on the floor's surface, Mr. Connor looked down at the splatter of raw egg that he was standing on. "Should I mop the eggs off the floor first?"

"I will call on Mr. Karcin to clean it up."

CHAPTER 7

Karcin Bane was halfway done his shift at the Hope Metal Badge & Button Company when Claire Auger entered into his boiler-room domain with her Ouija board and tarot cards. She was one of a string of girls at the factory that he was able to manipulate into having casual sex with him on a regular basis, even though they used to hang out together as kids. Claire was Karcin's girl of choice that week because he was having a hard time dealing with the death of his best friend at the factory, and she had a side-business as a medium. If only he was able to talk to Willy one more time. He figured that Claire's supposed soothsayer abilities were at least worth a try.

"Hi sexy!" Claire said, while placing her things on top of a large wooden wire-spool that Karcin used as a table.

Karcin had a reputation as a rough boy at the factory, with a motorcycle for transportation, an arm-sleeve of tattoos, several piercings, and a 'don't-take-crap-from-anyone' attitude. His muscular upper body and chiseled facial structure made him irresistible to the women there. Grunting, he benched the barbell two more times before Claire walked over and rubbed his crotch. He groaned irritably while returning it to the support bars on his weightlifting bench. "I freaking told you not to touch me when I have weights in my hands!" He sat up and grabbed Claire, forcing her legs to cradle him on the bench.

"Hmm, it seems like your hard body is getting even harder," she said, while lifting herself above him just enough to unzip his pants. While he wiggled them off, she did the same with hers and returned over Karcin, placing her hands on the suspended bar of weights like they were motorcycle handle bars. She lowered herself onto him. "Ohhh, Yes!" she bellowed loudly, while giving her legs a squatting workout of her own. "Do you like it, baby?"

Karcin continued to grunt until he let out one long moan. He lifted Claire off himself and began to maneuver his legs away from her.

"I'm not done, baby, work me," she begged, but Karcin wanted nothing to do with pleasuring her as he made his way to a draw in his desk, extracting a yellowed hand towel. He wiped himself before flinging the towel in Claire's direction.

"In-case you need to wipe yourself," he said, while standing over the obituary of his friend that was printed in the newspaper that sat on top of his desk. He was familiar with a few of the people that made the obit-section of the paper that week, including Hope's mayor and D.D. Divine, but the death of his friend sent him for a loop.

"You only get a pass because you are grieving," Claire said, "but next time you better make me come twice."

After re-buttoning his pants, Karcin placed his friend's obituary in the desk's top draw and then bent over to kiss Claire's forehead. "Just get me in touch with Willy and I'll do whatever you want."

"What about seeing me exclusively, Karcin? Your other floozies are nothing but sluts with very little to offer. I can hand you a future on a platter, or at least on a Ouija board."

"You know I can't be tied down, Claire. That don't work for me."

"Well, I don't know how much longer I can put up with you screwing other women. It doesn't make me feel very special."

"We can talk about it later. Let's talk to Willy now."

"I've only got twenty-five minutes left of my lunch before I need to punch back in. Maybe you should come to my place after work so I can be at the table I use for readings. We'll be able to talk to him longer," she suggested, while looking at the magazine pages of naked girls that Karcin pinned to a large bulletin board. He hung it in a back alcove where he kept his foldout cot for entertaining his female visitors. "What time are you getting out today?"

"The night maintenance guy is on vacation this week, so I'm hoping to get in some overtime. I could be there around seven or eight?"

"I have a reading booked for someone at eight. Be there by seven or forget it."

"I'll be there."

"If you can get there for six you'll be able to finish what you started," she suggested, while taking Karcin's hand and rubbing it against her still exposed erogenous zone.

"I need the money," he selfishly replied, before pulling his hand away from her and picking up a 5-gallon metal container full of overused mill oil. "I'll be right back," he added, before opening the overhead door to the loading dock.

"What the hell?" shouted Claire, as the outside light hit her eyes. "I'm still half-naked!"

"Chill-out. Nobody comes back here."

"Except your other little friends-with-benefits. Shut it!"

Karcin returned a few minutes later and washed his hands in the industrial sink while Claire ate a sandwich, sitting at his desk and reading Willy's obituary. "What's in the metal drum?" she asked.

"What *was* in the metal drum? Mill oil."

"What did you do with the oil? Is there some sort of large vat out back that you pour it into?"

"Yes, it's called The Black Bank."

"River?"

"Last time I checked."

"You dump oil into the river?"

"Not just oil, and it's not my call."

"That's really bad!"

"Just doing my job, the same way it's been done for the past century or two."

"No wonder why it smells so bad around here."

"Relax. It's not like anyone goes fishing in the Black Bank River, anyway."

"Nobody could if they wanted to!" Claire declared, as she got up from Karcin's seat. "Well, back to work for me. Remember, seven the latest. Six if you feel horny enough to do me again, but longer this time."

Once Claire left, Karcin sat at his desk, returned his friend's obituary to the top drawer before opening another one. He pulled out that month's copy of one of the erotically dirty magazines that he had subscriptions to. He heard a clink of metal when he pushed the drawer shut, so he reopened it to investigate. It was one of the two police badges that he snagged the last time that the Hope Metal Badge & Button Company manufactured the latest design of them for the Hope Police Department. He had given the other one to Willy, who worked in the factory, but on the manufacturing line that made buttons for military uniforms, mostly. He had begged Karcin to find a way to get a badge for him because Karcin's job as a maintenance person granted him access to all of the manufacturing lines in the factory.

"This must be a sign from Willy," Karcin thought, because he normally kept the badge in the desk's bottom drawer, along with his collection of several metal buttons that he thought looked cool over the years. Karcin remembered that Willy treated him to a night out at a strip joint as a reward for the badge. They both ended up at a no-name motel with strippers afterwards, as a result of Willy fraudulently flashing the badge around to the ladies that were dancing there. Both Willy and Karcin called in sick to work the next day, and when Willy finally made it home, his girlfriend Kylee Tarry was there in his driveway waiting for him. The smell of booze and perfume, and the lipstick marks still on his neck, were all the evidence Kylee needed to know that she had been cheated on. Although Willy begged and pleaded for forgiveness, she broke up with him then and there.

Karcin's heart sunk as he remembered how the rest of that next day went. Kylee had called Karcin in a desperate attempt to locate Willy. He had convinced Kylee that he would kill himself that night if Kylee went through with the break-up, and Willy's brother confirmed that Willy's gun was missing from his house. She picked up Karcin and they searched every bar he would frequent, and then every spot in Hope that Willy would potentially go, to pull the trigger of his gun. Eventually, they ended up back at Kylee's house where there was a message from Willy's brother that he had found him passed-out drunk in his car, with an empty bottle of Jim Beam and his gun sitting on the passenger seat. His brother took the gun and left him in the car to sleep things off. Relieved, Kylee poured two shots of whiskey from the bottle that Willy kept at her house, giving one to Karcin. Those shots lead to another one, along with several beers, until they found themselves naked, and very much engaged in a sex-romp in Kylee's bed. A day later, Kylee and Willie got back together. Karcin never said a word to him about being intimate with Kylee, nor did she.

"I wonder if he knows about that now," he thought to himself. "I'm sorry for that, Willy," he added, out loud.

Knock-knock... knock-knock-knock... Knock-knock

Karcin recognized the knock on the boiler-room door and put his smut magazine back into a drawer before walking over to a small locker near his sex cot. He pulled out three packets of a white substance before opening the door, narrowly.

"Three, right?" Karcin asked, without expecting an answer. "Sixty bucks."

A hand reached in, holding three twenty-dollar bills. Karcin grabbed the money and placed the three packets into the palm of the hand, which pulled away right after the transaction was made. Karcin closed the door quickly. Returning to the locker, he added the money to a large wad of twenties and tens.

"Man, what a long day this is," he thought, while looking over at the clock on the wall. He began to feel fatigue set in from the joint of marijuana that he smoked before he got to work. Karcin thought about setting-up his cot to take a nap, but figured he should stay near his desk phone in case any of the factory lines upstairs called for his maintenance help. Leaning back in his chair, he closed his eyes.

Several hours later, the boiler kicked-on and woke him up. His neck was sore, and his mouth was parched from sleeping so long with his head cranked back in his chair with his jaw open. He looked over at the clock and began to panic. It was already half-past six, and he still needed to take care of the trash and chemicals for that day's shift. Procedurally, he was instructed on his first day on the job, several years ago, to NEVER mix any of the chemicals together, even though that same training included illegally pouring them into the river. Karcin always adhered to that rule, but if he were to make it to Claire's for the spirit reading with Willy, he would need to cut some corners. He looked at the several canisters of various chemicals that lined two of the walls inside of the fairly small toxin room and decided to blend them in the large plastic bucket on wheels that was used for mopping the floor. He figured that rolling the bucket once or twice to the riverbank would be way more efficient than seven or eight trips of carrying one or two canisters at a time.

The first canister was more full than Karcin had expected, and as he aggressively poured its contents into the large bucket some of the acidic fluid splashed onto his face. He wiped his face with a nearby rag and felt an intense burning sensation before adding a second chemical. As it poured into the bucket, there was an instant flash.

The ceiling light felt blinding as Mother Madre removed a cloth from Bane Karcin's face. It took him several minutes to focus his vision on the woman standing over him. "I don't mind you napping, Mr. Karcin, but I have paged you several times to clean up a few messes," she said, while folding the cloth.

"I'm sorry, but I-"

"Disoriented? The boiler here at St. Perpetua Academy is quite old so it may have kicked out a puff of pollution. It may be good for you to take a walk away from the boiler room for a little while. Please follow me Mr. Karcin."

"I feel confused, Mrs-"

"Madre. Mother Madre," she corrected. "You'll feel better as we go along."

They made their way up a flight of stairs and down a long hallway toward the Hall of Truths. Bane saw his reflection in a doorway window and stopped. Mother Madre waited for his reaction.

"What is wrong with my face?" he asked, feeling the scars that covered most of it with both of his hands.

"Real beauty comes from within, Mr. Karcin."

She allowed him a minute to get acquainted to his surface appearance before continuing down the hall. Dr. Nihil came skipping and jumping from around a corner. Bane watched him moving about the hall like an ungraceful ballet dancer.

"What's with him?" Bane asked.

"That's Dr. Nihil, the Science Teacher here. He spent decades as a paraplegic in a wheelchair before he came to St. Perpetua Academy."

"He has a Doctorate? Must be really smart."

"Everything is relative, Mr. Karcin. He spent all of his years trying to disprove God, placing all of his beliefs in a theory that one explosion, or a big bang, created everything. Not exactly what I would call smart."

"Like, in a flash, there was some sort of explosion that made everything?"

"Sounds quite silly, right?" Mother Madre stopped walking for a moment. "Hold out your hands. Look at both sides of them. Notice the veins that you can see delivering just the right amount of blood to each finger. The bone structure and connected muscles that are communicated to from the brain and soul, by an elaborate system of nerves and strategic impulses, so that a person may achieve many amazing things with each of their hands. That *alone* would be hard to believe, statistically. That a single bang created the amazing human body. Now, let's throw in all of the various animals that are designed in exactly the most perfectly appropriate way for their environment. The giraffe with its long neck and legs, eating leaves from atop the tall trees throughout the plains, while below its hooves, thousands of perfectly designed ants work together as a team, or an army, to achieve each single goal. That's quite a bang, considering the thousands upon thousands of various species in existence that each has their own perfectly designed system on top of, or inside of the land. Let's now add the thousands more that exist in the fresh and salt-water environments. Gills, fins, micro-organic, whale-sized, housed in shells that are born-with or living in ones that they found. BANG BANG! Oh, that's right, there was only the ONE Big Bang. Imagine the odds. But wait! What about those creatures that live in the sky? Wings and feathers to fly, some trained to deliver, some trained to spy, all naturally perfect like you and I (or you and "me" if I want to be grammatically correct instead of using my poetic license in rhyming. My choice, all because of a bang). Nature, that's God's amazing work, or did a single bang create a crawling creature, several variations of it, actually, living on and in the land, that eventually climbs a tall tree past the giraffe and designs a tent, from which it will emerge as an elegant creature that can flutter and fly high above the land and trees, and when its cycle is through, can sweep close to the water and be snatched from a creature that begins under water as a swimming tadpole before growing into the ability to decide that a moth or butterfly would be better caught with its eyes and quick tongue just above the surface of the water, or from land, where it also thrives? Long sentence, but BANG! A perfectly intertwined life-cycle of billions of creatures on a planet that is perfectly positioned from a sun, allowing temperate conditions for all of the creatures to survive, along with the photosynthesis that allows vegetation, which allows for food, wood for shelter of many creatures, herbs to heal, fragrant flowers, and the eco-system of water distribution and oxygen recycling that allows it all to happen. Remember, though, that not all of those pretty and fragrant flowers were put on the planet solely for human enjoyment. Hardly. But rather, each having its purpose in the balance of life, like attracting bees and other flying creatures for pollinating. Each flower has a pattern on it, or a scent, or colors, which attracts exactly the right creature to pollenate it successfully. Did you know that there are flowers that grow in a leaf-covered flower bud at the end of a long stem, and there is a specific type of ant on each of those leaf-covered buds, that takes exactly the right amount of time to eat the leafy material from around the fragrant and attractive flower so that it's flowering coincides with its perfect pollinator's timing? Now THAT is nature working like a well-oiled machine. Wouldn't you agree, Mr. Karcin?"

"Yes, I-"

"BANG!" So you think? Have opinions? Feel emotions? Experience love? Not just lust, but real love? None of that came from an explosion, unless Mr. Nihil proves me otherwise.

"How would he even begin to?"

Mother Madre explained as she slowly walked toward the science lab, "For an explosion to create all that I just mentioned, and a billion more perfectly designed systems, beings, feelings, and miracles that we haven't even come close to understanding, the chances are not one in a million, one in a trillion, one in a quintillion, or even one in a septillion. If at all, it would be one in a number so high that you would never, ever, be able to fathom it." As they approached the science lab, Bane looked up at the changing numbers that were projected above the doorway. "But, Dr. Nihil still feels strongly about proving his life's work, or maybe just saving himself from being wrong, which would prove to eliminate his being saved at all. We have agreed to a simple little test, and have provided the doctor with a special table that counts the number of times that he drops the seventy-seven evenly weighted and duplicated sticks onto it, and measures the distance between each one. If ever those sticks land perfectly separated from each other by the same exact measured distance, we would rename the school after him and allow him to teach on the Big Bang theory here. As you must imagine, the chances of Dr. Nihil being able to drop the seventy-seven sticks, from as many angles and heights that he chooses, landing the same exact distance from each other are exponentially greater than some large explosion creating even one tiny insect. You can see that he has tried over nine-hundred-thousand times so far."

"Why is the number displayed out here above his door?"

"Because some people can't let go of the reality that they might be wrong, and there are still some souls here that are cheering for Dr. Nihil to be correct, oddly. They have been here at St. Perpetua almost as long as he has."

Bane peeked inside and saw Dr. Nihil suspended by a makeshift hammock positioned just so over a huge and strangely illuminated table. He positioned his wrist in an awkward position and slowly released his hand's grip on the sticks. It was apparent that the sticks weren't even close to being at the exact same distance from each other. He documented the various measurements in a notebook in an effort to piece together any trends whatsoever, then gathered the sticks and re-threw them onto the table sideways in frustration.

"His hands must be tired," Bane suggested.

"That is what he chose to do with his God-given hands, but it's what you've done with your hands, Mr. Karcin, that I'd like to discuss," Mother Madre stated, taking one of his hands and leading him back down the hallway.

There was a bothersome mixture of many voices echoing, which created a pulsating compression on Bane's ears as he entered the Hall of Truths. He wasn't going to say anything, but the farther he followed Mother Madre into the hall, the worse the pain got.

"I'm sorry, Madame-"

"Mother. Mother Madre."

"Why does it sound like there are a thousand voices echoing in here when there is nobody but us in the hall?"

"Those are voices from the Hollow of Lies outside that are seeping into the hall. Lies don't echo well in the Hall of Truths."

"It is painful on my ears."

"Those voices cause an awful lot of pain to the many desperate, or defiantly curious people on earth, that cling-on to any chance they might have in reaching those on the other side. The voices only know enough to gain the trust of the receivers before they become the voices of d-d-deceivers, sending them on a track in life that God didn't intend for them."

"On the other side of what? This wall of stained glass?"

"Well, actually-"

"Mother Madre, I can't take this pain in my ears anymore."

"There is a large pole on the floor along the wall that can reach the clasp at the top of the open window. You may close it if you wish, Mr. Karcin."

As he got closer, Bane could make out some of the words that were creeping into the hall...

I'M GETTING SIGNALS FROM YOUR LOVED ONE...

IT'S OK TO LEAVE YOUR HUSBAND…

THE SPIRIT SAYS KEEP AN OPEN MIND TO OTHER GODS…
MOVING AWAY FROM YOUR KIDS FOR NEW CAREER WILL BE
GOOD…

THEY SEND LIGHT AND LOVE…

Bane closed the window and felt instant relief. "Why does the
window only open in from the top, ever so slightly? It is *so* high up."

"That's so the ones sending the lies can never look in upon the
truth, only to distort it. Please take a seat, Mr. Karcin," Mother Madre
instructed while extracting her transparent screen from a fairly large
cardboard box that somehow made it onto the table in front of her.
"Before we begin, could you please get rid of this box for me?"

Bane looked around the vast and mostly empty hall and saw a
large trash barrel near the door he had just walked through, along with
a recycling bin. When he got a few feet from it, he tossed it over to
the recycling bin but it was too big and just glanced off the top rim
before landing near the trash barrel. Bane let out a grunt of frustration
then walked the additional steps to the box and threw it into the large
barrel.

"Shouldn't you b-b-b-break the box down, Mr. Karcin?"

"It's ok. I'll just have the dumpster emptied today, so one still-
assembled box won't affect anything."

"That sounds wasteful"

"That's a funny pun, Ha Ha," Bane chuckled, as he started back
toward the long table.

"There is nothing funny about pollution or litter, Mr. Karcin.
Turn around, break-down the box, and place it into the recycle bin."

"That would take a minute or so, and I know that you'd like to
talk right now."

131

"I'm sure that you have more interest in pleasing yourself than pleasing me. Break it down and r-r-recycle it!"

Bane quickly realized that Mother Madre was very much in charge of the situation, and he humbly took his seat once he did as instructed.

"Now, tell me all about the dream that you were having when I found you in the boiler room, Mr. Karcin."

"I don't really remember what I was-"

With a swipe of two fingers, Mother Madre's screen's glow changed color. "Are you sure you can't remember?"

"Wait! Yes. Yes, I *do* remember."

"Please tell me all about it."

"How far back to you want me to go?"

Mother Madre looked at her screen, tapping her finger against it. "Let's go way back. Please start from the tree-house."

"It feels like it actually happened. I was just a kid. My friends and I had a tree-house in the woods."

"What would you do in the tree-house?"

Bane felt embarrassed, so he answered, "We would play card games and stuff."

"I don't consider tarot cards a game at all. Shall we open the window again to listen in on the evil that such practices invite into the lives of those that dabble in that, Mr. Karcin?"

"No, Mother Madre. There was a girl that hung out with us who would always bring the tarot cards. None of us knew that they weren't good for us."

Would you pollute your body inside that tree fort?"

"No(esss)." Bane looked around the room to see if someone else said something, too, considering the conflicting echo sound.

"No? Was there a game that you would play regarding smoking?"

He wondered how she would even have a clue about that. "No(esss)."

"Mr. Karcin?"

"We had a game called 'How Long have You been Smoking?' where we would each take turns dragging on a cigarette while the others determined how long we each made it seem that we had been smoking for. You know, to look cool. We knew that we reached the pinnacle when the others would call you a Borba."

"A Borba?"

"There was a guy in town with the last name of Borba. He was well-known as a drug dealer, and he always had a cigarette hanging from his mouth."

"And that was considered cool?"

"It seemed so in my dream."

"Did you provide the cigarettes?"

"No(esss). Well, maybe most times."

"Tell me about the firecrackers, Mr. Karcin."

"Those I did NOT bring."

"But you did light them?"

"I did, but only a few."

"And you'd throw them from the tree-house, quickly, so they wouldn't go off in your hand?"

"Yes(oooh)."

"Should that have been a "No", Mr. Karcin?"

"Yes, that should've been a No."

"Please explain."

"I am feeling ashamed, Mother Madre."

"Well, that's a start. Please continue."

"Well, there was a brook that ran just alongside the tree-house. We would catch frogs." Bane stopped talking. Mother Madre allowed for a long pause until he felt equally uncomfortable by both the silence and what he knew he had to tell her, eventually. "In the dream, I had placed one of the firecrackers in a frog's mouth," Bane confessed, and after another long pause, realizing that Mother Madre was not going to give him a break, added, "and lit the fuse."

"How did that make you feel?"

"Bad(ood)."

"Bad enough that you didn't do it again, Mr. Karcin?"

Mother Madre allowed for another long pause, while she rested her chin on two fingers looking sadly down at her screen.

"I'm sorry, Mother Madre."

"I'm wondering if you are sorry only because your behavior is coming to light. Destroying life and lacking c-c-compassion are two extremely bad traits, Mr. Karcin. Was there anything hanging on the walls inside the tree-house?"

"Yes."

"Explain."

"We would hang magazine pictures on the walls."

"Of?"

"I'm embarrassed."

"Mr. Karcin, there are many ways that d-d-destroy the beauty that God has made, whether through the exploitation of a woman's physique, the calculated destruction of God's creatures, or the internal and external p-p-pollution of the human body."

"Pollution of the human body?"

"Roll up your sleeves, please, Mr. Karcin."

Bane looked at the many tattoos on him. "I don't remember getting these," he said.

"That's quite some detailed artwork, although the subject matter is all off, along with the "canvas" that it is on. A devil figure

134

embracing a naked woman? A skeleton making an obscene gesture? Poison anti-Christ imagery permanently staining your God-given body. How do you feel about your quote-unquote artwork today?"

"I don't really-"

"Let's jump ahead in your dream, to the boiler room."

"Oh, that's right. I also dreamed that I was working in a boiler room just like I do here."

"What were your duties there?"

"If any of the manufacturing lines went down I would determine what was wrong with the machines and I'd fix them."

"Anything else?"

"Yes, at the end of the day I would have to empty canisters of chemicals into the river."

"Polluting the river?"

"It wasn't my choice. I was ordered to do it by my boss."

"It was completely your choice. You could have chosen to find another job instead of engage in what you knew was wrong. Minimally, you could have chosen to challenge your boss on the practice of pollution, and if your concern had landed on deaf ears, challenge some authority higher than your boss, including an environmental official. The problem is that you were not concerned in the least."

"But if it was all just a dream-"

"Dreams often reflect one's core, Mr. Karcin, and your associated actions have had rippling d-d-damages that have reached far beyond what you could comprehend at this point."

"Does a God-made environment, including that in one's dreams, eventually heal itself, considering his perfect design as you mentioned earlier?"

135

"If it is God's will, it will, but sometimes over a very long period of time. What takes even longer to heal is the d-d-damage that is inflicted on people when p-p-pollution taints love, and even then, a scar will *always* remain."

Karcin touched his face, recalling seeing his reflection in the glass window earlier.

"Oh, the scars I am speaking of are much worse than yours, Mr. Karcin. They are felt deeper, last longer, and hurt more than any mutilations that physical infliction could bequeath."

"I'm not sure that I understand, Mother Madre."

"If you were to be truthful, you would eventually get to the part of your dream where you were selling drugs to others, worried about your profit but having had zero concern about the damage the poison you provided them with created in their bodies, minds, and relationships. Everyone that loves a person who got hooked on drugs feels pain, and the destruction is widespread. But, it appears that you didn't stop there," Mother Madre added while touching her screen again. "To engage in intimacy with another person's declared love is a sin that is not often forgiven by man or woman, and to do so against a friendship that has long been avowed raises some serious questions about character and loyalty. Lust and infidelity are very d-d-damaging poisons that spread pollution both deliberately and discreetly, all at the same time. There is no big bang that can instantly remove the d-d-destruction left behind in the wake of it all, but we can work through some things while you are here at St. Perpetua Academy. It all begins with facing and admitting who you truly are. Are you willing to do that, Mr. Karcin?"

"Yes, Mother Madre," Bane said, while rolling his sleeves back down in shame.

"It appears that you may need some help with that. Let's start with a song that Mr. Dyson has written."

The curtain on the stage opened, just as Mr. Dyson was tuning his guitar strings. "Oh, one moment, please," he requested.

"How long has he been here?" Bane asked, irritably.

"Relax, Mr. Karcin, he just arrived," Mother Madre assured. "Begin as soon as you are ready, Mr. Dyson.

TOXIC AQUA

I SEE THE SKY BLUE IN THE SUNSHINE
LIKE A TINTED PANE OF GLASS
BUT HELL IF I KNOW WHO BROKE THE WINDOW
ANOTHER STORE NEW ON THE CORNER
I LIKE TO SIT HERE ON THE GRASS
AND WATCH THEM BUILD ROWS WHERE MEMORY GROWS
NOW ONCE AROUND THE BLOCK
TAKES ME TWO TIMES AROUND THE PARK
BUT I DON'T FEEL BAD AT ALL
MY FAVORITE COLOR IS TOXIC AQUA
MY FAVORITE FOOD NO FARMER SOWS
I LOVE THE MUNDANES THEN TEST THE BLOOD STAINS
BUT I DON'T FEEL BAD AT ALL
SO GIVE ME YOUR NUMBER AND I'LL GIVE YOU A CALL
OH MY WOULD YOU LOOK AT THE TIME
I LIKE TO DRIVE MY BIG CAR
WITH THE AIR CONDITIONER ON
I THROW MY GARBAGE IN THE OCEAN
HEY PASS THE CAVIAR
IF THE GARBAGE MAN
DOESN'T WANT TO TAKE MY TOXIC WASTE
I'LL FLASH A HUNDRED DOLLAR BILL

AND HE'LL THROW IT IN THE BAY
AND I DON'T FEEL BAD AT ALL
IF YOU LIKE THE VIEW AND I BUILD A MALL
WE'VE ALL GOT TO MAKE A DIME
YEAH I'M SURE THAT I WAS THE ONE
THAT KILLED YOUR STARFISH WITH THE SUN
BUT I DON'T FEEL BAD AT ALL

"How would YOU know how I feel?" Bane angrily asked Devin once he finished singing the song.

"I DON'T know how you feel. I just wrote a song based on the words that were written on the other side of this scroll," Devin explained, while turning the scroll over. "Hey, what happened to the words that were on the back?"

"What are you, some sort of a-"

"That's enough, gentlemen," Mother Madre interrupted. "We all have our crosses to bear, here, so to speak. Mr. Karcin, this is Mr. Dyson. All of us are here to help each other, and in ways that we may not completely understand."

Devin came down from the stage and handed the scroll to Bane, then extended his hand for a handshake. Holding the scroll, Bane looked at Devin's outstretched hand then turned around.

Mother Madre added, "In due time."

CHAPTER 8

"We'll never do time, so best for you to keep your mouth shut!"

Those words kept running through Addison Ambry's mind like an evil ghost haunting every room of a large mansion while she paced through her tiny cottage in the woods. Her brain was running amuck with anger, sadness, and fear, as she aimlessly made her way around her piles of boxes, books, and artwork. A new painting sat upon her table, drying. She was able to suppress her thoughts and feelings for a long time and vent through her art, but it seemed that they were trying to crawl out of her skin, all of a sudden. Having the summer off from teaching school gave her too much time to think. How she wished she could just sit and hold her mother's hand one more time. It had been years since she passed away, yet Addison kept a scarf that she would often wear, in a large beacon jar. It still had her scent on it, so Addison would inhale memories of her whenever uncomfortable thoughts and emotions crept into her life. She decided to finally vent to someone. Grabbing the jar, Addison got into her car and drove to the cemetery where her mother was buried.

A funeral procession entered the burial ground ahead of Addison's arrival. She could see that mourners were gathered in the same section where her mother's grave was located, so she decided to park one section over and quietly walk slowly toward her mother's grave with the jar that held her scarf. The morning air was already warm on Miss Ambry's shoulders and she mentally noted the opposite effect that the cool morning dew had on her feet, as her open-toed shoes allowed the uncut grass to graze upon her toes. The moment felt refreshing to her in contrast to the stifled feeling that she felt inside of her small and cluttered house, so she decided to carry her shoes in her free hand to feel it fully. Lilacs were in full bloom, allowing Addison a fragrant jolt to her senses. Feeling more alive in that moment than she had felt in months, the irony didn't escape her while she contemplated the evidence of each former life under her feet. Looking at the scarf inside her jar, she suddenly wished the lilac scent would fade away. She walked among the gravestones like she walked about her piles of boxes, taking time sporadically to guess what, or in this case, who, was inside.

A faded teddy bear somehow survived what looked to be a several-year nap in all sorts of weather atop a grave, based on its appearance. Addison paused and remembered the young boy. He was only eight, but he passed away from cancer, even though the entire town was raising money and praying for him. As she read the headstone once again she did the math. "Wow, it's been twenty-seven years already," she said to herself in a whisper of surprise. "Everything goes by so quickly."

The next stone over belonged to the man that owned the old country store in Hope. He was old back then, Addison remembered, when she was just starting kindergarten. He had lived to be ninety-seven-years-old. No, she re-thought, he lived to be ninety-seven-years-*young*. She pondered on how even if a person lived to be ninety-seven, it is still just a blink of an eye, in relation to not only forever, but how the dying person must view it, regardless. "He was nice," she thought, remembering the elderly man opening one of the canisters of penny candy and allowing her to take one for free every time that she went into the store with her mother. She could still recall the squeaking of the old wooden floorboards, and various scents in each corner of the store. It gave her some relief that such a gentleman was only a few graves over from where her mother's resting place was.

She held the beacon jar even tighter as she stepped closer to her mother's grave. The minister's voice became audible, though muffled, and it reminded her of her own mother's funeral. She circled the grave once, thinking of those that gathered around that spot on that sad day over a decade earlier, all of which she hadn't seen since. Even though she hadn't contacted any of them herself, she still felt a little betrayed that all of the "We're here for you" people never were. God forbid if they ever *did* show up, if truth were told.

"Mother," she began, but stalled. She wondered if the funeral congregation could hear her single voice. Listening to the minister's voice, and a followed "amen" by the rest that was barely comprehendible, she decided that she could speak freely. And Addison needed to. "Mother, there is so much that has happened since your death that you don't know about, and much more from when you were alive."

141

Circling the grave again before sitting on the damp grass, Addison took her familiar spot just off to the side from where her mother was buried. Being her favorite place outside of school and her cottage, she would visit her mother's grave often. The difference was that she was actually opening up to her for the first time.

"The azalea shrub that we planted together is now the biggest one I've ever seen. It is beautiful, and that dove that built a nest inside of it still comes back every year. I sometimes wonder if it is an offspring of "our" dove, or if it's the original one." She paused for a moment, as if expecting a response. "Either way, I smile and think of you every time I see her. Sometimes I cry when I hear her coo." Addison unscrewed the top of the beacon jar and took a deep breath before continuing. "Actually, I cry often, mother. Your death has been a change in my life that has been very difficult to deal with. I miss your old stories about how grandpa came here from across the sea when he was just a boy, how he built our house when daddy left and made toys with the extra wood. I wish that he were here to make me a doll to hold. There isn't anyone in my life aside from my memories of you, and the children that I teach. At the end of each school year, I say goodbye to the twenty or so young lives that I had grown attached to. I would have thought that the annual ritual of goodbyes would have prepared me to eventually say goodbye to you. It didn't."

Crossing her legs in front of her, she sifted her fingers through the clovers, which competed with the grass that grew above her mother's body, picking one and studying its three leaves. She held it up to her nose and breathed in. She knew that it wouldn't have much of a scent, but she held it there for several seconds so as to buy some time before continuing her talk. Releasing it up to the sky, she was surprised by how far it traveled in the air, landing near the minister's feet, several rows of graves over. It was as if it was hand-delivered by the wind, but there was hardly even a breeze that late morning.

"A sad thing happened the other day, mother. I passed a man that was walking into the convenient store. He was swearing and looked very disheveled, and for some reason I watched him from my car before pulling away. I couldn't believe it, but he started knocking things off the shelves. The man behind the counter put his hands above his head and glanced quickly out the window. Our eyes met for a brief instant. He looked like he was desperately pleading for help with his facial expression. I will never forget it. Remembering what you always told me, I kept to myself and drove away." Addison picked another clover and rolled it into a green wet clump between her finger and thumb. "I read in the newspaper the next day that he was shot and killed by that robber. The world seems to be getting more and more sick, mother."

Addison stood up and paced around her mother's grave two more times before kneeling down at her spot. Her eyes looked down and a single tear hit a large blade of grass. It imposed upon a dewdrop, forming a larger bead that the grass would no longer support, forcing it to drip and sink into the ground.

"I apologize, mother, for what I'm about to tell you. I feel so ashamed," she said quietly, with a quiver in her voice. "It was just a week before you passed. I knew that I should have gone directly home after teaching that day, like I always did, especially because I knew that your health was declining. It was the last day of classes and the other teachers were teasing me because I never did anything outside of school with them, so I finally agreed to follow them to Smitty's Bar for a drink. The other teachers kept buying me drinks and I didn't want to be rude. Eventually, I felt sick and went into a stall inside the ladies room. I must have fallen asleep or passed-out, and before I knew it, I was woken up by the owner of the bar who was touching me between my legs. I screamed out, but the bar was already closed for the night so there was no one there to hear my cry for help, well, nobody that would help me. The man then forced me to bend over the sink and then he raped me. When he was finished, he traded places with a policeman while he stood at the door to keep me prisoned in there. As soon as I could, I ran out of the bathroom, grabbed my pocketbook and tried to dart out the front door. It was bolted shut. I turned around and the owner was standing right there. He grabbed my arm and said that if I told anyone that he would see to it that I was killed. I kneed him in the crotch, and was able to escape out through the back door near the men's room. A police car raced out of the parking lot. When I finally found my car keys, the front door opened and he shouted out "We'll never do time, so best for you to keep your mouth shut!" – Oh mother, I am so sorry."

Addison was crying uncontrollably as she ripped up a patch of clover and grass. "Argh!!" she screamed out while throwing the cluster of dirt and vegetation in anger before opening the beacon jar. She inhaled in-between bursts of cries, which were absorbed by the scarf inside. Startled by the voice of an elderly man, she looked up quickly. Her swollen eyes felt a stinging combination of salt and sunlight as a beam shined through an opening in the branches and leaves of a large maple tree nearby.

"I'm sorry if I startled you, ma'am," the elderly man said, allowing Miss Ambry to settle down a bit. "Is your name Addison?"

Once her eyes focused, she studied the man for a moment. He was well dressed, frail, and was slouching over a cane. She looked over to where the funeral was being held and saw that everyone but the cemetery workers had left. "I'm sorry sir," she responded, wiping her eyes, "should I know who you are?"

The man spoke fairly slowly, yet his oratory delivery sounded eloquent. "The very last funeral service that I performed was at this grave. I remember not being able to console the daughter of Mrs. Ambry once the service ended. I recall thinking that the woman's anguish went even beyond the grief of losing one's mother, similar to the distress that your face and body language are showing now. Would that daughter be you?"

Squinting her eyes while looking into his, she said "Minister Trickett?"

"Yes, this is me," he replied. "Ninety-three years old and still on this side of the ground."

"I remember you. Not a single word that you might have preached that day, but I can still remember that you did make me feel better, even though I was inconsolable at the time. I knew that you were close to retirement back then, already in your eighties, but I hadn't realized that my mother's funeral was to be the last service that you'd perform."

"Well, it was the last funeral service that I'd perform up until today."

"That was you speaking over that grave this morning?"

"Yes, it was. I guess you could say that my wife took me out of retirement."

"Oh, I'm sorry Minister Trickett. It was your wife who was being buried?"

"It was. My beloved darling finally gave up her last breath after a brave battle against cancer. Considering all of her suffering, it was almost a blessing. Selfishly, I wish she would have lived one day longer than me because I'm afraid of dying alone."

"I'm sure that she's in a better place now," Addison offered in condolence.

"I sure hope so," the minister replied.

Addison felt some disappointment in the wake of his words. "Shouldn't we *know* so, Minister Trickett?"

He looked behind him to see if the nearby wooden bench looked safe enough to still sit on. "Please, Addison, would you mind if we sat down for a moment?" He didn't wait for a response, but rather turned around slowly as he positioned his cane and body for a direct walk to the bench. When he finally arrived at it, Addison took hold under one of his arms and helped to lower him onto the bench top before taking a seat next to him.

"I am happy to see that my remark has you concerned, Addison," he said, while his fingers touched a rotted portion of the wooden seat. "You know, I was here for the dedication of this bench many, many, many moons ago, and have often sat here pondering the many shells in the ground while wondering where the souls that were attached to those shells went. I personally knew at least half of those that are now buried here. Some were great people that didn't believe in God, others committed some very bad sins but had professed Jesus Christ as their Savior. At the age of ninety-three, I still search for answers regarding particulars. Why do young children die? Why is there such a thing as death, regardless of age, anyway? As we look around here, we are reminded that the space between ages on earth is never that long." He glanced over at the two men that were shoveling dirt back into his wife's grave, and then leaned on his cane to bend over. After a failed attempt to reach the ground, Minister Trickett asked Addison to pick a clover for him. Holding it between his shaky fingers, he continued. "But, God has left for us reminders embedded in nature throughout the world that hope and genuine love should never be lost. When I hold this particular species of clover in my hand, I look at its three equally sized heart-shaped leaves and am reminded that there is a

Holy Trinity, with each Heavenly component as equally important as the next. What is important is to learn about, and *trust*, The Father, The Son, and The Holy Spirit. From there, all of the other questions will be eventually answered, if not on earth, then in due time."

In due time… The minister's words prompted Marshall Smith's voice to creep inside Addison's head again, which she involuntarily recited out loud - "We'll never do time, so best for you to keep your mouth shut!"

"Excuse me, Addison?" Minister Trickett responded with a concerning surprise.

"I'm sorry," she said, before bursting back into tears. She grabbed the beacon jar and started to run toward her car.

"Addison!" the elderly minister weakly shouted out.

Her leg fell into a sinking grave upon her next step.

"Miss Addison!" Mother Madre said in a whispered shout while sitting on the wooden toy storage bench in the corner of Ambry Addison's classroom.

Ambry's foot slipped off the footrest on the stool that she was napping on, and she felt her leg reach the ground just as she abruptly woke-up.

"Mother, I'm so sorry."

"It's Mother Madre, and that's quite alright, Miss Addison," she said while taking her transparent screen out from her satchel. "Won't you take a moment and sit with me here on the bench?"

"Of course."

Ambry hadn't sat on that bench before, nor had she looked around at her classroom from that corner's view. It felt uncomfortable to her.

"Miss Addison, what do you think about rearranging your classroom?"

"But I like it just the way it is, Mother Madre."

"We have recently wrapped up a study on classroom design for optimal learning and the committee chose your room to conduct the pilot run before we roll out academy-wide implementation."

"Please, I beg of you, Mother Madre. Not my room."

"Can you tell me about your dream, Miss Addison?"

"Oh, I don't-"

"Open up?"

"I just-"

"You must."

"Mother Madre, please, I-"

"The painting of your mother is amazing. She looks beautiful sitting in her rocking chair."

"But, how would you know-"

"And the way you painted her scarf, it looks like it is in motion, and the only indicator within the painting that suggests your mother is actually rocking in the chair. It looks very natural, just like your artistic abilities, Miss Addison."

"Thank you."

"Miss Addison, do you trust me?"

Silence

"How long have you been painting?"

"Since I was a little girl."

"Can you remember your very first painting?" Mother Madre asked while touching her screen.

"I don't believe that it was my very first painting, but the earliest one that I can seem to remember right now was of a boy in my class at school that I had a crush on."

"In your dream, it appeared that you had saved mostly everything throughout your life. Did you still have that particular painting toward the end of the dream?"

"No, it was gone toward the beginning of it."

"Please explain," instructed Mother Madre.

Silence

"Please, Miss Addison," Mother Madre insisted. "When you are ready," she added, while touching the transparent screen.

Ambry looked around her classroom from the vantage point of the bench on which she sat. The bench's seat stored children's toys inside of it, and atop of it sat a grown woman that suddenly acted like a child. She folded her arms tightly in front of her and began to rock back and forth for several seconds before releasing her arms and throwing one of her pointer fingers in the direction of a desk in the back row. "There!" Ambry burst out. "He was sitting there, and my desk was right here, where we are sitting now. I had carried a note with me for several weeks and I was building up my courage to give it to him. It didn't say much on it. Just the words 'I LIKE YOU'. Finally, one day when I finished my test early and was just sitting there, I decided that it was time, so I pretended that I needed to sharpen my pencil. The sharpener was right behind where he sat, and I slipped the note onto his desk. Just as he was opening the note, the teacher scolded me for possibly cheating during test time, and she took the note. She said something like, "Are you trying to get an A, or trying to get a boyfriend?" and the entire class laughed at me until the end of the class. I was so happy that it was the last class on a Friday, and I prayed that everyone would forget by the time Monday rolled around."

"And did they forget, Miss Addison?"

"They probably would have, had I not thrown away that painting."

"Of the boy that you had a crush on?"

"Yes. My mother was throwing out a lot of things that weekend, and I added that painting to the trash pile at the end of our driveway. I just couldn't look at it anymore."

"Did throwing it away help to ease the pain that you were feeling?"

"At first it did, but later that day I saw from our cottage window the boy from across the street who sold lemonade. It was too early in the season for the trees to have leaves on them so I could see that he was going through our trash. I went to tell mother but she said that whatever we threw away might become someone else's treasure. When I returned to the window the boy was already gone."

"And he took your painting?"

"I was sitting in class on that following Monday morning and the lemonade boy from the neighborhood came to our classroom from his homeroom. He said that the Easter Bunny probably forgot to deliver the painting to a student in the class. He recognized the boy in the painting so he gave it to our teacher. The teacher said, "Well, it sure *looks* like Randy," before she turned it over and read out loud what I had painted on the back- A.A. LOVES RANDY. The entire class started a chant about me loving Randy that seemed to go on forever, and Randy just started saying mean things out loud. Things like "Yuck!" and "She's Ugly!" It was the worst day of my life." Ambry said, before folding her arms tightly back up in front of her and resuming her rocking. A full minute of silence passed before she added, "No, I remember a few worse days."

"Can you describe what the inside of the cottage was like?"

"It was mostly used for storage. There was access to a bed, and space at the table for painting and thinking."

"Why do you think most of the cottage ended up being used for storage?"

Ambry rocked faster and began to shake her head no.

"Miss Addison?"

"Nobody is taking anything else from me. My trash becoming another person's treasure only to return to me in the form of torture and tragedy will never happen again."

"Unfortunate events occur from time to time in everybody's life, many of which we have no control over. Often times they become our life-lessons, while other times they arise out of another's malicious intent, or even a perceived understanding of what is when "it" actually isn't what it is at all."

"I'm not following, Mother Madre."

"For instance, the young boy that took the painting did so because he legitimately thought that the Easter Bunny lived in your cottage and the painting was clearly of a person that he knew. He initially went to the trash pile for a completely different item. What happened from there inside the classroom happens every single day in classes of that particular grade. Unfortunately, that is how children act at that age, but as a result, it is often the point when children learn *how* to act in certain situations. I would say that your teacher is the one that acted most inappropriately by not only allowing the ridiculing and bullying, but also actually exacerbating it. Unfortunately, you allowed that moment to change the course of your life. You didn't necessarily do anything wrong, but it would be good for your soul to have an understanding, and maybe a release of the past and some s-s-secrets, so that it may float more freely."

"In my dream, it seemed like I preferred things just the way they were. I didn't need or want any changes, and I didn't want to create change in anyone else's life."

"Everything changes, Miss Addison. Everything n-n-n-*needs* to change. Stagnation doesn't s-s-serve God, nor does it help fellow mankind. It appears that the biggest change in your dream was the death of your mother. Would you agree?"

"I do miss her so," Ambry said, as she stopped rocking and repositioned her hands so that they cradled her shoulders. "I mean, the dream felt so real. It's like I still miss her."

"How did you deal with your mother's passing?"

Ambry smiled slightly and tilted her head to the side, then answered, "I would visit her grave on every sunny day."

"What would you say to your mother when you visited?"

Silence

"Miss Addison?"

"I would just kind-of sit there. I didn't tell her very much when she was alive, either. She would listen to her records often, and would sometimes talk about flying away for a nice vacation on some imaginary Saturday. I would just listen. I loved it when she would recite poetry to me. I really miss that a lot, even though it was just a dream."

"You would never talk to her?"

"Not about anything too serious. Sometimes I would open up to her under my breath when we walked through the train station together. She would take me there for afternoon tea and croissants at the station's bistro. It was always loud in there so I knew she wouldn't actually hear me speak while we walked."

Mother Madre touched her screen. "What did you happen to tell her when you were at the graveside in this recent dream?"

Silence

"Miss Addison, the idea that someone might still be living their life had you not kept a secret hidden does need to be addressed. Whether a clerk at a store, or a young child in a classroom, observation and e-e-e-empathy need to drive what words we choose and when we should use them. When we m-m-*must* use them. God provided us with eyes for seeing and a voice to be utilized for j-j-just causes, be it to profess love, teach others, offer praise, sing a song, to soothe, or to alert."

"I am understanding that now, Mother Madre."

"One must also l-l-love themselves, which includes seeking help or reporting incidents when they happen to you, too."

Ambry began to weep uncontrollably.

"Miss Addison?" Mother Madre inquired. She touched the screen again and gasped as she looked at it with shock. Pulling Ambry up from the toy bench, she held her in her arms as they both wept.

When Mother Madre felt Ambry's body stop shaking, she handed her a clump of tissues. As she wiped her eyes, Mother Madre lifted the seat of the bench and reached into the storage space inside of it and pulled out a beautiful wooden doll. It was dressed exactly like the painting Ambry had done of her mother. Mother Madre handed it to her, and Ambry slowly sat back down on the bench, staring at the doll in her hands. The wood smelled like the cottage in her dream. She cradled it, positioning the doll's scarf just under her nose.

Mother Madre joined her back on the bench. She looked around the classroom, and then back at Ambry before saying, "Maybe we'll just move this bench, and leave the classroom the way it is for now, Miss Addison." Mother Madre folded up her screen and returned it to her satchel before pulling out a scroll. Walking away from the bench, she explained how she was going to have Mr. Dyson sing a song for her so he could use his God-given voice to share with Ambry the concept of change, but suggested that she'll simply leave the scroll of lyrics on top of her desk, right next to the coloring sheet of an angel that still sat there.

Ambry inhaled the scent of the doll while rocking back and forth. "Would you mind reciting the words to me, Mother?"

"Madre. Mother Madre. Of course I'll recite them, Miss Addison."

EVERYTHING CHANGES
TELL ME ONE MORE TIME THE WAY
THAT GRANDPA CROSSED THE SEA TO STAY
AND WENT TO WORK WHILE HE WAS STILL A BOY
HOW WITH HIS TWO BARE HANDS HE BUILT HIS HOME
JUST THE SAME WAY THAT HIS DAD HAD SHOWN
HOW WITH THE EXTRA WOOD FOR YOU HE BUILT SOME TOYS
HOW HE WALKED TO SCHOOL FOR MILES IN THE SNOW
FOR I ONEDAY WANT THIS CHILD I HOLD TO KNOW
'CAUSE EVERYTHING CHANGES
SOON EVERYTHING'S GONE
THE SPACE BETWEEN AGES
IS NEVER THAT LONG
EARLY MEMORIES FOR YOU
INCLUDE TRAIN STATION AFTERNOONS
GAMES YOU PLAYED – THOSE YOU WOULDN'T DARE TO TRY
FOR ME THE VINYL RECORDS PLAYED
AN AIRPLANE RIDE ON A SATURDAY
NIXON TIED HIS TONGUE AND ELVIS DIED
DO YOU REMEMBER HEARING HOOFPRINTS ON THE ROOF
WHEN AMAZING THINGS WERE SO MUCH LESS ALOOF

BUT EVERYTHING CHANGES
SOON EVERYTHING'S GONE
THE SPACE BETWEEN AGES
IS NEVER THAT LONG
WE ALL HAVE DAYS THAT WE HOPE AND PRAY WILL NEVER END
WE ALSO FACE THOSE DAYS THAT DROP US TO OUR KNEES
THEY'LL HAVE US BEGGING PLEASE
WE NEVER CRIED OVER THINGS WE'VE LACKED
ALTHOUGH SOMETIMES SAD WHEN THINKING BACK
WHEN WE REALIZE HOW QUICKLY TIME MOVED ON
BUT YOU TAUGHT ME THINGS THAT REALLY COUNT
ARE NOT THE ONES THAT WE FRAME AND MOUNT
BUT THE ONES THAT HANG ON FAITH IN LIFE BEYOND
MY THANKFULLNESS AND LOVE DIDN'T ALWAYS SHOW
SO THE REASON FOR THIS SONG IS SO YOU'D KNOW
'CAUSE EVERYTHING CHANGES

Ambry stood up and gently placed the doll on top of the bench, as if she were putting it to bed for a nap.

"If you don't mind, Mother Madre, I'd like to keep this bench right here," she suggested, before taking it upon herself to begin repositioning all of the other desks.

"I do like that bench right where it is, too, Miss Addison," Mother Madre replied. "I do."

CHAPTER 9

"*I* do," insisted Mr. Connor. "Clearly, I have the best credentials to teach the new ethics class."

"No, again, *I* do!" argued Officer Williams. "I am an officer, so clearly I am more qualified to teach ethics than you are."

"You never taught a class in your life!"

"You call what you do *teaching*? Screaming and yelling at students is more like it! Plus, I could use the extra money more than you."

"How would *you* know what I need? I *teach* how to make money. You don't even know what to *do* with it!"

Mother Madre came around the corner and walked over to Mr. Connor and Officer Williams. "That's enough!" she ordered. "What is this all about, anyway?"

Both men pointed to a flyer on the bulletin board behind them, which advertised a job opening for an after-school ethics class teacher. Mother Madre ripped the paper from the board and instructed the men to follow her down the hall. "What makes *either* of you think that you are qualified to teach ethics?"

Hearing Mother Madre through her open PTO office door, Miss Kylee came out of her room and exclaimed, "Maybe *I* should take the ethics teacher job!"

Mother Madre stopped in her tracks, but continued to look straight-ahead instead of look at Kylee while she addressed her in response. "Kylee, this is *not* some appointed-for-no-good-reason job, but rather a position that is based on *real* m-m-merit. Back inside your room, and I will talk to you about this job posting flyer when I finish up with Mr. Connor and Officer Williams."

"But, I-"

"As I said!"

Officer Williams and Mr. Connor looked at each other and made faces of concern as they continued down the corridor behind Mother Madre, and into the Hall of Truths. Both men knew that she was extremely aggravated, and didn't dare say a word as she led them to two strange configurations that sat on top of the long table in the massive room. She pulled out two seats in front of the two structures and signaled them to sit down.

"You have both claimed to be experts in ethics, so it's time to play a little game called Moral Compass, sometimes referred to as The Ethical Foundation Game. Have either of you played the game before?" asked Mother Madre.

Each of the men shook his head no, while trying to determine what the two piles of material in front of them were all about.

"You can see that there is a fairly large compass resting on top of a foundation made from multiple materials. Each foundation's cornerstones are made from Jerusalem stone, which is a certain limestone that has been used to build structures since ancient times. In-between the c-c-cornerstones are blocks of lodestone, which are magnetic due to it being comprised of magnetite, and were used to make the first compasses. Wedged among the lodestone are crucifixion spikes that date back a few thousand years. Woven throughout each foundation are branches of thorns."

"I think I just saw a bug borrow into mine," Officer Williams said.

"Those are locust, which do live within and around your foundations," Mother Madre confirmed. "You will each be answering a series of questions and sharing stories throughout the game, which may or may not force you to take a piece away from your f-f-foundation. If any portion of your compass touches the top of the table, or if your compass no longer works, you l-l-lose the game," she explained, as she pulled two magnetic wands from her satchel and placed them in front of the two men. "Your hands should sit flat on top of the table unless otherwise instructed. Shall we get started?" she said, while holding her open satchel just above Officer William's line of vision. "Please pull out a question and read it out loud."

Officer Williams placed his hand inside the satchel and felt a stone tablet. "There is just one single stone tablet," he said.

"Please pull it out and read it aloud," Mother Madre instructed.

The tablet was lighter than it appeared, and the letters were chiseled into the face of it. "It spells REGRET," Officer Williams stated, while holding the tablet up as proof for Mother Madre, and his opponent at the moment, Mr. Connor.

"Thank you, Officer Williams. Place the stone tablet off to the side, and please, just a reminder to leave your hands on top of the table in front of you" Mother Madre said. "Now, you will be given access to three various regretful memories. You must quickly think

158

about them and chose one regret that you are willing to share with us."

"Like, something I did bad?"

"That you regretted doing."

"Does it have to be, like, really bad?"

Mother Madre cast a look of disappointment in Officer Williams' direction and said, "Chose one of the three memory options, please."

"Ah, here's one! Ha-Ha! This was the summer that my folks let my best friend come to the beach house with us. It was a lot of fun, up until the teachers went on strike at the end of the summer, and we stayed at the beach for another few weeks. We had done all of the surfing that we wanted to do, along with all of the fishing, clamming, and even sneaking into the fancy hotel's pool several times." Officer Williams paused and looked at Mother Madre as if expecting another look, or maybe a penalty. "We were so bored. Eventually, all we did was walk around with the neighborhood dog, named Wing-nut. Either we'd be hiking to buy candy at the General Store, or we'd go down inside the old bunkers at the coastal campground. We'd play 'How Long Have You Been Smoking?' in there. It was super dark, but during a certain time of morning the sun would shine through a vent at the top of the hill that the old army bunker was buried underneath. That was our spotlight for the game. I even got voted as a 'Borber' a few times! Ha!" he reminisced. "I'll never forget the day when I lit the fuse of one of my friend's firecrackers in there. It was SO loud that our ears rang for a week. I think that Wing-nut became permanently deaf that day. After that, he never came anymore when we called his name."

"And you felt r-r-regret at that moment?" asked Mother Madre.

"No, there's more to the story. I haven't gotten to the regretting part yet."

"No, you will stop right there, Officer Williams." Mother Madre ordered.

"But, I haven't gotten to the good part yet."

"Oh, I'll let you continue once you perform this task. Take your magnetic wand and point it at the lodestone block that has REGRET written on it."

Officer Williams looked at Mr. Connor, who nodded at him and said for him to do as she said. He said something under his breath as he pointed the wand nearer to the stone until there was a magnetic connection. He slowly tugged back in effort to disturb as little of the foundation under the compass as he could. A second block attached itself to the REGRET block. "Hey! That's not fair! It's pulling more than one block."

"You r-r-ruined more than one ear on that dog, Officer Williams." Mother Madre said, and then sat there for a few silent moments so Officer Williams could think about the harm that he caused to Wing-nut. "The magnetic properties of the wand will increase with the s-s-severity of your actions. Place the two lodestone blocks off to the side with the stone tablet and continue with your story, please."

Officer Williams set the wand back on top of the table. He frowned as he looked at the damage to his compass's foundation before beginning again, "My mother was getting upset that we were just walking around the town and not going to the beach anymore, so she demanded that we went with her that afternoon. While she was making sandwiches for us to eat at the beach, she kept asking us why we were speaking so loud, and not hearing what she said the first time she said things. We just laughed about it and got into her car. When we got to the beach, we told her that we were going to go for a walk along the shore, and then just abandoned her on the blanket. She

160

warned us that we had better take a swim, too, or else there would be no beach house the following summer. Well, once we got out of her sight, my friend noticed a sprinkler watering the lawn of a business across the street from the beach. He suggested that we just run through the sprinkler to make it look like we went swimming. None of us wanted to jump into the ocean's salt water. We were just done with it at that point in time. After we crossed the street, we noticed an old man sitting at a picnic table outside of a grocery store. We decided that it would be fun to see if we could get the man to go into the store to buy some food for us, so we came up with a story and then headed his way. Our conversation went like this:

"How are you, sir?" I asked, loudly.

"Oh, you don't need to speak so loud, young man. I may be old, but my hearing is still good. I'm OK, thank you," he answered.

"You will need to look at us when you talk so we can read your lips."

"You are deaf?" he asked.

"Close to it. We go to a summer-school for the deaf," I said, and then my friend added that we hadn't seen our teacher since she dropped us off at the beach early in the morning, and that we were starving.

"Oh, I see," the elderly man said. "Sit down if you'd like. Where are you boys from?"

My friend said "the beach", and I said "Hope", at the same time as each other. I kicked him under the picnic table and explained that we stay at the beach during the summer and live in Hope during the other seasons. He seemed very interested in our story, and when he asked why we didn't know sign language yet, I told him that was why we were going to summer school. We played out our hunger act until he went into the supermarket and returned to the outside table with a loaf of bread and some bologna from the deli. While we made and ate sandwiches together, he told us about his life. His wife had passed away at an early age and he raised his son alone. He explained that he was living on welfare money, and resided in an apartment building for the poor in the city. Describing how he hadn't seen his son in years, the frail man told us a story of how he finally received a letter from him, asking for money. He said that the note simply said, "Out of Mon(ey), No Fun, Your Son," and that he wrote back, "I'm Sad, Too Bad, Your Dad." Looking at the return address, he couldn't believe that his son lived only an hour away from his apartment and never visited him. I could tell that he felt lonely. Transportation by bus was free to the old man, so he would try to make it to the beach a few times per month and feed the seagulls. He said that it took just about two hours each way because of all of the bus stops and transfers. I remember that his eyes watered when he said that it was going to be his last day at the beach because his health was declining quickly. He pointed to the bus stop just a few feet away, and said that the last few times that he went to the beach, he would walk from the bus, to the supermarket to buy bread for the gulls, then to the picnic table that we were sitting on, and he would stay there until he would take whichever bus came before it got too dark to return to his apartment safely. I just looked at my friend, who was starting to devour his second bologna sandwich. We both placed our food on top of the picnic table. Everything seemed to get really quiet, and even the wind stopped blowing for a second."

"How did you feel at that moment, Officer Williams?" Mother Madre asked.

"I felt a deep regret. My friend did, too."

"Did you do anything to remedy the situation?"

"I'd like to think so. My friend and I decided to ask the man if he wanted us to help him across the street to sit on the beach for a while. He declined at first, saying that there would be nobody to help him get back to the bus stop. We ensured him that we would sit on the beach with him for an hour, and even dip our feet into the water together before helping him back to the picnic table near the bus stop. It was a special hour for me, because I could see how special it was for Leo. The man's name was Leo," Officer Williams stated. "Wow, how did I just remember his name when I can't even remember my best friend's name?" Officer Williams looked at the compass in front of him as he paused in thought. "I remember that I was praying to God for Leo, and asking for forgiveness while I lay in my beach-house bed that night, hoping that my friend couldn't hear me quietly weep. Within a minute or two, we were both crying openly and talking about our afternoon with Leo."

"I am pleased to hear that you and your friend had learned a valuable lesson about honesty, generosity, loneliness, and c-c-compassion, and I'll bet that your company might have made it one of Leo's favorite afternoons on the beach." Mother Madre said, before redirecting her attention to Mr. Connor. Holding her satchel just above his eyes, she instructed him to pull a stone tablet from it.

"What? Shouldn't he have to pull away another block from his foundation first?" Mr. Connor protested. "That was a mean thing to pull on the old man."

"Officer Williams explained that he p-p-prayed for forgiveness, and I believe that God has already done that," explained Mother Madre, as she pulled the satchel away and touched her screen. "Can you provide us with a story of how you have f-f-forgiven another person? Please choose from the three memories that you can now access."

163

"Absolutely. I returned home a day early from a business trip that I was on and found two shot glasses on my nightstand that smelled like tequila, and a pair of men's underwear under the bed that my wife and I shared in this particular memory. I was shocked, and went to a divorce lawyer the next day once she admitted to sleeping with someone else. A stranger to me, no less, in *my* bed."

"So you did *not* forgive her?"

"After some marriage counseling, I finally did forgive her and called off the divorce."

Mother Madre waited a full minute in silence before asking, "Is there more to the story, Mr. Connor?"

"No(essss)." A locust quickly crawled out from between a few lodestones of Mr. Connor's compass foundation. It scurried up the pointer finger of one of his hands and a scorpion-like stinger pierced the backside of that hand and latched on. "OWWWWWW!" Mr. Connor began to scream while trying to shake the locust off his hand. "OWWWWWW! GET IT OFF ME! MOTHER MADRE – PLEASE! OWWWWWW!"

Mother Madre showed no sympathy while she watched Mr. Connor deal with the pain for several seconds more. Finally, she touched her screen and the locust burrowed back into the foundation. "Lies hurt others very much, Mr. Connor, and t-t-truth is that it always comes back around to sting the l-l-liar harder. Let me ask again, is there any more to your story about forgiveness?"

"Yes(essss)."

"Continue then, please, Mr. Connor."

"So, I called off the divorce, and although things weren't quite the same since she cheated on me, I thought that we were working on our marriage in a positive manner. Eventually, it came out in one of our counseling sessions that I wouldn't let the matter go, and we did eventually divorce anyway."

"Mr. Connor, it appears that you did not actually f-f-forgive her. Although not very easy to achieve, f-f-forgiveness is one of those absolute pillars that are necessary to maintain a p-p-p-peaceful and everlasting existence."

"But, I felt so betrayed."

"Have you ever said the words 'Forgive us our trespasses as we forgive those that trespass against us'?

"Of course. That is part of 'The Lord's Prayer.'"

"So, you expect God to f-f-forgive you without you actually forgiving others yourself? Nobody has been b-b-betrayed more than The Lord, yet he forgives all who truly seek it. Please remove one of your foundation's Jerusalem cornerstones with your fingers."

"Yes, Mother Madre," he said, while slowly extending his hand toward the foundation and retracting it quickly from fear.

"As long as you don't lie, there is no need to worry about the locust," Mother Madre ensured.

"I forgive you for holding up the game," Officer Williams jeered, as Mr. Connor was still slow in taking away one of his foundation's cornerstones. "You should have just forgiven her and you wouldn't be losing this game. I'm guessing that you weren't an angel while on your little business trip. Did you cheat on her yourself?"

"No(ooooh)!" shouted Mr. Connor in anger.

"Gentlemen!" Mother Madre injected, as she tried to stop the back-and-forth banter, to no avail.

Mr. Connor continued, "But I'd bet that *you* did cheat on someone, Officer Righteous."

"No(essss)," Officer Williams said. When he heard his unmatched echo, he pulled his hands from the top of the table and watched as a locust ran in a figure-eight pattern on the table in front of his foundation.

"Pulling your hands from the table is against the rules, Officer Williams. Return them to the table or forfeit the game," instructed Mother Madre.

He placed his hands back on top of the table and held his breath. The locust ran back between a few stones of the foundation. As Officer Williams let out a breath of relief, the locust scuttled back out from between some stones, followed by a second one. "AAAAARGH!" he screamed. "OWWWWWW! PLEASE MAKE THEM STOP! PLEASE!"

Both locusts hid back inside the foundation of the compass that sat in front of Officer Williams. He stared at his hands while his face gave evidence that the pain inflicted by the locusts remained.

"The hurt that is inflicted by a l-l-l-lie always l-l-l-lingers, Officer Williams," Mother Madre confirmed. "Now is a good time to review your infidelity," she added, before touching her screen. "Well, at least there is only one memory to choose from, that included physicality, anyway. Please begin. Hands on the table."

"I had a suspicion that my girlfriend had cheated on me with a friend of mine, but I couldn't prove it. Considering that, I felt that I had a free pass to do the same. I guess that I looked at it like an insurance policy in case she actually did cheat on me, or if she ever would have done so in the future. I remember that I was returning from a defense training class and stopped in at a restaurant a town or two over from where I was living. The restaurant was crowded and the wait for a table was long so I decided to eat at the bar. There was a woman that was also eating at the bar and we struck up a conversation. Before we knew it, it was closing time. I felt a bit inebriated and accepted her invitation to stay on her couch because she lived just around the corner."

"Was she single?" Mother Madre asked?

Officer Williams looked at his hands before replying, "No. She was married, but had explained that the marriage was essentially dead, and that there was no romance left between them."

"So you drove to her house and slept on her couch?"

"No, she drove, Mother Madre."

"And you slept on her couch?"

"Not exactly. One thing led to another, and before we knew it I was in her bed with her."

"You slept with a married woman?"

"Yes."

"We will address that in a moment. Did you use protection while engaged in sex with that woman?"

"No, Mother Madre. I had not expected to meet someone that night."

"Officer Williams, please extract the branch of thorns that is sticking out of your compass foundation."

As he grabbed hold of it, a thorn stuck into one of his fingers. He watched as a drop of blood formed and then hung from that finger. It seemed to have a reflection of the lady's smiling face on the surface of the drop, and when it finally hit the tabletop the smile in the reflection turned into a frown and the drop quickly evaporated. A second blood drop formed and the reflection appeared to be that of Mr. Connor's face, which was frowning as the drop clung to Officer Williams' finger, and then smiling as it, too, quickly evaporated off from the table. Not mentioning what he just witnessed, he continued to tug at the branch of thorns. It dragged several lodestone blocks and crucifixion spikes with it, causing the compass to dip dangerously.

"Can I replace the blocks and spikes that the branch dislodged from the foundation, Mother Madre?"

"Absolutely not. Your unprotected sex was completely r-r-r-reckless, and the act had the potential of r-r-ruining, and possibly ending, the marriages and lives of others through disease and deceit, similar to the way thorny bushes and vines can invade then impede the growth of a garden or forest, choking each plant or tree until it completely d-d-dies a slow d-d-d-death. The branch of thorns had twists and turns that you couldn't see as you pulled it out, which caused much destruction. Very apropos, considering your r-r-reckless actions. Now please stack the lodestone blocks off to the side, along with the crucifixion spikes."

Officer Williams stacked the blocks just as Mother Madre had instructed, but when he gathered the few spikes that were pulled away from the foundation, he felt an immense burning pain throughout his hands and feet that increased throughout several pulsations, as if from a hammer's continuous striking. His efforts to let go of the spikes were futile, as his hands seemed to be paralyzed, or at least immobile for several minutes. Finally, the pain ended and he was able to place the spikes near the lodestone blocks.

"Can you imagine the p-p-p-pain that Jesus Christ endured while being nailed to the cross so that all of these sins that we are talking about today could be wiped away from our records? Now *that* is pure love and forgiveness. Officer Williams, please explain what happened after your sinful night had ended."

"I felt terrible. For the next several weeks, I asked God for forgiveness, and even begged him to take my life in exchange for ensuring that my girlfriend wouldn't get any sexually transmitted diseases from what I had done."

"Please pick up your wand and extract two more lodestone blocks from your foundation, Officer Williams."

"Shouldn't he need to take away more blocks than that? The woman was married!" Mr. Connor angrily suggested.

"Why don't you mind your own business," Officer Williams replied.

"Maybe YOU should've minded YOUR own business before screwing someone's WIFE, you jerk! I should kill you myself!"

"Take away two Jerusalem cornerstones Mr. Connor," ordered Mother Madre.

"Nobody confirmed that it was YOUR wife, Conner, but if it was, I should have taken your house and all of your belongings, too, you bastard!"

"Take away four lodestone blocks, Officer Williams."

"J-Christ, this is bullshit!"

"Using The Lord's name in vain? Take away another cornerstone and branch of thorns, Mr. Connor."

Both compasses hit the top of the table at the same time, just as Mother Madre was folding her screen. "Well, it appears that neither of you are q-q-q-qualified to t-t-teach ethics right now. The fact that both of you were concerned about making extra money by teaching the after-school ethics course, more than the actual subject matter, disqualified you right from the start. What could you use the money for here anyway? What would you possibly purchase?"

Silence.

"The Moral Compass game is obviously over, but each of you has amassed quite the pile of stone blocks. How far do you care to take this feud? Whoever feels that they are more p-p-pure than the other may cast the f-f-first stone," she added.

The two men sat there quietly in shame.

169

"You are both dismissed from the Hall of Truths. On your way back to your classroom and officer station, please ask Miss Kylee to see me in here when you pass by her office." Mother Madre requested. "And tell her not to delay."

Mother Madre collected all of the materials from the Moral Compass game and placed them inside her satchel. She fluffed her satchel into a pillow and rested her head on top of it.

Marjorie Murphy was already standing near the classroom door when the Hope High School dismissal bell went off. She darted down the hall because she had thought up the perfect plan. Her target, Hailey Crown, was already several steps ahead of Marjorie in the hallway, but she didn't want to make it look obvious that she was trying to reach Hailey. Worse than that, she didn't want to look desperate. Both girls had made it as the final two candidates for Class President, and Marjorie's personal polling suggested that she was going to lose, and lose badly. Marjorie was well liked by her peers in her debate class, and some of her history classes, but Hailey was popular throughout the entire school. Even though Marjorie believed that she had more leadership skills than Hailey, she knew that she also had more political skills. Dirty. Rotten. Politics. And it was time for her to put those skills to work.

"Oh, Hailey, I've got some news!" Marjorie shouted out. Everyone loves to be 'in' on something, and by loudly blurting that out, it instantly gave Marjorie a social advantage, and piqued the interest of her opponent enough to get her to turn around and wait-up for Marjorie.

"Hey Marj, what's up?" said Hailey, pleasantly.

"Look, I know that it's getting close to the election. I just want to say that if you win, I'll support you one hundred percent."

"That is so sweet to say, Marj. Thank you, and you know I'll do the same. Anything I can add to college applications can only help. I'm sure that my grades aren't as good as yours. You are so smart. Well, Good luck to both of us!" she said cheerily.

As they started to descend the large stone staircase leading out from Hope High, Marjorie continued, "You know, we could make this election a lot of fun for the student body. Spice it up a little."

"How would we do that?"

"Maybe tomorrow, you say something negative about me, and I'll say something negative about you. That always gets attention."

"But, I don't want to say anything bad about you, Marj."

"Nothing too bad. Just something like, you heard that I haven't paid my student dues yet so how could I even consider running for President?"

"I don't know. I guess."

"And I'll just say something like you haven't even taken the leadership course yet so you aren't qualified. You on board?"

"I *guess* it would make it more interesting," Hailey responded, hesitantly.

"So remember, we don't take any of this personally, right?"

"Right! Of course not!"

"OK. What we need to do now is each choose a friend to become the people that you and I communicate to each other through, that way nobody will know that we are faking it. Nobody from the student body should ever see us talk to each other unless we are sneering at each other. Starting tomorrow morning, I'll speak through my friend Liz. Who do you pick?"

"Oh, I don't know. Maybe Joy."

"Great! Let the fireworks begin!" Marjorie said, while extending her arm for a handshake.

"I'm not sure I like this," Hailey said, while shaking her hand.

By the end of the next day, some classmates were talking about how inexperienced Hailey was, while others were saying that Marjorie should pay up or drop out of the race. There was even a small fistfight over the two candidates that erupted between a few friends on one of the busses as it was leaving the school. As a first step, it was the exact result that Marjorie was hoping to achieve. On the third day, Marjorie arrived at school an hour and a half early and hung up campaign posters on the school walls, for *both* parties. One poster design had an unflattering photo of Hailey Crown with the words 'Hailey – Not smart enough to wear the crown of Class President', and the other poster design was a photo of Marjorie holding as many gold coins in her arms as she could, with the words 'Marjorie "Midas" Murphy – She takes but doesn't give, so don't give her your vote!'

Liz alerted Joy of the posters once she spotted her getting off her bus. She reminded her that it was all in good fun, and that it was the first time in Hope High's history that the class presidential election created that much attention. Liz handed Joy a letter from Marjorie that explained a twist in the plot that should happen the next day. It would be an after school 'Secret Summit Meeting' between the two candidates that would be promoted through the school as "Two Candidates Working to Bring Unity back to Hope High" and harmony back between the two class presidential hopefuls. Liz told Joy that they should meet again the next morning where she will let her in on the secret location for the summit. Joy agreed, and the two parted ways for the day.

By the next morning, the school had been divided by politics, and the hate spread beyond the candidates. Even some teachers began to spread propaganda, and arguments could be heard in Hope High's main hallway coming from the teacher's room. Students hovered around a bulletin board where a poster announced the 'Secret Summit Meeting', which was to happen at an undisclosed location after school. It would be held just before Marjorie and Hailey were to give their campaign speeches to the school the following day, so the intrigue and interest pertaining to the class presidential election reached an all time high.

That afternoon, Marjorie and Liz got to the secret location half an hour before it was scheduled for. The site was located in the woods near the supermarket, up the path and on top of the hill. There were a series of large rocks there that were perfect for sitting on, just above the poison ivy, seemingly arranged by nature to hold such secret meetings as the one that was about to happen. Liz was poised upon one of them while Marjorie ran a mini microphone and wire through her sleeve to a recording device that she had tucked into the back of her pants.

"Now remember, don't move at all during the meeting," Marjorie instructed, as she walked around the rock that Liz was sitting on in effort to make sure that no wires were showing. "As soon as we see her walking up the path, I'll turn it on. The key will be for me to get her permission to allow us to record her."

"How do you plan on doing that?"

"Trust me."

Finally, Marjorie heard some cracking branches under walking feet. "Here we go," she said to Liz, while hitting the record button. She started walking down the hill to meet Hailey halfway. "Where's Joy?"

"She had practice after school, so it's just me," Hailey explained.

Marjorie escorted her to the rock directly across from Liz, telling her that it was the most comfortable of all the boulders in the forest. "Can you believe the attention this election is getting?" she asked Hailey.

"I know! But, I have to admit that I'm glad that we are shifting the focus from hate and division to healing and friendship. I don't hate you, in reality, so the attention never really felt all that great to me."

"I agree, and like you said before, no matter who wins we will support the other. Thankfully, neither of us have anything to hide. I mean, I would allow my words to be recorded during our summit to prove that I have nothing to hide, or no ill will against you."

"Me, too," said Hailey.

"That you are honest enough that you'd be ok if someone recorded our summit, too?"

"Of course! I have nothing to hide."

"That's awesome! Good! I'm glad that we are cordial enough to speak kindly and freely to each other, unlike Jasmine in math class. Do you know that I heard her calling you a loser today?"

"She did? What a jerk she is!" Hailey said.

"She's a what?" Marjorie asked.

"If she said that, then Jasmine is a jerk. I've done all I could to help her in that class. I was even her tutor last semester."

"Oh, that's nothing," continued Marjorie. "Robin was telling everyone in gym class that you are were as graceful as a rhinoceros when she saw your ballet recital last week."

"Are you serious? She told me that she loved it. I never realized that Robin is two-faced. I mean, I worked so hard on learning that dance. It was perfect. I'm sure of it. It's like saying that Timmy Mardo can't even run, although he is Hope High's track star, or saying that

Dyson Devlifar couldn't sing a note to save his life even though he won the school's music competition. I just don't get it."

"Don't let it bother you, Hailey. You're above them. You are a finalist in the run for class president. You should feel proud of all that you have accomplished at Hope High. Ever since our freshman year, I admired you."

"You did?"

"Absolutely. I've always wished I were more like you - as pretty, as talented, as kind to others. There's a reason why you are so popular."

"That is so nice of you to say, Marj. I hope you know that I admire how smart you are in classes. Your GPA must be through the roof!"

"Thanks, Hailey, but Principal Jacobs messed up my last report card. She is unfit to be the principle at Hope High."

"It must have been an honest mistake. Principal Jacobs always seems to look out for each student's best interest."

"Who?"

"Principle Jacobs. You just said that Principal Jacobs is unfit to be Hope High's principal."

"Maybe you are right. Must have just been an honest mistake. Well, I'm glad that we had our little summit."

"Me, too. Is there anything specific that you wanted to talk about regarding the election, Marj?"

"Nah, this was just to create a buzz around school. Let the best candidate win!" said Marjorie, before leading her back down the hill, away from the rocks.

"Why isn't Liz leaving?" asked Hailey.

"She's going through some personal stuff right now and probably just wants to chill out before going home. I should probably head back up there and check on her. I'll see you tomorrow."

"Speech Day tomorrow! I'm a little nervous. Did you finish writing yours yet?" Hailey asked.

"Not yet, and I'm sure it will take me the rest of the night."

"Me, too. Good luck, Marj!"

The following morning, all of the student body sat at their desks in anticipation. Class president campaign speeches were going to begin over the intercom once the morning announcements were complete, and you could hear a pin drop in each classroom as the speeches began.

"Hello Hope High faculty and student body. My name is Hailey Crown, and I am running for Class President. I'd like to begin by thanking Principal Jacobs for the support that she has given my opponent Marjorie and me throughout this election cycle, and for the opportunities and leadership that all of Hope High's students benefit from as a result of Dr. Jacobs being our principal. She is a role model to me, and I would strive to live up to the high standards that Principal Jacobs has set for herself, and those around her, if I were to be elected as your Class President. I also want to extend well wishes to Marjorie, with whom I had a nice conversation with yesterday during our secret summit. You can all feel confident that whomever you elect as your class president will work hard during all of our days here at Hope High School. Again, My name is Hailey Crown, and I would appreciate your vote."

"Thank you, Hailey," said Principal Jacobs over the intercom system. "Now we will hear from Hailey's opponent, Marjorie Murphy."

"Thank you, Dr. Jacobs, Hope High faculty, and fellow students. I am Marjorie Murphy, and I am running for Class President. Before this speech is over, you will all agree that I am most fit to lead our class as we navigate our paths from where we are today straight through to graduation day. In effort to be a great leader, I b-b-believe that one must understand and r-r-respect those that elect them to office. Unfortunately, my conversation with Hailey yesterday highlighted our d-d-differences, which included her aversion toward some of those that she would potentially be elected to lead. Here are just a few samples of what she had to s-s-s-say about her classmates," Marjorie said, and then proceeded to hold the recording device up to the microphone and play some of what Hailey said: *"Jasmine is a jerk - Timmy Mardo can't even run - Dyson Devlifar couldn't sing a note to save his life. Robin is two-faced"* Marjorie paused the device and continued to speak into the intercom's microphone, "And, speaking of someone being t-t-two-faced, it appears that she has a certain way to describe Principal Jacobs when she is in front of her versus when she is not. Take a listen." Marjorie pushed play on the device one more time, *'Principal Jacobs is unfit to be Hope High's Principal.'* Marjorie placed the recording device inside her pocketbook before continuing her speech, allowing the students, and the principal, to absorb what they had just heard. "In addition, I'd like to address the assertions that she and others have made against me regarding not paying my class dues as of yet. Unlike many here at Hope High, my family d-d-does not have much money. My mother works three jobs and still struggles with making ends meet. We have been w-w-w-working hard and saving up to pay for expenses that others have an easy time taking care of. How dare she call me 'Midas' during the campaign? What Hailey is ignorant to is the ch-ch-charity work I get involved with on weekends when she is trying to charm people with her ballet dancing. Twice I had

177

earned the money for class dues, and twice I ended up g-g-giving that money away to strangers in our community that appeared to n-n-n-need the m-m-money more than me, or even Hope High for that matter. For those who may still remain critical of me, you may rest easy in knowing that I recently p-p-paid my class dues in full because I sold the stamp collection that my grandmother and I had worked on, and that she left for me upon her death. I cried at her gravesite after s-s-selling it, but I know that she would've understood, having been Class President here at Hope High two generations ago herself. My dear fellow students, please cast your vote for me tomorrow during Hope High's Election Day. You won't be let down, d-d-disappointed, or talked about behind your b-b-b-backs. Thank you."

By the end of the next day, Marjorie was sworn in as Class President. The first thing that she enacted was a school talent show to help reunite the student body. It would be held in the auditorium during school hours in two weeks. All of the students were happy with Marjorie's idea because they would be out of class for two full periods. Unfortunately for Marjorie, her inaugural honeymoon was short lived because she had promised Liz a role as 'Assistant to the President', but ended up giving it to Marshall Smith's sister, thinking it would get her closer to Marshall because she had a crush on him. As a result, Liz became upset and provided the original recording of the secret summit meeting to Principal Jacobs so she could see how it was taken out context during Marjorie's speech. As a result, the presidency was taken away from Marjorie and given to Hailey.

Many students signed up for the talent show, and the structure that Marjorie put together for it remained. There were three judges that sat on the side of the stage while the students performed, which included Marjorie, and if a performance was terrible or if a student signed up an act as a joke, a judge could press a buzzer and that person would be eliminated from the competition. Most students had serious acts, such as juggling, singing, playing an instrument, and acrobats. Class clown, Billy Brown, pretended that he had a flea circus on stage until he was buzzed off, and his friend Justin Pierce was buzzed off the stage after he tried performing a song out of armpit farts. The only other person to be buzzed off the stage was newly appointed Class President, Hailey Crown. She was halfway through an elegant ballet dance when Marjorie Murphy buzzed her performance. It seemed to go on forever as Marjorie held her hand on the buzzer for a prolonged length of time. Hailey ran straight from the stage to the girl's bathroom in tears.

A few hours later, the Hope High dismissal bell rang. Marjorie found herself feeling very alone in the crowded hallway leading outside. Much of the students shunned her once they learned about her election scheme, and by the end of the talent show, mostly all of her classmates thought she was downright bitter and rude. She exited the building and saw Marshall Smith open his passenger-side car door for Hailey to get in. As she stood there watching from the top of Hope High's outdoor stairs, Liz approached her.

"Have you heard? Marshall asked out Hailey today. Don't you think they make a gorgeous couple? He *loved* the way she danced," Liz announced, enjoying every word.

Marjorie yelled out "That BITCH! I hope she DIES!"

"I HOPE SHE DIES(lives)!"

"Mother Madre?" Miss Kylee inquired, as she entered the Hall of Truths and pulled out a chair to sit down on.

Mother Madre lifted her head from her satchel and looked around. "Ah, Miss Kylee. Have you been here a while?"

"Yes(oooh)," Miss Kylee looked puzzled when she heard her conflicting echo.

Mother Madre took the transparent screen out from her satchel, looked at Miss Kylee with a disconcerted stare, then folded it again and returned it to the satchel. "Miss Kylee, when did I ask you to design and post the flyer for the Ethics Class Teacher position?"

"I'm not(am) sure, Mother Madre. Maybe a week(onths) ago?" Miss Kylee gave a confused glance. "Why do some echoes-"

"TWO months ago, Miss Kylee. Two MONTHS!"

"I could've sworn-"

"There has been a new teacher in that position for over a month. You must have seen him in the teacher's room by now."

"Oh, Mr. L'Heureux?"

"Yes," Mother Madre responded, shaking her head in disbelief.

"He seems like a really nice per-, wait, do we like him?"

"Do you ever have even just one s-s-single original thought or opinion, Miss Kylee?"

Silence

"Are you actually th-th-th-thinking, Miss Kylee?"

"Oh, I'm sorry. No(oooh)."

Shaking her head again, Mother Madre said, "Just g-g-go back to your office, Miss Kylee."

Miss Kylee stood up without pushing her chair in, and began walking toward the exit of the cavernous Hall of Truths.

"Did you forget to do something, Miss Kylee?" Mother Madre asked, after waiting for her to almost get to the door.

"No(esss), Mother Madre. I was(n't) going to ask you for another assignment to prove myself."

180

"Stop the lying, Miss Kylee. Sit back down," Mother Madre commanded. "Lies are very d-d-damaging, to others, and to yourself."

"But mine are usually just white lies."

"There is no such thing as a white lie. A lie is a lie, and I am afraid that you have lied, and made up excuses, so many times that you actually believe them. That is when it gets to a very d-d-dangerous point. You can no longer discern between r-r-right and wrong, and it is creating some serious scars on your soul. You must address the battle within yourself before any healing can begin. Very simply put, there is a battle in yourself between r-r-right and wrong. Most people have such battles going on, but at least can tell the difference between good and bad before making g-g-good or bad ch-ch-choices. You need to understand this and battle against it. Mr. Dyson will perform a song for you and then hand you a scroll of the lyrics. I've said this before, you need to work on *you* before I will give you any additional assignments."

The stage curtain opened and Mr. Dyson began the song.

THE BATTLE IN YOURSELF
THE BATTLE IN YOURSELF
THE BATTLE IN YOURSELF
THE ENEMY BEHIND THE LINE
THE BATTLE IN YOURSELF
THE BATTLE IN YOURSELF
THE ENEMY INSIDE YOUR MIND
YOUR HEAD IS SAYING MAYBE
BUT YOUR HEART IS SAYING NO
NERVOUSLY YOU QUICKLY LOSE CONTROL

YOUR HANDS ARE REACHING UPWARD
BUT YOUR FEET ARE SINKING LOW
YOU FEEL IT PASSING FROM THE HEAD TO TOE
THE BATTLE IN YOURSELF
THE BATTLE IN YOURSELF
THE ENEMY BEHIND THE LINE
THE BATTLE IN YOURSELF
THE BATTLE IN YOURSELF
THE ENEMY INSIDE YOUR MIND
THE WAY THAT YOU ARE FEELING
DOES THAT COME FROM THE SKY?
OR IS IT COMING UP FROM THE GROUND?
IS IT THE TRUTH OR IS IT ALL A LIE?
DO YOU PICK IT UP OR PUT IT DOWN?
THE BATTLE IN YOURSELF
THE BATTLE IN YOURSELF
THE ENEMY BEHIND THE LINE
THE BATTLE IN YOURSELF
THE BATTLE IN YOURSELF
THE ENEMY INSIDE YOUR MIND

"Catchy song, Mr. Dyson, but maybe you should work on your own battles and mind your own business," Miss Kylee commented.

Mr. Dyson handed the scroll to Miss Kylee, and then began to say, "Listen, I'm only given a certain amount of infor-"

"Thank you, Mr. Dyson. I'll take it from here. I imagine the negative reactions after your performances are quite different than the adoration you may have gotten used to in your dreams," Mother Madre suggested. "Please close the door behind you."

Once Mr. Dyson left the Hall of Truths, Mother Madre walked around the entire long table, apparently in deep thought, while Kylee read over the scroll a few times. Finally, she sat back down, leaned-in toward Miss Kylee, and spoke quietly, "I will be spending some time in St. Perpetua Academy's chapel. Please let the others know that I am not to be disturbed. That is your assignment, Miss Kylee. Do that right away, and then work on fixing you."

CHAPTER 10

"What are you working on, Mr.?"

Bane Karcin didn't expect that anyone would be standing behind him while he worked on the boiler. He lifted his head quickly, banging it on a pipe as he turned around. "Ouch!"

"I'm sorry!" the young boy said, and he began to run away.

"Wait!" shouted Mr. Karcin. He rubbed the back of his head and then looked at his hand for any evidence of blood. "How did you get down here? Shouldn't you be in class?"

The boy stood with his back to Mr. Karcin. His head was hung low, and Bane noticed a teardrop disrupt a pile of sawdust in front of the child's feet as he walked toward him. The movement in the boy's shoulders confirmed that he must have been crying.

"I'm Mr. Karcin. What is your name, young man?"

After wiping his eyes with his sleeves, the young boy turned around without looking up and said, "Simeon, but my friends call me Sim."

"Well, nice to meet you, Sim," Bane said while extending his hand for a handshake. The boy looked up until his swollen red eyes met Mr. Karcin's, and he shook his outstretched hand. "Why all this sadness?"

Sim reached into his back pocket and pulled out a carelessly folded paper. He unfolded it and tried to iron it against his leg with his hand before handing it to Mr. Karcin.

"Ah, your report card. Mind if I take a look?"

Sim looked back down and shook his head no, and then put an arm up above his head as to if protect himself. Bane noticed the action with concern, and then focused his attention on Sim's report card.

"Oooh, I see," said Bane with empathy. "Is it the 'F' in Science that has you worried?"

Without breaking his gaze on the sawdust all over the floor, the young boy shook his head yes, and then slowly turned and looked up at Mr. Karcin as he hesitantly lowered his arm.

"I tried my best, but the tests are too hard for me to pass," Sim said, with evidence of his sorrow affecting the tone of his voice.

"If it makes you feel better, I never did very well in school, either. Work that came from books just never clicked with me," Bane said, trying to comfort the boy from his anxiety.

"What other kind of school work is there?" Sim asked.

"That's the problem," Mr. Karcin answered. "Not enough schools offer classes on the trades."

"The trades?"

"Trades are things like plumbing, which is what I'm working on now, or carpentry, electricity. Things like that."

"I wish they had classes like that here at St. Perpetua."

"Maybe we can start one right here and now. What do you think?"

"That would be great, Mr."

Bane walked over to his phone to contact the main office. "Oh, Hi Miss Kylee. I was trying to reach Mother Madre."

"I'm sorry, Mr. Karcin, but Mother Madre will be unavailable for a while."

"Oh, I see. Please do me a favor, and if anyone comes looking for Simeon, you may let them know that he is with me working on the boiler."

"You got it."

Mr. Karcin walked over to his locker and rummaged through it, pulling out a tool belt, a wrench, and a hammer. "Alright, Sim, here are your first supplies for this classroom. Put this belt around your waist and we'll get started."

Sim looked at how Mr. Karcin wore his belt, but it wouldn't stay suspended above his tiny hips as he tried to wear it.

"Bring it over here to the workbench and I'll add a hole to make it fit tighter. Actually, *you* will add the hole," Bane suggested, as he kicked a footstool into position just in front of the workbench.

Sim's eyes seemed to light up as he stood on the stool and accepted a hammer and leather-punch from Mr. Karcin.

"Now, watch me first," Bane said as he took a piece of scrap leather and held a leather-punch against it. "This is a leather-punch. You will want to make sure that it is positioned exactly where you want your hole, because once you make it you can't take it away." He tapped the punch lightly, and then gave it a good whack. "Voila!" he said, showing the new hole in the leather scrap. "Ok, now it's your turn. Mark the belt where the new hole should go, and always measure twice." Mr. Karcin waited patiently for him to complete that step, then assisted in positioning it on top of the workbench. "Now, place the leather-punch into position. Give it a few light taps so you get a feel for the hammer and punch, and then a good wallop."

The young boy did as he said, then came down hard with the hammer right on top of his thumb. "OWWWWWW!" Sim began to cry again.

"Ooo, that must have hurt, Sim. Hang on," Bane said before walking to the small refrigerator near his desk to pull an ice pack from the freezer. "One thing about the trades is that they may hurt now and then. Here, hold this against your thumb."

Once the crying stopped and the pain subsided a bit, Sim asked, "Why are you caring about me so much?"

Bane paused for a moment. He didn't really have an answer. He thought harder, and still wasn't sure, but offered, "Because I was once like you." Picking up the tools that he gave Sim to use, he gave the leather-punch a hard hit with the hammer, and held the belt out for the young boy to see the result. "That should help it fit better. How's your thumb?"

"Hurts."

"It'll feel better soon. Do you still want to learn a trade, or would you rather head back up to your classes?"

"I wanna stay here, please."

"Ok, let me see that thumb. Can you bend it like this?" Bane said, while demonstrating with his own thumb. Sim was able to bend it. "Good! Let's get to work. For today, I just want you to watch."

Sim followed Mr. Karcin over to the boiler, and they both knelt down near some pipes. Bane explained how he had already turned off

187

the water supply so that he could work without worrying about a flood while he changed out a leaky coupling. As Mr. Karcin did each step of the process, Sim looked on intently, and asked questions when he needed clarity. Mr. Karcin, himself, enjoyed the experience, and explained to Sim that as long as it was okay with Mother Madre, he'd be willing to show him a new skill each day.

"Do I need to return to classes now, or could I stay here for a while longer? My thumb is still sore, and I'm not so sure that I'd be able to write right now, anyway."

"I'll tell you what, "said Mr. Karcin, "that chair over there reclines. Lay back and keep the ice pack on your thumb for a while. It's break time for me, and I need to check on something. Sim did as he suggested, and closed his eyes.

"Why did you need to write a check for something?" Sim's father said to Sim's mother in a scolding voice.

"I had no choice," she replied. "It is Sim's birthday tomorrow and the tool kit that he talked about all year long was on sale for half-off. I had no cash, but I did have the checkbook with me."

Sim's father swiped the back of his hand across his mother's face, forcing her to fall back onto the couch. "There's a reason why you had no cash. It's because we *don't* have any until my next paycheck comes in, and even then, most of it will be going to a carpenter to fix the leak in the roof, unless you like the rain dripping in on the kitchen table! Now I need to pay a bank fee for a bounced check on top of it!"

"But, it is Sim's birthd-"
SLAP!

Sim ran out from his bedroom and curled up next to his mother who was weeping. "Stop hitting Mom!"

"Why must you always have such rage? Look at how scared your son is," Sim's mother said, with fear of retribution.

"Do you want another slap, woman?"

"If you do, I'll finally call the cops on you!"

Picking up the phone, Sim's father held it out to her. "Go ahead! Call the damn cops! When they get here I'll be sure to tell them all about you writing out bad checks!"

"Just leave for work and leave us alone!"

"And you can shut the check-book and shut your mouth before you earn yourself a fat lip!"

Once he left and slammed the door behind him, Sim hugged his mother and they both cried. Eventually, she told him to get ready so that they could visit his grandparents. That always cheered up Sim, who looked up to his grandfather more than anyone else in his life. As a matter of fact, his grandfather was the only male in his life that ever paid any attention to him.

"Make sure you feed your gerbil before we leave, Sim," his mother added.

Sim moved the reading book that leaned against the broken cage latch so his gerbil wouldn't escape, and poured a capful of rodent food into the small bowl inside. "There ya go, Ben," he said, before grabbing his jean-jacket and jumping into his mother's late-model car.

"Not a word to your grandparents about this morning, okay?"

"Sure, Mom."

His grandparent's house was the largest single-family dwelling on their street, and was built by his grandfather and great-grandfather. Sim's favorite place in the house was his grandfather's woodshop in the basement. It also happened to be his favorite place on earth.

189

There were jars of every size nail and screw that one could imagine, an uncountable number of tools that hung on hooks along a full wall made of pegboard, a workbench with a vice mounted to it, and shelves with assorted pieces of wood. To Sim, it was a space full of possibilities, with limitations created only by one's lack of imagination, which was never a problem for him. As soon as Sim stepped foot into his grandfather's basement, the scent of freshly cut wood sent his creativity into high gear, and on that particular morning he set out to build a new gerbil cage for Ben.

As per usual, His grandfather allowed Sim to head into the basement to start in on whatever inspired him that day, before heading down himself to assist and to teach. By then, Sim had already nailed half of a box together, albeit with unmatched angles, edges and gaps.

"What are you building today, my friend?" Grandpa asked, while walking around his workshop, selecting tools here and there.

"I'm building Ben a new cage."

"Ben?"

"My gerbil. His cage is broken."

"Oh, I see," Grandpa related, as he opened a drawer and pulled out a pad of paper. He reached for the pencil that he kept tucked above his ear and sat at his Tuesday-night poker-game table. "Maybe we should sketch out a design for the cage before we gat started. Sound good?"

"Sure Grandpa."

"Do you have a design in your head?"

"I was just going to build a box with a door."

"Would you like to make it even more fancy than that?"

"Of course!"

Grandpa's hand fervently danced back and forth as the sound of the pencil on the paper colored excitement and hope in Sim's eyes. After two minutes, he held up the sketch so Sim could see it. "What do you think?"

"Wow!" Sim looked over the sketch, which included a Gambrel-style roof made of wood and screen, a metal-mesh front door, and an inside loft with a ramp for Ben to climb up to it. "Do you really think we can build it like that, Grandpa?"

"If we take our time and do it right, we sure can, Sim!" Grandpa said, before jotting down several items from his workshop for Sim to gather while he chose the best planks of wood for the job.

Late that afternoon, the main structure had been built when Sim's mother called down the stairs for him to wrap it up because they needed to go home so she could prepare dinner.

"Do you think we can build some more tomorrow, Grandpa?"

"I was planning on it, Sim!"

By the end of the next day, the mostly completed cage sat upon the workbench with various clamps attached to it.

"Can I bring it home, Grandpa?"

"We need to let the glued areas dry, Sim, and then we will paint the outside of it tomorrow, so I'd say that you can bring it home in two days."

Sim's shoulders dipped, and he said, "ok" in a disappointed tone.

"Patience, my young carpenter. Quality work takes time."

"I know. I love you, Grandpa."

"And I love *you*. More than you will ever know, and forever."

The following weekend, his raging father, who found his gerbil running behind the toilet in the bathroom, woke Sim up in the middle of the night.

"What the hell is your gerbil doing out of his cage?"

191

Sim was disoriented, and tried to figure out quickly what his father was talking about before he might get slapped by him. He turned on his bedroom light, which made him squint his eyes as he surveyed the new gerbil cage. Ben wasn't inside, and once his eyes adjusted, Sim could see that the gerbil had chewed a hole through the wood in a corner of the cage. While he scrambled about the bathroom and down the hall in attempt to catch Ben, he heard his father talking to himself, and saw him walk toward the back door with the new cage.

"How stupid to make a rodent cage out of wood. Just more garbage for the town dump!"

"No, Dad! Don't throw it away! I made that with Grandpa!"

"Well, you can tell Grandpa to come clean up the mess outside."

"What mess?"

"THIS mess!" Sim's father said, before throwing it down on the cement landing outside the door. He picked it up again and hurled it to the ground a second time, which ensured that it was beyond repair, even for Grandpa's carpentry skills.

Crying hysterically, Sim continued his search for the gerbil through his watery eyes for almost an hour more before instructed by his mother to jump back into bed. He decided that he would run away the next day, so he quietly packed his pillowcase with an extra set of clothes.

The next morning, once his father left for work and his mother was getting ready in the bathroom, he snuck out of the house with his pillowcase, along with the tackle box and fishing pole that his grandfather had given him for his birthday. Just as he got to the street, his father's car pulled back into the driveway.

"Where are you going, Sim?" his father shouted, as he quickly got out of his car.

Sim began to run.

"HEY, GET BACK HERE!"

"Get back here!" Bane Karcin said, while crawling around the boiler room floor on his hands and knees.

Trying to get his bearings, Sim woke up and straightened out the recliner. "What's going on?"

"Looks like we have a visitor. I saw a mouse run out from behind my desk."

Sim got on all fours himself and assisted in the search. "I'll bet that it ran out through this hole in the corner," he announced, before standing up and bumping his head on a pipe. "Ouch!"

"Same pipe that I banged *my* head on!" said Mr. Karcin.

Sim touched his head where it hit the pipe and felt wetness. Looking at his hand, he started to cry when he saw blood.

"Let me take a look," Bain said, while parting Sim's hair. "Not too bad, but it wouldn't be a bad idea for you to go up and see the nurse so she can clean it up."

Once Sim left the boiler room, Bain sat down on the recliner. Surveying the floor once more for the mouse, he finally pushed back on the seat and closed his eyes.

Karcin Bane ran around the boiler room at the Hope Metal Badge & Button Company with a broom in his hand while the company's president's secretary stood naked on Karcin's weightlifting bench.

"I swear, it was carrying a freaking fish in its mouth. So gross!"

193

"It's gone. Ran around the rusted fire door into the warehouse. It's their problem now," Karcin said. "Plus, I'm buck naked and so are you. Still have time for some loving?"

"Ugh," she answered, looking up at the clock. "Mr. Prez has a meeting in ten minutes that I need to take dictation for."

"Say that word again."

"What? Dictation?" she asked, while putting her panties on.

"Drop the 'tation', *and* your panties." Karcin said while rubbing his anatomy against the young secretary.

"Ohhhhh, that feels *so* good, but I can't!"

"Come on, I'll write you a tardy note," he insisted.

"*Stop* Karcin, I *can't.*"

CLANG! OWWW! OWWW!

Karcin quickly put his pants on so he could investigate the noise and wailing outside. The secretary grabbed her clothes and hid in the back alcove as the brightness of the outside unapologetically invaded the dark space as Karcin poked his head out.

A boy was running in a sporadic pattern, swatting the back of his shirt and screaming "It hurts!"

Karcin noticed that his gasoline can had been kicked over in the boy's melee. He ran to him and ripped the shirt from his body, exposing two bees engaged in an ongoing sting operation. Swatting them away, Karcin surveyed the boy's back, which had a dozen or so swollen sting marks on him, one with the stinger still pumping into the child.

"It hurts! OWWW! It hurts!"

"I know. Try to hold still so I can pull this stinger out," Karcin said with concern, as he pulled out his Swiss Army knife that had tweezers attached. "Got it." He looked at the red sting marks while the boy cried and took his shirt over to the gasoline can. Most of the gas remained inside, and he dipped a corner of a sleeve into it. "This might burn a little at first, but it should help to take the swelling down," he said, while patting the gasoline-drenched shirtsleeve on the bee stings.

"OWWW! OWWW! STOP! OWWW!

"What is going on out here?" the secretary asked, while stepping outside from the boiler room.

"This kid just got stung by some bees," Karcin answered.

"What are you putting on him? Gasoline?"

"Isn't gas the same thing as witch hazel?"

"Seriously? Not even close! I'll run upstairs and get the first aid kit."

The boy's crying began to subside as Karcin set two large plastic buckets upside down for them to sit on. "So, where did you get stung?"

"On my back," the boy answered.

"I know you were stung on your back, silly. Where were you when you got stung?"

"Over there."

"In the shed?"

"Behind it. I was fishing."

"Did you catch any?"

"Sure. I caught four, but I don't know what happened to one of them. They are over there near my tackle box.

"So the rat *did* have a fish in its mouth!"

"What? Rat?"

"Oh, nothing. What's your name?"

"Simeon, but my friends call me Sim."

"Nice to meet you, Sim. I'm Karcin. I work here. Where did you learn how to fish?"

"Right here. My grandfather takes me fishing sometimes after church on Sundays. He always makes me throw them back in, though."

"Why aren't you throwing them back today?"

"Because I need to eat them."

"You *need* to eat them?"

"Uh-Huh."

"Why, just because you like fish?"

"Because I ran away."

"Oh, I see," said Karcin, as he walked over to the shed and pulled out a small hibachi grill. As he attached the small propane canister to it, he re-confirmed, "You said that your Grandfather brings you here?"

"Yup."

"Do you know how to scale a fish?"

"Scale?"

"Let's go get those fish of yours."

About an hour or so later, Sim's grandfather pulled up behind Hope Metal Badge & Button Company, and was relieved to find him sitting at an old wooden cable spool that Karcin used as his outside summer table.

"Grandpa!" shouted Sim.

"Who loves you more than you will ever know, and forever?" Grandpa shouted back.

From that point on, Sim would visit Karcin most workday afternoons during that summer. He eventually learned the best spots around the factory grounds to find worms, the many ways to tie various fishing knots, and how to fillet a fish all by himself. Once a week, the boy was given a rag and some polish and he'd clean the chrome on Karcin's motorcycle, and at the end of Karcin's shift, Sim would be given a ride on it around the factory parking lot. Karcin found that he liked having the little guy around, but he wasn't only teaching him good skills. He would take advantage of Sim as a helper in dumping chemicals, or sweeping the loading dock whenever one of his female friends arrived for some private time.

Sadly, by the next summer, young Sim was diagnosed with a rare form of cancer, and passed away within months of his diagnosis. Karcin was asked to be a pallbearer at his funeral, and did so without giving any thought to the contribution he may have been responsible for regarding Sim's cancer cause. All he knew was that the boy had looked up to him, and that he may have provided him with the best summer of his short life. As he helped to carry the tiny wooden casket, he looked down at some words that were carved next to a cross: 'I love you, Sim. More than you will ever know, and forever. Love, Grandpa'.

Karcin's teardrop landed inside the cross, encapsulation the sawdust that remained within the carving.

CHAPTER 11

Mr. Connor paced up and down the hall. He felt complete bewilderment, which his face clearly projected. Hoping that he'd run into Mother Madre, he kept passing by her office, and then return past his classroom before turning back around just after the music room and retracing his steps for the second, third, fourth, and on up, to the ninth time. The dream that he just woke-up from wouldn't leave his mind, nor did he want it to before he had an understanding of its meaning.

"Getting your exercise in, Mr. Connor?" Mr. Dyson asked, as he leaned out through the music room door.

Mr. Connor turned around.

"Hey, your face is full of perplexity. Is everything ok, man?"

"I really don't know. I had a dream that I can't seem to shake, and I'm not sure that I should. It just feels like there's some sort of unfinished business that I need to tend to."

"You are a true workaholic, Mr. Connor. It's Always business before pleasure with you."

"No, not that sort of business, Mr. Dyson. It seems extremely important, yet very personal."

"I'm a good listener if you feel that you need to talk about it and get it out of your head."

"Thank you, but I was hoping to run into Mother Madre. She always seems to have some insight on whatever happens to arise."

"That's true, but I heard that she was going to be unavailable for a while."

"Really? I've been up and down these halls, I don't know how many times, and saw nothing posted about that."

"Mr. Karcin told me when he came in to clean up some broken glass earlier. It does seem strange that nothing was added to the bulletin board about it. The offer still stands if you'd like to talk and chill in my room for a bit."

"I really would like to talk about this, but I don't need to hear some judgmental song after."

"Honestly, I wasn't being judgmental at all before. I had no idea the song had anything to do with you, personally. There's an opportunity for me to make tenure, and I need to write a series of songs in order to do so. I am usually given the subject to write about from Mother Madre. Seriously, come on in."

Mr. Connor entered the room hesitantly, looking at the various instruments scattered throughout Mr. Dyson's music room. "Wow, I've never been in here before. Do you know how to play *all* of these?"

"Most of 'em," Mr. Dyson answered, "but I don't know how to play the harp. I'm not actually sure where that even came from."

"So cool. I'm not musically inclined at all, but I do love music."

"It's never too late to start taking lessons. I always say that musicians get better and season with age, whereas athletes decline with age. I'd be willing to show you some chords on guitar or piano when we both have time, if you'd like. Music can be very therapeutic, for the listener and the composer, and I'm guessing that you could use some with whatever is bothering you. The floor cascades in stages, so watch your step.

Mr. Dyson took a seat in the front row of chairs, and Mr. Connor continued over to the piano.

"May I, Mr. Dyson?"

"Of course, but I thought you said that you were not musically inclined?"

"For some reason, I know this one melody. I'm not sure where it came from, but it plays on and on in my head."

Mr. Connor played the single notes of the melody and his eyes began to well up with tears.

"That's beautiful. Is it an original piece?"

"Again, I have no idea where it comes from. I don't even know how or when I would have learned that, but it has been haunting me since my last dream."

"Can you remember it?"

"It's strange because I usually don't remember my dreams unless Mother Madre prods me to do so, but this dream felt so real. Yes, I remember it vividly," Mr. Connor said, before playing the melody once more, which pulled another tear from one of his eyes.

"Here, take a seat. I'm all ears if you feel like telling me about it."

"Thanks. Not even sure where to begin. I remember standing in line with a young girl so we could get our picture taken. It was in a school gymnasium, which was all decorated for a father-daughter dance. She looked beautiful, and kept calling me daddy. I was calling her Honey-Bunch, so I'm guessing she was my daughter in the dream. There was some guy in line next to me with his daughter, who explained how his older stepdaughter had just graduated college and he was relieved because she was moving to the other side of the world for a job. He explained how he didn't want to have her living with him and his wife. The guy wouldn't shut up. He started telling me how uncomfortable he felt because a few fathers down in the line was the soon-to-be-ex-husband of his newest client, who had hired him to be her divorce lawyer. He told me how the guy just went up to him and defended himself by saying that he wasn't a bad guy. The lawyer then went on to say, "Sure, but you were screwing your secretary." I could tell that the lawyer guy wasn't someone that I would ever be friends with, and I sure didn't want him tainting my daughter's mind with his inappropriate conversation, so I told my daughter that she should go hang out with her friends until I got to the front of the line. The poor girl walked over to our table and rested her head while the disgusting lawyer continued to spew nonsense from his mouth. I asked him to hold my place when we neared the front of the line so I could get my daughter, and by the time I returned, he not only took my place, but cut the father in front of where I was so he could take a quick photo because he wouldn't be staying long. That father tucked a twenty-dollar bill in his pocket that the lawyer had given him, and I tucked back into line with my Honey-Bunch a few people back."

"What a jerk."

"He sure was. Anyway, my daughter and I went back to our table after our photos were taken because the food was being served. She didn't touch any of it, but rather pushed her plate away so she could rest her head again. I asked her if she was ok, and she just said that she was a little tired. After dinner, the dancing began. Eventually, she lifted her head and said that she loved the song that started playing. I suggested that we dance to it, and she said that she felt too weak and might have been getting sick. I picked her up and held her close while slowly doing some dance moves on our way out of the gymnasium. When I tucked her into bed that night I promised her that we would dance to that song twice at the next father-daughter dance."

"And that's the melody you were just playing on the piano?"

"It was. Within my soul, it feels like there's an un-kept promise whenever I hear it in my head. Whoever Honey-Bunch was, I feel that I owe her a dance. Two, actually."

"That's actually very sentimental, man. You're not just a crude business teacher after all."

"After all?"

"Come-on, man. You've got to know that you are hard on the students."

"Do you want to hear the rest of the dream?"

"There's more? Of course I do."

"It was the morning after the dance and a young boy, who appeared to be my son, jumped into my bed. He must have only been three years old or so, but it may have been the strongest hug I had ever felt. I think I said something like "What's up, Bud?" and he asked me why I didn't see God. I responded by saying we *do* see God through things like the frog pond where we like to explore what God made, through the songs that the birds sing, and through smelling the flowers that grow all around. And then, I realized that he was asking why *I* didn't see God, specifically. He started telling me that God was in his bedroom, so I asked him what God had said to him. His response was that God told him that he liked his toy motorcycles, which he was collecting. I thought it to be the perfect icebreaker to say to the young boy, so I asked him if he said anything else. The boy hugged me even tighter and asked me if I was going to miss him when I'm in Heaven."

"Woah, that's heavy stuff, man. How did you answer?"

"I told him that I'd be his angel right there beside him."

"You're going to make me cry, now."

"In my dream, I felt shaken by it. I seemed to be a smoker, and had glimpses of being outside in the snow to smoke while the young boy looked out at me through the house window. I decided then and there that I was going to quit smoking. Later that day, I ran into someone in a department store that I hadn't seen since High School, but all I could think about was death, and what my son had said earlier. Feeling numb to the present moment, I recall having nothing at all to say to that person aside from some generalities. He must have had things on his mind, too, as his words were also shallow. It made me wonder if anyone ever actually listened to anyone else. I mean, ever."

"I'm sorry, what were you saying?"

"Ha Ha! Funny. But, honestly, we both ended the conversation at the same time, with the same words – "So anyway," with no words to follow it up with."

"And you feel bad that you had nothing to say to that friend that you ran into?"

"Actually, no. Not at all. Well, maybe I feel bad that it was a glimpse of how thin many friendships really are. That, unless it is a relationship by blood, most will be only as deep as the help or gifts that one or the other may bestow upon the other, and when any of those dry-up, for whatever reason, so often will the relationship. In this case, I feel some undeniable tug on my soul that the young boy was someone who relied on me for love and direction, just like the young girl in my dream. What I feel bad about is promising the young man that I'd be his angel. I feel a certain connection to him at the soul-level, and somehow feel a sense that I abandoning him, but I also get a feeling that it's out of my control. Like, it feels that death is circling me, or something. Does that make any sense?"

"As long as it makes sense to you. That's what really matters."

"Oh, ok, so it *doesn't* make sense to you."

"That's not what I said."

"Did you actually listen, or do you want to say 'So anyway' and continue on with your day?"

"Dude, not only did I listen, but I can re-cap what you just told me in a song."

"Seriously? You could write a song about my dream?"

"I already did. It's all right here in my head."

"Really?"

"I'd play it for you but you did say that you didn't want to hear a song afterward."

"I'm sorry about that. Would you please play it for me?"

Mr. Dyson looked over to the ink and feather near the Bible and saw that there were some blank scrolls there that he hadn't noticed before. "Sure, I'll play it for you, and will even write the lyrics out on a scroll for you to take with you," he said, while picking up an acoustic guitar from an instrument stand and then sitting back down next to Mr. Connor.

SO ANYWAY

SO ANYWAY SHOULD I TELL YOU ALL ABOUT MY DAY?
LIKE SOMETHING BOUGHT WHILE AT THE STORE?
IF YOU FIND IT STRANGE I HAVEN'T FOUND A WORD TO SAY
I'LL CHOSE A THOUGHT FROM A MILLION MORE
I RAN INTO STEVE WHO SAID HE'S LEAVING TOWN
HE SAID HE COULDN'T STAY – I DIDN'T ASK WHAT FOR
WHAT WAS I STARTING TO SAY? I BOUGHT THE CLOTHES I WORE
SO ANYWAY
SO ANYWAY I HEAR THAT YOU ARE DOING WELL
YOU'VE GOT A FEW KIDS – I'VE GOT MY OWN
I PRAY MY BOY AND GIRL
GET TO SEE THEIR DADDY GROWING OLD
THEN SAVE MY SOUL WHEN MY TALE IS TOLD
SUDDENLY IT SEEMS LIKE LIVING A DREAM
NEVER WAKE UP UNTIL SOMEBODY SCREAMS
HAS IT EVER BEEN SEEN
THIS THING THAT KEEPS CIRCLING ME
MY SON WOKE UP SAID GOD WAS THERE
HE HELD ME REALLY TIGHT AND WHISPERED IN MY EAR
WILL YOU MISS ME DAD? – WHEN YOU'RE IN HEAVEN?
I SAID I'LL BE YOUR ANGEL RIGHT HERE.

"Mr. Dyson, you really *were* listening. Thank you, my friend."

205

"You're welcome, Mr. Connor. Feel free to drop by whenever you feel the need to talk. I'll scribe the lyrics onto a scroll and drop it off at your classroom in a little while."

Although Mr. Connor felt some relief from talking about his dream, he felt even more of a need to connect with those children, somehow. Heading back toward Mother Madre's office in an additional attempt to find her there, he poked his head into Miss Kylee's room.

"Knock-Knock," he said, while looking around her barren office.

"Oh, hi there!" Miss Kylee replied, turning around from facing her empty desk.

"I hope that I didn't disturb your work."

"No, I wasn't really doing anything. Come on in."

Mr. Connor took a seat on the spare chair near her desk. He spent several seconds taking in the empty walls, shelves, and even the wastebasket in the corner.

"Can I help you with something?" she asked.

"Yes. Um, I'm sorry. I was just checking to see if you might know where Mother Madre might be. Have you seen her?"

"You're like the fourth person that asked me that. She is in the chapel, but doesn't want to be disturbed."

"Do you think that it might be worth making a notice of her unavailability and hanging it on the bulletin board so that others can know about it without disturbing you?"

"Oh, I don't mind."

Mr. Connor took yet another look around her empty office in disbelief, then asked, "So, what exactly do you do here at St. Perpetua?"

"I'm head of the PTO here, and the assistant to Mother Madre when needed."

"What sort of activities does the PTO do?

"Well," Miss Kylee drew a blank for several seconds, "I know that we're going to have a meeting soon. I just need to finalize the design of the flyer for it."

"Could I take a look at what you've designed so far? Being a business person, I am always curious to learn what marketing approaches other people take."

"Yeah, um, it is designed in my head. I just need to get it laid out on paper before the meeting."

"I sure hope that you'll get it posted some time before the meeting so others can actually know about the meeting well enough in advance so they may plan and prepare for it, especially if part of the meeting's strategy is to allow for input from members during the meeting. Otherwise, I would guarantee that nothing would actually get done."

"Good point."

"So, you aren't doing anything right now?"

"Nope"

"Then, why don't I help you get started on the flyer? Marketing is my specialty."

"Um, ok, I guess."

"We can begin by sketching out a draft," Mr. Connor suggested. "Do you have any paper?"

Miss Kylee pulled open the drawer in her desk and took out an unopened ream of paper. "Mother Madre gave me this, and all kinds of writing and drawing materials when I first came to St. Perpetua."

"That was a while ago. What have you-, ah, forget it. Let's get started. So, what is the purpose of the next PTO meeting?"

"I'm not even sure."

"Did you say that you are in charge of the PTO?"

"Yeah, I'm the President!"

"Ummm, oooookay. Let me ask it this way - What are your goals for the next meeting?"

"Maybe to ask everyone what *their* PTO goals are?"

"Well, it's a start. We should come up with a catchy headline for the flyer that reflects that objective. Something that we could tie an associated graphic to on the flyer. Can you come up with something?"

"Hmmm. Maybe, 'Come Share your Ideas'?"

"Ok, that's a start. But what sort of graphic would you put with that? Is it fun or exciting enough? Could we expand on it?"

"Like, how?"

"Is there another line that we could add to 'Come Share your Ideas' that would rhyme or something?"

"How about 'If You Really Care, Then You'll Share Your Idea.' That rhymes, right?"

"Sure it rhymes, but it may sound judgmental to others. What do you think of 'We're All Ears — Come Share Your Ideas!', and we can have a graphic of a large ear with examples of some ideas spiraling into it? That way, it is fun and clever, and it gets potential meeting-goers to begin thinking up ideas that they may want to bring up."

"I love that idea!"

"Great! Then, you will need to include pertinent information to the flyer. Of course, 'PTO Meeting' needs to be right up there with the catchy headline, and make sure that you add place, date and time. Sometimes less is more, or else it becomes too cluttered or distracting and the intended message may get lost."

"Thanks Mr. Connor. I feel like I just took one of your business classes, but without all of your yelling."

"Am I really that bad?"

"No disrespect, but when you are teaching, I can usually hear your manic rants all the way from your classroom to my desk in here."

"I guess that we all have some things to work on here at St. Perpetua. You know, I never really knew how loud or unfair I was until Mother Madre pointed it out to me. Good luck with the flyer!"

As he left Miss Kylee's office, Mr. Connor heard Officer Williams' voice coming from the hall behind him.

"Hey, Mr. Connor, wait up."

"Oh, here we go," Mr. Connor said under his breath, just before stopping and turning around.

"Look, no hard feelings from the Moral Compass game. Deal?"

"Deal. It sure proved that neither one of us are any better than the other when it comes to ethics. Where you coming from?"

"Just doing my rounds, making sure that the doors are locked. Take a walk with me?"

"Sure. Why not?"

"I've been looking for Mother Madre. Were you just with her?"

"No, I was helping Miss Kylee design a flyer. I heard that she is in the chapel, and not to be disturbed."

"Shouldn't she post something about that?"

"I'm guessing that someone dropped the ball on that."

"Wouldn't be the first time!"

"Ha-Ha, you're not kidding."

There was an unusually long pause while the two continued down the hallway before Officer Williams spoke again, "Can I lay something on you that I need to get off my chest?"

"Yeah, sure."

"I'm not even sure what it all means, if anything at all, but I had a dream that felt too real to ignore.

"The same thing happened to me. What was yours about?"

"It wasn't pleasant at all," Officer Williams began, as he tugged at one of St. Perpetua's external doors to make sure that it was secure. "There was a carnival happening in a town's center and I was working a detail as the officer on duty."

"Carnivals are usually pleasant, aren't they?"

"Not that one. At first, it seemed like it was going to be a dream-come-true day for me, but it quickly turned into a nightmare," the officer said, before pausing again and pulling on another door's handle.

"Go on."

"In the dream, I only had gotten a few hours sleep after getting home from a barroom. Smith's? Smithers? Smithy's? I can't remember the name of it, but there was some sort of anniversary party for the chief of the town's police department. Everyone was hootin' and a hollerin' all night long, and Chief was buying rounds of shots for all the guys. Eventually, he announced that it was open bar. The next morning, half the force called in sick so Chief called me to work the carnival."

"Oh, man, all of those carnival bells, whistles, loud games and rides. I can see how that would be a nightmare after a long night of drinking. I'll bet that you couldn't wait for your shift to end."

"Actually, I was very excited in my dream, at first, because it was to be the first detail that I worked where I actually had a police-issued badge and pistol. Up until then, I was simply a traffic cop. Chief said that he had no choice but to trust me, considering that most of his force were nursing hangovers."

"Sounds like a big step in a cop's career."

"It would have been. *Should* have been, had I not messed up so bad," Officer Williams admitted.

"What, did you go on a spinning ride and puke all over your uniform or something?"

"I wish it was that innocent. The day sure started out that way. The carnival was well attended and everyone seemed to be having a great time. In my dream, I could actually smell the popcorn and taste the cotton candy while a carnival worker twirled each paper cone inside of the mesmerizing machine that created an instant fluffy nest of pink and blue sugar. There was an occasional shout of victory when someone won a stuffed animal, and I watched as they carried around stuffed animals larger than themselves all day long. Their carnival "wealth" became a burden, and I thought about that being relative with general life. To break that thought came the inevitable cry of a child standing above a failed ice-cream cone experience, melting on the ground at their feet while a parent consoled. Maybe *that* was the treat – the parents' outward display of love. Screams came from a pirate ship ride as it reached its highest altitude, and laughs filled the air as an audience gathered around some juggling clowns. The scene was a perfect carnival day, and the respect that I felt while walking throughout the crowd was incredible. I finally felt like a real cop."

"It sure sounds like it. So what went wrong?"

"My break had just ended and I needed to use the bathroom, so I made my way to the row of porta-potties just past the House of Horrors. As I was making my way past that haunted house, the carnival worker that was taking tickets there was engaged in an argument with a woman who was apparently working for the carnival, also. She was holding the hand of a young girl that appeared to be her daughter. It sounded as if they had broken up, and that she was going to be getting an abortion. It was loud and heated, and very inappropriate for the carnival's clientele. I decided that it would be best for me to stay out of it and let them work out their differences, plus I really needed to use the bathroom. Just after I closed the door to the porta-potty, I heard a gun shot. I looked out through the screen toward the top of the porta-potty and saw that the carnival worker at the House of Horrors had fired a warning shot. The crowd had backed away, and the worker had grabbed hold of the young girl. The female carnival worker was screaming hysterically for someone to call the cops, while the male worker shouted, "If it's ok for you to kill my baby, then maybe it's ok for me to do the same to yours!"

"Man, that's crazy! Did you spring into action?"

"No. That's the problem," Officer Williams said, with a tone of disappointment of himself in his voice. "I completely failed. My mind raced, and I reached for the gun but my hands were shaking so badly that I never pulled it out."

"So, how did you deal with the guy?"

"I didn't. I cowered. All of a sudden, I felt like I didn't want to be a cop anymore. Figuring I'd be an instant target in my uniform, I was afraid to get shot so I sat on the toilet, hiding in the porta-potty. In my mind, I justified it by convincing myself that one of the full-time cops should have been there instead of calling out sick that day from drinking too much. If they hadn't gotten so wasted I wouldn't have been in that position."

"What ended up happening to the young girl?"

"Well, I didn't look through the screen again because I didn't want to get noticed, but I could hear the guy as he continued to yell profanities at the girl's mother, calling her a carnival-slut and accusing her of sleeping with some motorcycle stunt-rider that had apparently just been added to the traveling amusement show. It must have gone on for twenty minutes or so, until I heard Chief's voice. He had a bullhorn, and was attempting to talk the guy out of doing anything stupid. He kept saying something like 'Let the girl go and we can work out the situation. By taking the life of a born human, you'd be just as guilty as her taking the life of an unborn human. Nobody wins.' Chief said a lot more than that, but that was the gist of it."

"Was he successful in talking him out of it?"

"It seemed to have taken a long time, but the guy finally freed the child just as I heard additional police arriving on the scene. Eventually, they got the gun away from him and placed him under arrest."

"You must have been relieved."

"Honestly, I felt like a complete jerk. An absolute coward. I sat in the porta-potty a bit longer and eventually heard Chief's voice grumbling from the next porta-potty over. Considering that he was the one who got everyone drunk the night before, including me, I decided to play it up by forcing myself to throw up, which was my excuse for not dealing with the situation. After explaining that I would have been ineffective and could have possibly compromised the situation and made it more dangerous based on my condition, he stripped the holster and pistol from me and said that I'd be a traffic cop for the foreseeable future."

"It sounds like he went easy on you."

"I'm still trying to figure that out. He added something like, 'And if you *ever* mention anything that you may *not* have heard last night to anyone, I'll fire you on the spot.' Then, after that he said, 'and stay the hell out of bathroom stalls.'"

"What did that all mean?"

"Who knows? At one point during that night before, I was using the men's room at the bar. While I was in the stall, I heard Chief walk in with who may have been another cop. He was saying something about making sure that nobody gets prosecuted, and that the Mayor already knew all about it and was cooperating to clean it up. I just figured it was just some after-work police banter about a case, and thought nothing of it, until I flushed the toilet and left the stall. While I was washing my hands, Chief said something like 'If you like your job, you won't say a word about this to anyone.' Again, I just thought that it was some case that may have had some sort of court-ruled gag-order attached to it. Now that I'm thinking of it, I'm wondering if there was something more to the story. Something dark and sinister."

The two men continued to walk for several steps without saying anything. Finally, Mr. Connor said, "I'm not sure what it all means, but it sure sounds like it was quite the disturbing dream."

"It certainly made me feel inadequate as a cop. Mr. Connor, please, I need you to be honest with me. How do you think I'm doing as an officer here at St. Perpetua?"

"You're doing fine. I mean, there aren't a lot of major issues that arise here, but you do a good job keeping the halls safe."

Just as Mr. Connor said that, a student came running from around the corner. Officer Connor grabbed him just as he was about to slip on the wet part of the floor that Mr. Karcin was washing just a few feet away.

"See?" reiterated Mr. Connor. "You saved that young student from a potential broken arm or sprained ankle."

"Thanks. I really needed to hear that right now, Mr. Connor," he said, before turning his attention to the student that was running. "Where are you off to in such a hurry?"

"I heard that Miss Addison is doing car-ture drawings," the out-of-breath student said.

"I believe you might mean caricature drawings?" Officer Williams corrected.

"I guess so. I saw my friend Sim's and it was really neat. He was holding a hammer and a huge nail. It looked just like him, but in a funny way."

"Come on, I'll take you to her room so you won't run and slip on the wet floor."

"I'll catch up with you later," Mr. Connor said to Officer Williams. "Keep your chin up. You're a great officer!"

"That means a lot to me. Thanks Mr. Connor."

Officer Williams and the young student heard laughing coming from Miss Addison's room as they approached her door. There was a string tied from one end of the classroom to the other with dozens of caricatures of the students hanging from clothespins. Several students walked back and forth, pointing and laughing at the cartooned drawings of them. A child sat in a chair facing Miss Addison as she sketched away on drawing paper attached to an easel. She finished up the over-exaggerated facial features of the student's face before adding a tiny body in a ballet outfit to the large head. Some of the pupils that were looking over Miss Addison's shoulders laughed as she unclipped the paper from the easel.

"Ta-Da!" she said, while turning the paper to face the child. "What do you think?"

The child's face lit up and she joined the other kids in laughter before getting up from her seat.

"Is that it?" Ambry asked.

"No, you have one more subject to draw, Miss Addison," Officer Williams said, as he and the boy walked over to her. "This is quite a talent that you have," he added.

"Oh, I hadn't seen you two standing there. Of course! Take a seat young man," Miss Addison instructed. "What do you like to do?"

215

"I had a dream that I was riding a bike with some friends, and I was really good at it!" the student declared. "I was able to do all kinds of stunts on it, like riding it with no hands, popping a wheelie for the length of three houses on the street, and even jumping it off of a ramp!"

"A bike it is!" said Miss Addison, who wasted no time with the strokes of her black marker on the thick drawing paper. A moment later, and again, "Ta-Da!"

"COOOOL!" the young student said in awe, as in his head he envisioned actually jumping over some busses with his bike, just like she drew him. "The big helmet and cape is really neat!"

"I'm glad that you like it. Is that it for drawings?"

"What? You mean the adults don't get to have a caricature done of themselves?"

"Of course we do, Officer Williams," Miss Addison explained. "Take a look up there. That one's mine."

"Hmmm, I wouldn't have taken you as a Jeep type of girl. That's awesome," Officer Williams said with a smile on his face, which faded fairly quickly as he tilted his head and took in the drawing deeper, mentally.

"Take a seat!"

Miss Addison studied his facial featured for several seconds and then began to draw.

"Do you want me to smile? Not smile? Turn my head to the left?"

"You're fine just like that, Officer Williams. I'm actually done drawing your face, and am now doodling your uniform… Now your cap… Now your gun." Ambry did a few strokes more and stopped, jumping back from the paper in a startled jolt. "I can't," she said, as the marker hit the floor.

"I imagine that your hand must be so sore by now after drawing all of those kids. No problem. We can finish another time," Officer Williams suggested, feeling uncomfortable himself, as he glanced back up at the drawing of Miss Addison and her Jeep.

Once everyone finally left her room, Miss Addison walked over to the one that she drew of herself. Why *did* she draw a Jeep? She wondered. She then walked back to the drawing of Officer Williams that still hung on her easel, and stared through it for a long time. Eventually, she split her glances between that drawing and the coloring sheet of an angel that remained on her desk since she arrived at St. Perpetua. Picking up the marker from the floor, she made her way to the angel coloring sheet and turned it over. On the blank side of the sheet, she began to draw a beautiful young girl. Without thinking about it conscientiously, she drew a ripped dress as her clothing. The girl was holding schoolwork in her hands that had an A+ and a heart written on it. Miss Addison held it to her heart as she walked to the display of caricatures that was strung across her room, and added it to the one space left on the string of artwork, which was right next to the drawing of herself.

Inside St. Perpetua's chapel, Mother Madre was kneeling under a cross, just in front of a multi-tiered wall of candles. Finishing a prayer, she raised her head and lit an additional candle, completing the lighting of one third of the candles along the vast wall, which provided enough light to illuminate the entire chapel. She looked at the row of pews behind her and decided to lie down and take a nap, or dig deeper into her truth, rather. Using her satchel for a pillow once again, she pulled her feet up onto the pew and closed her eyes.

"Oh, I'm not sure that I should have another drink, Marshall. I'm feeling pretty good already." Marjorie said, while Marshall Smith got up from the couch and walked over to his liquor cabinet.

"The last few drinks were to convince you of the deal. This one is to celebrate it."

"Now wait a minute. You still haven't agreed to my k-k-kickback percentage. Ten percent, or you can take changing Smitty's zoning to allow gambling right off the table."

Marshall returned to the couch with two glasses of brandy. "Of course you'll receive a kick-back, Marjorie, but come on, ten percent?"

Marjorie accepted the glass from Marshall, who in turn raised his up to cheer the agreement. "No clinking until I hear ten percent. Period, Marshall. This is my reputation on the line if the public ends up revolting against gambling in Hope. Rezoning your business property is a big risk."

Marshall took a few steps toward the fireplace and prodded the logs with a long metal poker to re-engage the flames. "Who cares?" he said. "It's on the outskirts of town near the river and the factories. It's not like I'm setting up some casino next to the elementary school or anything."

"Ten percent. You are poised to make a lot of money by allowing off-track gambling at Smitty's and you know it. One percent less and this conversation is over."

"You look sexy when you get all business-like. Okay, okay, ten percent it is, but we renegotiate in five years."

"If we renegotiate in five years, I promise that it won't be in your favor, Mr. Smith," Marjorie said, while raising her glass.

Marshall's glass met Marjorie's and the two each took a large gulp. He reached for Marjorie's free hand. "Come on, I think that it's time for us to consummate our agreement."

"Are you sure that your little ballerina wife won't be home until tomorrow?"

"I'm positive. She called earlier to tell us that she advanced to the semi-final round, so it will be tomorrow at the earliest. The day after that if she wins that round."

"How old is she? Is it odd that she continues to compete in dance at her age, or is it just me for thinking so?"

"She still enjoys it, so I encouraged her to get involved with the adult competitions. Plus, it gets her out of the house so we can do more of this."

"If you like it better when she isn't here, why are you still married to her?"

"It's complicated, with having a daughter and all."

"I'm sure that Angela would adjust just fine. Parents get divorced all the time, Marshall. Think about all that we could get accomplished if we were together as a couple. Your business isn't going to grow as a result of Hailey's fading tutu."

"Getting a divorce would be too costly. I don't really want to sign away half of Smitty's Bar to her."

"That's a good point, but if you are serious about this deal she will be out of the picture by the next town council meeting."

"And if not?"

"If not, then you can raise prices on beer at Smitty's to make more money. I'm not playing around with this. Consummate *that* deal?"

Marshall unbuttoned Marjorie's shirt and threw it on top of the couch before pressing his lips against hers. Soon, her bra sailed past her shirt and landed on the floor in front of the fireplace.

"What if Angela wakes up?"

"She sleeps like a log. Come on, we've got a deal to seal."

Marjorie followed Marshall into his bedroom. They had crossed that infidelity line together before, but never in the very bed that he slept with her archrival, Hailey Crown-Smith. By the time she jumped onto the bed, she was completely naked, and working on getting Marshall unwrapped. She had waited for that moment since her high school days, and she was going to do everything in her power to make sure that every drop of his passion was fully absorbed by her body.

As they held each other on top of the bed after, they chatted about different things they could do with all of the gambling money that they projected would come in. A vacation in the tropics, or maybe a vacation home somewhere. His and Her sports cars. Maybe a boat.

THUD - The front door of the house closed.

"What the hell?" Marjorie said in a loud whisper while jumping out of Marshall's bed.

"Honey?" Hailey's voice came from the foyer.

"Oh no. Sneak out through that sliding door," Marshall said in a panic, as he quickly pulled his pants on.

"But my shirt is out there."

"Here, wear this t-shirt. Go now!"

The next night, Marjorie, Marshall, and Hope's police chief gathered after hours at Smitty's Bar.

"So, to make sure that we are all on the same page, we will rule Hailey's death a suicide," Chief reiterated. "None of us can waver from this story ever. Agreed?"

"Agreed," said Marjorie, "and I receive ten percent of the entire business for as long as it is in existence."

"Agreed," said Marshall, "and I sign the deed of Smitty's over to you, Chief, over the next few years once we know that we are free and clear to do so without raising any flags."

"That's right," Chief confirmed. "Marjorie, we will work out a way to have the ten percent funneled to you through some undetectable account, and Smitty, I will draft up a pre-deed promise for you to sign. From this point forward, no mention of *any* of this to anyone."

Mother Madre woke up and knelt back down under the cross, hanging her head in additional prayer. By the time she left the chapel, two thirds of the candles had been lit.

CHAPTER 12

Mother Madre walked into her office and found her mailbox full of message memos. The stack of them made it apparent that several staff members at St. Purgatory had not been informed of her unavailability. She sifted through the papers, and then headed down the hall.

"You want to sand *with* the grain of the wood," Mr. Karcin explained to Sim, as Mother Madre approached.

"What's going on here?" she asked, while placing a hand on one of the boy's shoulders.

"My new friend Sim is helping me to refinish these two front doors of the academy. The old varnish is faded and flaking off."

"Then, it sounds like a job well-worth doing," she replied.

"I'm not sure if you received my memo yet, Mother Madre, but I'd like to speak with you about a special project that I want to do with Sim."

"I'm listening."

"I think it would be great if I could have permission to build a tree-house with Sim."

"You mean outside of the school?"

"Well, yes. In a tree. The young boy is thirsty for knowledge of woodworking, and I believe that he would learn a lot from doing the carpentry work while being able to enjoy that boyhood experience."

"Although I do like concept, Mr. Karcin, and appreciate that it appears you have taken this boy under your wing, nobody has been allowed to leave the walls of St. Perpetua during enrollment periods."

"Mother Madre, I really do think it would do wonders for the youngster, and it could also be a pilot program for future students with similar interests and propensities in the future. Would you please consider it?"

"Propensities? You've been expanding your vocabulary, Mr. Karcin."

"I'm guessing that I wasn't the best student, and Sim seems to be a lot like me when it comes to book work. I truly think that he really does have the aptitude to do some amazing things with his hands, Mother Madre. He's learning how to use tools, and even helped me fix some plumbing earlier. Oh, and you should take a look at the amazing cross that he whittled out of some old wood I had laying around in the school basement."

"Whittled, Mr. Karcin?"

"Yes. With his own hands."

"With his own hands? Holding a knife?"

Silence.

"Please explain to me, Mr. Karcin, how a boy got access to a knife here at St. Perpetua Academy."

"It was mine, Mother Madre, but I did take time to show him how to use it properly, and explained how a knife should be utilized for only the right reasons."

Looking at her screen, Mother Madre seemed to be studying something at length before she spoke again. "If we were to g-g-grant your request, would you be able to p-p-promise that you would stay on one specific side of the building, n-n-n-never to venture off beyond there?"

"Of course. I don't see why we would need to leave a specific area, as long as there were trees there for us to build the tree house in. We would obviously need some lumber and supplies, but maybe Kylee could bring it up when the PTO meeting happens so we may receive some donations toward it."

"Kylee? PTO meeting? No. I'll find the funds for your new tree-house program, Mr. Karcin. There will be several full-grown trees on one side of St. Perpetua Academy, which is the ONLY side of the building that you are allowed to be on. I look forward to checking out the tree-house once it is built. I think that it's a wonderful idea!"

"Thank you so much, Mother Madre!"

"Yes, thank you ma'am," Sim added.

Mother Madre squeezed the boy's shoulder, and then continued her stroll down the main corridor of the academy. Passing Miss Addison's room, she slowed her steps as she peered in at the numerous drawings that were strung across her room. Regaining her original gate, she arrived at Mr. Dyson's music room, entering without slowing.

Mr. Dyson stood up from the piano bench after the last note of the melody that he played on the keys faded, and he rushed over to the feather and ink pedestal, carrying a scroll that he had been singing lyrics from. He signaled to Mother Madre that he would need a moment to get the song's final syllables onto the scroll before forgetting them.

As soon as Mr. Dyson returned the feather to its holder, Mother Madre wasted no time before speaking, "Mr. Dyson, is there any chance that you have f-f-finished the song that I last provided some details for?"

"Mother Madre, the last time you provided details, they were for three different songs."

"The details about the young girl. *That* song."

"Great timing. That's the one I just finished. Very sad, yet full of hope. The ink is still drying on the scroll."

"While it dries, I need to ask you to p-p-perform it in a few moments outside Miss Addison's room. You'll find a piano waiting for you there."

"Yes, of course."

A moment later, Mother Madre entered Miss Addison's room. She hadn't noticed the teacher standing behind the easel. "Miss Addison?"

Startled, Miss Addison dropped the wooden doll that she was holding. "Oh, I'm sorry, I didn't hear you walk in, Mother Madre."

"That's a shame," declared Mother Madre. "One of her arms broke off," she added, while reaching down and picking up the two pieces."

Miss Addison reached out without reservation and regained possession of the doll and its detached limb from Mother Madre, cradling both in her hands as her arms gently swayed back and forth. She took a step away from Mother Madre, facing her back to her as a tear formed and landed on the doll's scarf. She quickly raised it to her face and inhaled while Mother Madre briskly walked to the far end of the drawings that were strung above her head. Slowly, she paced back toward Miss Addison, taking in all of the caricatures of the children. When she got to the end of the display she said, "These are really something, Miss Addison. I'm sure that all of the kids l-l-loved being the subject of your amazing artistic t-t-t-talent."

"They seemed to," Miss Addison replied, keeping her answer short so that Mother Madre wouldn't detect that she was crying.

It was a failed attempt, but Mother Madre continued on as if she didn't notice, by saying, "I don't r-r-recognize this particular student, Miss Addison."

Miss Addison felt like she had no choice but to turn around and look. Her face was drenched in sadness, and she swiftly turned back around, again fixating on the doll in her hands. Its face suddenly resembled the unknown girl in the drawing. She looked back at the drawing, then over to Mother Madre, whose eyes were already fixed on Miss Addison but shifted quickly back to the drawing when their eyes met. The pause that followed was long.

"Mother Madre, this may sound strange to you, or to anyone for that matter, but I feel like I am grieving something or someone that I don't even know, but I feel like I need to find a way to receive some closure on it. I know this all sounds crazy. Oh, Mother Madre, is that it? Am I going crazy? Have I *already* gone crazy?" Miss Addison went to cry in her hands and hesitated while she thought about placing the doll parts down to do so. Instead, she held them against her cheek as if to baptize it with her tears. "Do you think that there's a special doll house in Heaven for the broken ones, so to speak, Mother Madre?"

"I can't imagine there *not* being one, so to speak, Miss Addison. Look, it has been a long day, and that's a lot of drawings for one teacher to do," Mother Madre said, while unfolding her screen. "I like where you moved the toy-chest bench to. One gets a clearer p-pprospective from up there on the reading-area platform. Why don't you take a rest on it while I watch over your doll for you."

"Well, I guess I should try to get a little rest before my next class. Would you mind *holding* my doll? I know it sounds silly, but I don't want it just tossed somewhere."

"I p-p-promise you that the doll will be well looked after, with v-v-very much care."

Miss Addison transferred the doll into Mother Madre's arms as if it were a real baby. She stepped up onto the reading-area platform, glanced back at the doll, and then sat down on the toy-chest bench and closed her eyes.

A church bell rang overhead. Miss Addison looked up to see an open steeple, tall above her head. The crisscrossed rafter woodwork fascinated her for a moment before she pondered how the bell wasn't very loud, considering the direct access that she had to it. Noticing that she was sitting in the balcony of a large church, she looked at the morning sunrays as they dragged colors from the stain glass through which they pierced. The pews were filled with an equal mixture of very young children and adults. Miss Ambry contemplated how she never saw such a large church like that even close to being at full capacity. Considering how well everyone was dressed, she guessed that they were there for a wedding. She began to get excited at the thought of it. It had been a long time since she had been to a wedding. "Wait," she thought, "Have I even been invited to a wedding, ever?" It didn't matter. She was finally at one. All of the flowers that surrounded the altar created the largest collective bouquet that she had ever seen. Her excitement grew when a pianist began playing from the other side of the balcony's partition wall near where Miss Addison was seated. As the congregation stood and turned around, she scanned the pews below, feeling that some of the children looked familiar. She couldn't wait to see the bride finally emerge down the isle from underneath the balcony. "She must look so beautiful," Miss Addison thought, "because everyone is already crying."

Suddenly, a small casket appeared below, as it was slowly being escorted toward the altar. Miss Addison gasped. It was the smallest casket that she ever saw. Outbreaks of audible crying erupted from the people in attendance, first the children, and then the adults. The pianist played and sang his song from the balcony while the sadness from below mixed within each note, pulling both toward the ground like a piece of paper floating on heavy air, swaying back and forth, until landing at the ground near the preacher's feet. Once the echo of the last note completed its reverberation, the preacher signaled that it was ok for the congregation to sit back down.

"It's a morning like this that reminds us that evil exists upon the earth. It's a morning like this that may have many of us questioning our faith in God. But, I assert to all of you, my brothers and sisters, that this is a morning to test our very faith in God, to rejuvenate our trust in The Lord, and to rejoice in the gift of eternal life, which comes from God's love and grace."

The preacher paused, taking a moment to circle the small casket that lay in state in front of the congregation. Plucking a small flower from the arrangement that was draped over the casket, the preacher held it to his nose and inhaled, and then let out an exaggerated exhale.

"Everything changes, and everything passes, each in its own time. Each in *God's* time, actually. The beauty with God's time is that it never ends. The issue that we have as humans is that we cannot even begin to fathom eternity. Everything that we are exposed to has a finite amount of time attached to it. The tread of a tire has only so many miles before it goes flat, the paint on a house weathers only so many storms before it peels, a song has only so many verses before it fades, ballet shoes have only so many dances before it wears away, this flower that I hold has only so many whiffs of fragrance to release before it wilts, and a human has only so many breaths before it gives its soul back to God. We tend to believe that we are owed at least seventy, eighty, even ninety years or more of life here on this planet, and some are granted that. The reality is such that some aren't. There is no easy way to accept that fact, considering our limited capacity for understanding "forever". That, no matter how great the pain here on earth, it is a flash compared to the beauty and comfort that awaits us on the other side of that flash. Romans 8:18 reads, "For I consider that the sufferings of this present time are not worth comparing with the glory that is to be revealed to us." Brothers and sisters, I believe that those words have never held more importance and significance to us than they do right now, right here, on this very morning."

Looking out over the sea of mourners that packed the large church, the preacher paused. He turned back toward the casket and pulled yet another flower from the bouquet. That time, he chose a pink carnation. "If there is a young girl here today with the name Keturah, please raise your hand so I may see where you are sitting." A child's arm went up along the aisle in the forth row of pews from the casket, hesitantly, while her mother patted her leg in support. The preacher walked over to the girl and handed the flower to her.

"I understand that you were Angela's best friend in school."

The girl nodded.

"I also believe that pink is yours and Angela's favorite color, is that correct?"

229

The girl nodded again, and then looked up at her Mom, who smiled back at her through her tears.

"Keturah is a very pretty name," the preacher continued. "Did you know that Keturah means 'fragrance' in Hebrew?"

The girl shook her head no, and then inhaled the aroma of the pink flower in her hand.

"I can promise you, Keturah, that the sweet memories of your friendship with Angela will remain in your heart and soul long, long after the scent of that flower fades. Longer than every flower that you will ever smell in your lifetime. I can also promise you that your friend now has a home in Heaven that lasts forever. Do you know how I know that?"

The girl shook her head no, slowly and less vigorously than the first time, as she didn't want to stop smelling the carnation under her nose.

"I know that because young Angela believed in God. Evidence of that exists from her very own words, which she wrote in a journal that she kept hidden under her mattress. It was found the day after the tragedy, and it spelled out a faith in God better than I could ever preach about it. I'd like to read some excerpts from it, so we may all have a better understanding of a young life full of suffering and sadness, yet also of hope, forgiveness, and faith. I believe that we will all learn something from young Angela's words."

Returning to the sermon podium, the preacher opened the journal and flipped through a few pages. He put on some reading glasses and began to share Angela's words.

"Dear Mom, it has been a few weeks since you went to Heaven. I miss you so much. I know that I'm going to see you some night in a dream. You're probably getting used to everything in Heaven right now. Did you get to see God yet? I bet he'll have you dance for all of the angels. Daddy's gonna be in soon so I'll write more later. The only good thing is that he hasn't hit me again since you left."

Pausing to take his glasses off and wipe his eyes, the preacher sifted through a few more pages and then continued to read.

"Today we had an ice cream social at school. I knew that you were there with me because my teacher brought chocolate/strawberry/vanilla ice cream, *and* black raspberry! Only you knew that black raspberry is my favorite flavor. Daddy was mad when I got home because some of it dripped on my dress, but he only slapped me twice. I miss you so much!"

The preacher shook his head as he turned the page. He paused, shook his head again while glancing over Angela's words, wiped a tear, and then flipped the page once again before continuing.

"My teacher, Miss A., is really nice. Sometimes I feel like she looks after me since you went to Heaven. She brought in dolls for us to dress today. The boys got pine-wood cars to paint. Keturah was taking a long time to clean up the reading-area. It was her day to clean up after reading time and it was so messy so I helped her. We got to the bin of doll clothes after everyone else. There was only one pink dress left. You know how we both love pink. I think you'd be proud of me because I remembered what you said about it being better to give than to get, so I let her have the pink one and I was going to dress my doll in a blue dress. Well, Keturah's Mom must have told her the same thing because she kept telling me to take the pink one. We ended up both dressing our dolls in purple ones to be the same. It might be our new favorite color. Joking. It will always be pink for Keturah and me."

The preacher paused while the audience shared a therapeutic laugh. He looked over at Keturah and winked before allowing the laughter to fade and displaying a serious look on his face.

"But when I got home, Daddy was mad about something and he broke one of the arms off the doll. I wish I knew what he is always mad about. There must be a lot on Daddy's mind. I guess he misses you, too, but not as much as I do. Did you get to meet God yet? Can you ask him if there is a house in Heaven for broken dolls, and where people can stay without getting hit?"

The congregation became solemn, once again, as the preacher read the next page.

"Thank you so much for visiting me in my dream last night, Mommy. I believe you, and miss you too. I won't be afraid. My teacher was going to fix my dress after school today but Daddy showed up. Ok, well maybe I am a little bit scared. During dinner tonight, he didn't say anything about hitting me this morning. He didn't say anything at all, except to make sure that I drank all of my juice. It tasted funny. Like, really really bad. I don't want him to come in and hit me tonight. Can you please ask Jesus if he can watch over me, and maybe help my tummy? It doesn't feel good and my mind feels-"

Looking down, the preacher took off his glasses, folded them, and placed them on top of the podium. "That's where her journal ended." He paused for a moment while the church wept. Eventually, he lifted his head, and spoke directly to the people.

"Brothers and sisters, allow me to recite Mathew 19:14 – 'Jesus said, "Let the little children come to me, and do not hinder them, for the Kingdom of Heaven belongs to such as these."' These are words spoken to us directly from The Bible. I promise you that there sure is a house built for broken dolls in Heaven, and Angela is there right now, feeling no more pain, along with her mother, and also with her teacher, Miss A., as you all are aware of by now. God rest their souls."

Miss Addison gasped again, covering her mouth with one hand while looking down and touching her body with the other.

"We are reminded in Psalm 34:18, that 'The Lord is near to the broken hearted and saves the crushed in spirit,' and for all of us gathered here today, including the body of our loving young Angela, Mathew 5:3-4 states, 'Blessed are the poor in spirit, for theirs is the Kingdom of Heaven. Blessed are those who mourn, for they will be comforted.' Angela feels pain no more, but rather a glory and eternal life that can only be found through Jesus Christ. Amen.'"

The pastor slowly stepped away from the podium and sat on a large chair near the altar. He lowered his head into his hands. Up on the balcony, Miss Addison took her tear-drenched hands from her face and looked up just as the church bell began to ring again.

The school bell rang, waking Miss Addison from her dream. She felt mentally exhausted as she rose from the toy-chest bench, but didn't hesitate before walking over to the drawing that she did of the unidentified girl. Unclipping it from the string, she brought it over to her desk and wrote the name Angela on it.

Mother Madre walked back into the room, holding the scroll of the lyrics that Mr. Dyson had sung while Miss Addison slept. "Angela," she said. "That's a pretty name."

"Oh, isn't it, Mother Madre? Look how beautiful she was."

"Was?"

Mother Madre unrolled the scroll and added it to the drawing on top of Miss Addison's desk. Her eyes darted back and forth across it before she quickly rolled the scroll back up and handed it to the mourning teacher. "This scroll of lyrics will help you to achieve the closure that you were seeking, Miss Addison."

"Thank you," Miss Addison said softly, looking at it rolled up in her hands. "May I also hold onto my doll?"

"Your doll's arm is going to be fixed, first, Miss Addison. Is that ok with you?"

"Yes, Mother Madre," she replied. Taking a moment to build her courage up enough to ask, Miss Addison finally came right out and began to inquire, "Um, Mother Madre, is there a chance that I already-"

"Oh, Miss Addison, look around the room. What is m-m-missing?

"Missing?"

"Missing. The students?"

"That's right, the bell already rang," Miss Addison agreed. "But, Mother Madre, did I actually already-"

"Not now. I n-n-need to go l-l-learn where the student p-p-population is," Mother Madre said, while rushing out of the room."

Miss Addison held Angela's drawing out in front of her, then walked back over to the string and rehung it. She couldn't help but stare at it and wonder what it all meant. Was she actually Miss A.? If so, did she know about anything in advance? Could she have prevented anything by speaking up instead of keeping everything in? She wanted more closure so she decided to unroll the scroll and read the lyrics on it before the students would arrive, if at all.

BROKEN DOLLS

SHE CLOSED HER EYES FOR HANDS SHE NEVER HAD TRUSTED
BUT WOULDN'T DARE TURN AROUND TO SHOW DADDY A FROWN
ON A FACE DISGUSTED
THE CHURCH FOLK NEVER SEE EIGHT WAYS TO SUNDAY
SHE'S TOLD TO SAY THANKS AND SMILE WHEN THEY TELL HER
YOU'RE SUCH A LOVELY GIRL
SHE COULD NOT TELL A SOUL THE SECRETS SHE HOLDS
WHAT HE DID TO HER MOTHER TOO
SHE LIES AWAKE EVERY NIGHT – PRAYS WITH ALL HER MIGHT
WHISPERS MOMMY
I WISH I WERE THERE WITH GOD AND YOU
IS THERE A HOUSE BUILT IN HEAVEN FOR BROKEN DOLLS?
IS IT THE BEST PLACE YOU EVER SAW?
DO YOU FEEL PAIN NO MORE?
I'M MISSING YOU…
IN CLASS HER TEACHER SENSED A TRUTH WAS HIDING
SHE SAID I KNOW HOW TO SEW THOSE RIPS IN YOUR CLOTHES
IF AFTER SCHOOL YOU'LL FIND ME
AS SHE FIXED HER DRESS THE TWO BEGAN TALKING
BUT BEFORE SHE GOT PAST THE QUESTIONS SHE WOULD ASK
AN ANGRY DAD CAME STALKING
WHERE THE HELL HAVE YOU BEEN? – YOU'RE IN TROUBLE AGAIN
HE RIPPED HER DRESS AS HE DRAGGED HER OUT
NEIGHBORS HEARD A SCREAM – HER MOM CAME IN A DREAM
PICKED HER UP - AND SAID WITHOUT A DOUBT
THERE'S A HOUSE BUILT IN HEAVEN FOR BROKEN DOLLS
I'M GOING TO CARRY YOU THROUGH THAT DOOR
YOU'LL FEEL PAIN NO MORE
I WAS MISSING YOU…
THE VERY NEXT DAY TWO CARS PULL AWAY
EACH WITH A PERSON IN THE BACK
ONE HEADS TO JAIL THE OTHER TO A CHURCH

WHERE A PREACHER TELLS A CONGREGATION
THAT DON'T KNOW HOW TO REACT
HE SAYS THERE'S A HOUSE BUILT IN HEAVEN FOR BROKEN DOLLS
SHE'LL BE CARRIED RIGHT THROUGH THAT DOOR
SHE FEELS PAIN NO MORE
THE GOOD BOOK'S TELLING YOU
THERE'S A HOUSE BUILT IN HEAVEN FOR BROKEN DOLLS
SHE'LL BE CARRIED RIGHT THROUGH THAT DOOR
SHE FEELS PAIN NO MORE
I PROMISE YOU

"Miss Kylee! Get out here NOW!" Mother Madre was beyond upset, as she stood outside Miss Kylee's PTO office door, holding a flyer that advertised an event.

"What is it, Mother Madre?"

"You tell ME! What IS it?" asked Mother Madre in a rage.

"It's Dr. Nihil's event. He asked if I could design a flyer for his one-millionth try to prove the Big Bang Theory. Do you like it?"

"Are you k-k-kidding me?" Mother Madre grit the words through her teeth. "Where was the n-n-notice that I asked you to post when I was going to be unavailable?"

"I was going to-"

"And where is the p-p-posting, or any information whatsoever, regarding the PTO meeting?"

"Oh, I do have a design for-"

"And I find THIS trash hanging on b-b-bulletin boards and every other classroom door?"

"But, it's his millionth try, Mother Madre," Miss Kylee pleaded.

"Do you even think, Miss Kylee? Is his millionth try to be celebrated? I actually say YES! Celebrated because a self-declared expert claimed that he could disprove that God created all, but f-f-f-failed miserably over the course of one MILLION tries! I guess we can celebrate what we already know, but we actually do that already, every day through worship and prayer, or at least we should. Is THAT how *you* are celebrating?"

"Well, I was just instructed as to what should go on the flyer."

"Confirming to me that you d-d-DON'T think."

"But it is kind of cool that he is hitting a million. He worked so hard. My arms would be so sore."

"Wow. Just, Wow." Mother Madre said, while shaking her head in utter disappointment.

"You should see the science lab. I did all the decorating with streamers and balloons."

Mother Madre paid her no mind after that, and sped down the hallway toward Dr. Nihil's science lab. The numbers displayed above the doorway were two digits away from the millionth mark. Most of St. Perpetua's students were crammed into the lab and waiting for the one-millionth try.

"Oh great! Mother Madre is here, students!" Dr. Nihil exclaimed, while he cranked a dial on some device that cradled the seventy-seven equally weighted sticks.

"What is happening here, Dr. Nihil? I have a lot of empty classrooms scattered throughout St. Perpetua Academy right now, and I think I just f-f-found where the students are all at."

"Well, they are all excited to be here to witness my one-millionth attempt at proving the Big Bang Theory."

"Proving the *one* big b-b-bang?"

"Yes, Mother Madre, could you imagine?"

"Wait, trying to p-p-prove, as you say, the p-p-proposed one big bang with a one-*millionth* try? I would say that n-n-nothing would be proven but the existence of God. I do take issue with the students being f-f-fed propaganda that has most-obviously already been d-d-disproven. Deception regarding what to be excited about versus what to stand up against has taken quite a serpent's poisonous turn, Dr. Nihil, and I'm afraid that your have become one of the many snake-charmers that utilize trickery over reality. Hopefully this one-millionth try will c-c-convince you that you are wrong about the so-called big bang, and more importantly, that you should turn your studies toward p-p-p-p-proving Jesus Christ's resurrection. What could be more important than that?"

"That's just not how scientists' minds think."

"Well, I'm afraid that those thoughts may be short-lived, unless you scientists discover the m-m-miracle of God, which doesn't take a scientific doctorate d-d-degree to experience. Quite the opposite, actually, although God made all sciences, ultimately."

"We shall see. It is time for number 999,999."

"Hmm, flip that over and you have yourself a double-dose of evil numbers. How appropriate. Fire away! No p-p-pun intended."

"In my time, Madre."

"Mother Madre, Dr., Mother. Madre. And *your* time is limited, if you, yourself, actually believe in your dark goal."

Dr. Nihil put on a blindfold for effect in front of the students, and shouted out, "In the name of science, nine-hundred-thousand, nine-hundred and ninety-nine!" His hand let go of the seventy-seven sticks, which led to an eruption of laughter when twenty or so of them landed on the ground. "That was strictly for calibration," he said, while taking off his blindfold and pecking at the ground to recover them. "And now, boys and girls, ONE MILLION, on the count of three. One – Two - Three!"

Each student threw a handful of confetti into the air as Dr. Nihil released the seventy-seven sticks.

Mother Madre snickered as one of the sticks slowly rolled to the edge of the table and fell to the ground. "Maybe next time, Dr. Nahil. Students, please get to your real c-c-classes so you may earn a real education."

Dr. Nihil looked around at all of the confetti on the floor, tables, and scientific instruments. "Mother Madre, would you call Mr. Karcin to come clean up the science lab?"

"Absolutely not. Maybe you can impose a scientific change of inertia on all of those confetti pieces by picking up a broom and d-d-doing some sweeping of your own for once."

CHAPTER 13

Mr. Karcin sat as his desk in the boiler room with Sim. He had a pad of paper in front of him and had just finished sketching a few trees onto a page. Sim was all smiles and full of excitement as they talked through the tree-house planning stages together.

"One thing we know for certain," Mr. Karcin explained to Sim, "is that every tree-house needs a good solid foundational floor on which to build the walls, regardless of the design or style of it." He continued to sketch some wooden framework in-between the trees that he had just drawn. Handing a piece of paper and a pencil to Sim, he asked, "Is there any design that you are thinking of in your head?"

As soon as Sim picked up the pencil, he began to draw. He faced the drawing toward Mr. Karcin and asked, "What about this?"

"A Gambrel-style roof? I like it!"

Soon, the two were outside St. Perpetua Academy, on the side of the building that had a small forest of trees growing there. A pile of lumber was neatly stacked near four tree trunks that were perfectly spaced apart for the tree-house's foundational floor. There was also a ladder, a toolbox, a level, a handsaw, and a tool-belt that had Sim's name written on it.

"I think you're right, Sim. These four trees will be perfect as the four corners of the tree-house. Now, what's the first thing that we'll want to build?"

"The floor's frame?"

"Exactly. The frame is very important. If that frame is at all crooked or weak, everything that is built upon it will also be crooked or weak. We should get a measurement from tree to tree so we can know how long the outer-frame boards need to be. See if there is a measuring tape in the tool box."

Sim started digging through the medium-sized toolbox. "Wow, there's lots of stuff in here," he declared, while digging further. "Found one!"

"Good, now hold it against this tree and I'll take the end of the tape measure and bring it to that tree so we can know how much to saw off the first board. When I get there, lock the tape measure when I say so and tell me the number of inches."

"Ok, I won't move."

Mr. Karcin walked the end of the tape measure to the opposite tree from the one that Sim was holding the tape measure base against. Sim was looking up in amazement at how tall the tree was.

"Alright," said Mr. Karcin, "lock it there and tell me how many inches it says."

Sim wasn't sure what Mr. Karcin meant by 'locking it', but he looked down to read the number of inches just as the several yards of extended metal tape came retracting back toward him at a high rate of speed, pinching his thumb when it got to the end."

"OWWW!"

"You didn't lock it in?"

"I don't know what that means."

"Sim, if you don't know what something means, you need to ask, especially while working on projects, such as construction, where lots of tools will be used. It is too easy to get hurt if you don't understand how things work, and how to use everything safely." He walked over to Sim and said, "Let me see the damage," while examining his hand. "Just a pinch. I think you'll be just fine. Ok, hold the tape measure against the tree trunk again." Mr. Karcin began to walk, allowing himself to get about halfway before walking excruciatingly slow. "Forget anything Sim?"

"I don't know. I don't think so."

"Ok," Mr. Karcin patronized, then walked faster until he reached the opposite tree again. "I'm here, so lock it and take the measurement."

"No! Don't let it go!"

"What did you forget?"

"To ask how to lock the tape measure."

Mr. Karcin smiled and chuckled as he made his was back to the eager boy. After a quick lesson on tape measures, they were able to collect the necessary data from tree to tree. Eventually, they used the measurements to mark four long boards. Mr. Karcin pointed out two nearby trees that had low branches, which could be used as saw horses.

"I don't see any horses," Sim challenged.

"Ha Ha! Not *that* kind of horse," he replied, while instructing Sim to grab an end of a long board. Once it was suspended across the two branches and positioned for sawing, Mr. Karcin instructed Sim to re-measure their markings.

"But we already measured and marked the boards."

"The rule is to measure twice, and cut once. If, for whatever reason, we were off on our numbers, the second measurement should catch it before we might have cut the board in the wrong place, which creates a lot more work and waste than taking an extra moment to double-check measurements."

Sim and Mr. Karcin worked tirelessly, leveling and nailing boards into place, securing critical weight-load points with lag-bolts, using a chalk-line so that Sim could nail flooring boards with confidence into wooden studs below that he couldn't see. It was a learning experience for Sim, and a bonding opportunity for both of them. They sat on top of the finished flooring, with the feeling of accomplishment.

"Wow, Mr. Karcin. This is so cool. It feels fun to be up in the trees."

"You've put in a good day's work. Hopefully you've learned some new things as we went along."

"I sure did, and there's probably so much more to learn, too, once we begin to build the walls and roof."

"Everything we do has the potential of being a learning experience, Sim, and you are proving yourself to be a very intelligent young man. Well, we should head back into the school for now. The next stage of the project will be the walls, like you said. Maybe we can sketch out where you'd like the windows to be, now that you've been able to get the perspective from up here."

"This has been my favorite day at school, ever!"

Back inside St. Perpetua Academy, Mother Madre attached a hand-written notice of her unavailability on her office door before heading back into the chapel with her satchel. The first two-thirds of the candles along the chapel's long wall were still burning from her previous reflection visit. She lit the remaining candles with a symbolic hope that the glow would help to battle the darkness that she was about to reveal to herself. She bowed her head and said a prayer to God, asking for forgiveness for what she might learn during her slumber. She slipped into a pew and closed her eyes.

"Jumping the gun a little, aren't you, Marshall?"

"Marjorie, what are you doing here so early? And, how did you get in? Did I actually leave the kitchen door unlocked again? I'm in a fog. Wild night last night."

Mayor Murphy walked around the gambling machines that Marshall Smith was in the middle of setting up. She looked over at a second crate of machines on a wooden pallet in the corner. "My God, Marshall, how many machines do you plan on putting in here?"

"Considering this is the new gold-rush, I'm going to install as many as I can fit into Smitty's Bar without having to take *out* the bar. Maybe I should rename the place Smitty's Saloon, you know, like a return to the wild wild west!"

"Speaking of wild, how wild *was* last night, and with who?"

"Don't tell me that you're going to get all possessive on me, now that we share some hot and steamy nights now and then."

"Steamy nights? Hmmm. Well, at least I'd rather be your steamy night than some juvenile-based wild one."

"What are you getting at Marjorie? Shouldn't you be preparing for tonight's town counsel meeting? We've got a lot riding on it. Like, *every*thing riding on it."

"Sure, let me get right to w-w-w-work while you p-p-party into the night with whoever tickles your little fancy at the time. Is that it? Keep me barefoot and pregnant, yet also keep me working?"

"My little fancy? Barefoot and pregnant? What is up with you this morning, Marj?"

"Did you not hear me? I'm pregnant, Marshall."

"Wait! What? Pregnant? Are you being serious right now?"

"I'm as serious as a heart attack."

"Marj, I think you're giving me one. I thought you were on the pill?"

"I was, but speaking of heart attacks, I had to change my heart medication and I couldn't be on the pill at the same time due to potential complications."

"Complications? What do you call this?"

"Oh, is that what this child is to you? A complication?"

"What about your other meds? You're acting all crazy right now. Are you off those, too?"

"Well, I'm not going to fill my body with a cocktail of medications while I have a baby growing in me."

"Marjorie, you can't be serious. You're not thinking straight. I can't have another baby right now. And what about you? Wouldn't you and me having a relationship make the public suspicious of any deals that we might have made?"

"I knew it! It's all about the deals. You never really cared about me. You just care about your bottom line, your profit, and not going to jail."

"Marjorie, please. We can't have this baby. I'll pay for the procedure."

"WE can't have this baby? WE? Until I see your legs up in stirrups while a doctor coaches you in-between breaths to push, it is *not* WE! I am having this baby, and you are supporting it, or our deals are off."

"Marjorie, *please.*"

"Marjorie, *please*? Was it Hailey, *please*? No! It was all about how wonderful it was to bring Angela into the world, even though you seem to have a not-so funny way of showing any love for her.

"Look, Marj-"

"No. *You* look, Marshall. By the time I'm done developing those old factories across the street into modern dwellings, and maybe a farmers market district, Smitty's Bar will be nothing more than an eyesore."

"And then what? You'll force me to spend money to renovate the outside of Smitty's to match your pretty and fake façade?"

"There would be no chance for renovations, Marshall. It would just be gone. No more Smitty's Bar."

"You know you can't do that, especially now that Chief Parker has a vested interest in the business."

"An interest based on you not going to jail, so he can eventually have you sign the bar over to him. Who holds the better hand right now?"

"Smitty's has been part of Hope's culture and history for generations. You can't just wipe that away. Look, I think that Chief Parker should be here for this conversation. He should know what's going on."

"The Chief will have as much stake in the business as you will have if this baby isn't born. Zero."

"How can you say that?"

"Can you say Eminent Domain?"

"What are you even talking about? You can't just take this property because you want to."

"But the town can take it if it makes sense regarding the good of the public, and as a matter of fact, one rendition of the development plans of the factories has a street rotary right where we are standing. Bye-Bye Smitty's."

"You are evil!"

"And you are in a heap of trouble if we don't work out a deal, right here, right now."

"Marj. Please. I'm begging you to get back on your meds so we may continue this conversation with a semblance of sensibility."

"And harm this baby? I don't think so, Marshall. You have 24 hours to give me an answer as to how you'd like to live your life moving forward. The development plans and your little gambling zoning will move forward during tonight's meeting, regardless. The difference will be if Smitty's Bar remains in existence and you remain free, or if the newly zoned property formerly known as Smitty's becomes the new Hope Casino, which is a very real possibility within my development plans. As a matter of fact, if this baby is born, we may be able to call it Smitty's Casino, allowing your family name to live on in Hope, and making you more rich than you have ever imagined."

"But, Marjorie, a new baby is not an option for me right now. Is there anything else that we could work out? Anything at all?"

The Mayor walked around, inspecting all of the gambling machines that Marshall had prematurely invested in. She then looked down at her body, rubbing her stomach with her two hands as if already holding and massaging her baby. "If you're asking me to kill this baby, I expect an eye for an eye."

Mother Madre walked over to the brightly illuminated wall of candles and snuffed each one of them out, one by one, by holding a thumb and finger on each candle's wick and not letting go until she prayed The Lord's Prayer:

OUR FATHER WHO ART IN HEAVEN
HALLOWED BE THY NAME
THY KINGDOM COME
THY WILL BE DONE
ON EARTH AS IT IS IN HEAVEN
GIVE US THIS DAY OUR DAILY BREAD
AND FORGIVE US OUR TRESPASSES
AS WE FORGIVE THOSE WHO TRESPASS AGAINST US
AND LEAD US NOT INTO TEMPTATION
BUT DELIVER US FROM EVIL
FOR THINE IS THE KINGDOM
AND THE POWER
AND THE GLORY
FOR EVER AND EVER
AMEN

CHAPTER 14

During Mother Madre's time in the chapel, some of the St. Perpetua staff began to ask questions among themselves. Nobody could seem to remember ever leaving the academy, although it didn't feel unnatural not to do so. And who were the people that they had dreamed about? Were the scenes in the dreams just lessons to be learned, or were they something more?

"Mother Madre, Do you have a moment?" Mr. Connor asked as he entered the principal's office. After she turned around to face him, Mr. Connor noticed how drained she looked. "Or, I could come back later if now is not a convenient time."

"No, please do sit down. What's on your mind, Mr. Connor?"

"Mother Madre, is it possible that-"

"What is that in your hands?" Mother Madre interrupted.

"This is a song that Mr. Dyson wrote for me. Well, the lyrics anyway. I had a dream that I just can't seem to clear out of my head. As a matter of fact, it keeps tugging at me to act on it, somehow."

"May I read the lyrics?"

"Please do, Mother Madre." Mr. Connor handed her the scroll, while his hope swelled that she might be able to give him some insight. The feeling he had of missing the two children in his dream was becoming unbearable.

Mother Madre unfolded her screen once she read the lyrics. She appeared to be reviewing something before speaking. "Mr. Connor, I believe that we all do get a glimpse of what we may perceive as God, or what God may have in store for us in his good time. It's usually just a matter of recognizing it when it happens, like your, um, the boy in your dream did."

"But, do you think that maybe we get to experience a glimpse back? You know, like after we d-"

"With God, all things are possible, Mr. Connor. When did Mr. Dyson write this song for you?"

"Right after I had a dream about that boy, and there was also a segment about a girl at a father/daughter dance that I-"

"Yes, I see that."

"I don't understand. How would you be able to s-"

"With God, all things are possible, Mr. Connor."

"Do you think that God would allow me to-"

"Mr. Connor, I need to tend to something. Would you mind heading over to the Activities Room? I will join you there in a moment."

"Sure, should I bring anything with me?"

"Just an open mind, Mr. Connor."

Once he left the room, Mother Madre called Mr. Dyson to the principal's office for a chat. She inquired about what they spoke of in an effort to gauge how much knowledge of St. Perpetua the staff may have gained during her time in the chapel. After praising Mr. Dyson on writing such an appropriate and sensitive song for Mr. Connor, she asked how close he was in completing the latest song that she had recently given him the concept and title for.

"I'm pleased to report that I've finished the song, and already know the lyrics by heart. It sounds more and more like a prayer to me every time that I sing it."

"That's wonderful, Mr. Dyson. If you could write three more prayer-style songs, we can take a look at finalizing your music teacher tenure status."

"How exciting! I do enjoy writing songs like that, and I may even compose *more* than three additional ones," Mr. Dyson said, with enthusiasm.

"Excellent. Please head over to the Activities Room and wait for me there. I'd like for you to perform the song before the activity that I have planned for the staff in a little while."

Mother Madre picked up the phone to contact Miss Kylee, but after holding the receiver in her hand for a moment, she hung it back up without dialing her extension. She picked it back up and dialed the boiler room instead.

"Hello, Mr. Karcin?"

"Yes, Mother Madre?"

"Are you in the middle of anything?"

"I was just going to start in on fixing Miss Addison's broken doll with Sim."

"Please put that project aside for the time being and meet me in the Activities Room."

251

"I'll head that way right now."

Mother Madre hung up and dialed Miss Addison's room. There was no answer so she hung up and then dialed again. Still, nobody answered. She picked up her satchel and walked to Miss Addison's classroom. When she arrived, she found her sitting on top of her toy-chest bench with a blindfold over her eyes and earplugs in her ears.

"Miss Addison," Mother Madre tried. "Miss Addison?" She walked about the room, noticing that each student's desk had their caricature drawing on it so the students could enjoy them when they arrived back at class. The drawing of Officer Williams remained on the easel. Taking a step up onto the reading-area platform, she spotted a rolled-up drawing in Miss Addison's hands. As she tried to slip it out of her hands, Miss Addison jumped and pulled her blindfold off.

"Oh, Mother Madre," she said, while pulling her earplugs out of her ears. "You startled me."

"Did I wake you, Miss Addison?"

"Unfortunately, no. It seems that no matter how hard I try to fall asleep I just can't."

"Are you feeling tired?"

"No, not really."

"Then why the quest for sleep?"

"I feel like I need to get back to my dream, but earlier, so I can change things."

Mother Madre unrolled the paper and looked at the drawing of Angela. "Unfortunately, Miss Addison, there is nothing that you could do to change what you saw in your dream. Everybody is called back to God in his time. There may be some things that you could change in a different dream, but not right now. We are congregating in the Activities Room and I'd like for you to head there."

On the way to the Activities Room, Mother Madre instructed Officer Williams to follow her. When they arrived, the others were sitting at a large round table in the center of the room, engaged in friendly conversation, talking about things that they liked about each other, and the progress that they had noticed in the students at St. Perpetua Academy.

"Welcome to what I call 'Jigsaw Afternoon'," Mother Madre said as she entered the room. "This activity is a crucial part of your curriculum here at St. Perpetua. It is to grow your empathy, and acquire a better understanding of the impact that you've had on others."

She opened her satchel and pulled out five medium-sized boxes, each with a staff-member's name on it, and each one containing several puzzle pieces inside. As she placed a box in front of the person associated with it, she continued, "People that we've interacted with may not remember the words that we might have said, or what we might have done, but they will never forget the way that we made them feel. Inside each of your boxes are puzzle pieces that correlate with various people from your past. Each piece represents a different person. As you hold each one in your hand, you will feel some of the emotions that specific person felt as a result of your actions and/or relationship with, or around, them. You will not be able to release each puzzle piece until that feeling has subsided. If you attempt to place the piece down before the emotion fades, it will not fit into the puzzle, and you will need to pick it up again, at which time the full emotion will double in strength. Understood?"

Everyone nodded their heads while looking around the room at each other.

"I have asked Mr. Dyson to write a theme song for this activity as part of his requirements for achieving music teacher tenure, just as I had instructed him to write and perform songs related to some of the stories and dreams that you have all shared with me. Whether you liked each song or not when he performed them for you, I think that it would be nice to share a round of applause for Mr. Dyson for the thought, time, and talent that he put into each of those very personal songs."

Everyone politely clapped and cheered for him.

"Thanks everyone," Mr. Dyson said. "I never thought I'd enjoy writing and performing for one person at a time, but I can tell you that I learned a lot about myself through all of *your* songs, and actually appreciated, and grew fond of, the single-person audiences. Thanks for putting up with me."

The others responded with quips regarding how talented he was, good tunes, private concerts are the best, could have been a rock star, etc.…

"Ok. Enough already," he said, while blushing from the praise. "This one is kind-of like a prayer."

JIGSAW AFTERNOONS
WOULD YOU POUR YOUR LOVE
IF I LEARN TO FIX THIS HOLE THAT DRAINS MY CUP?
TO KEEP PROMISES
AND GIVE YOU BACK THE SECRETS THAT I KEEP
WAKING ME UP BEFORE I SLEEP
SHAPES AND PIECES BUILD MY LIFE
THE WAY A PUZZLE GROWS
EACH ONE HAS A TIME AND PLACE
SOME ARE PEOPLE THAT I KNOW

BUT I'VE LOST A FEW OR LET THEM GO
THOUGH MANY DIFFERENT WAYS I'VE BEEN UNKIND
I'M A TRUSTING CHILD WHO ONLY WAITS FOR YOU
TO HELP ME FIT THE PIECES I CAN'T FIND
ON JIGSAW AFTERNOONS
THIS MORNING I SURRENDER
I THINK I MIGHT BE HURT
IF I HEAL BY AFTERNOON
I'M SLIPPING INTO THE DITCHES I HAVE DUG
AND SWEEPING THE DIRT UNDER A RUG
BUT IF I PAVE MY PATH WITH STONES I GRIND
I MIGHT AS WELL FILL CRATERS ON THE MOON
THE SUN WON'T SHOW ME FORWARD OR BEHIND
ON JIGSAW AFTERNOONS
I BELIEVE IN A RESURRECTION
ASHES TO ASHES – DUST TO DUST
BUT I CAN'T PERCEIVE
THE THINGS THAT I'VE BEEN SEEING HERE ON THE STREET
HOW CAN ANY OF US BECOME COMPLETE?
I WAS NEVER GOOD AT PIN-THE-TAIL BLIND
BUT SOMETIMES IT'S LIKE I'M FEELING AROUND FOR YOU
TO HELP ME FIT THE PIECES I CAN'T FIND
ON JIGSAW AFTERNOONS

The staff applauded, while enjoying the camaraderie that they all felt for each other at that point. Mother Madre let them take in the moment before speaking again.

"That's very good D.D., um, I mean Mr. Dyson. I think that the song drives the point home that sometimes it isn't until we n-n-*need* something that we finally decide to p-p-p-pray, and then quite often, we break the silent p-p-promises that we made to God as soon as the problem that we asked relief from goes away. We tend to do the same with our fellow people. Treat them well while things are going our way, or until we get what we want from them, while not thinking of how our lack of sensitivity or empathy makes them feel. When one feels how others felt because of their actions or non-actions, that's when they question if they'd ever be good enough to get into Heaven. My friends, I have one word for you – g-g-g-GRACE."

Mother Madre walked around the circular table, personally taking the lids off the top of each staff member's puzzle box. Once she had all of the lids in her hands she said, "Once you begin your puzzle, there is no going back. The puzzle must be completed, and the pieces will remain connected, never to be taken apart again." She handed the cardboard box lids to Mr. Karcin. "I think you know what to do with these."

"I sure do," he said, while getting up and breaking each lid down before placing them into the recycling bin in the corner of the Activities Room.

Once Mr. Karcin sat back down, Mother Madre opened her satchel again and unfolded her screen while she continued, "This will be an intense exercise that will feel uncomfortable at times, unbearable at times, jubilant at times, and somber at times. In addition to sitting, if you feel the need to stand, lay down, etcetera, during any part of this activity, you are allowed to do so. Jigsaw Afternoon doesn't finish until every puzzle has been completed." She looked around the table as the nervous and skeptical staff looked around at each other. "Are we ready?"

"As ready as I'll ever be."

"Bring it on."

"I've got this."

"Oh, I don't know about this."

Pause…

"Miss Addison?" Mother Madre asked.

"Yes, Mother Madre. I think I'm ready."

Holding the screen in her hands, Mother Madre began circling the table. "You may begin. Please pick up your first puzzle piece," she instructed.

Instantly, there was shouting, crying, and laughing. Officer Williams was standing in a crouched position with his legs bent. Every time his legs straightened up he screamed. Mother Madre glanced at her screen and said, "Those underwear wedgies sure can hurt, Officer Williams."

Mr. Connor was drenched in sweat, while nervously trying to explain something as if inside some boardroom with a tyrant of a boss. "It's extremely difficult to work effectively under that kind of management, Mr. Connor. Good luck with your presentation," said Mother Madre.

Miss Addison erupted, "HELP ME – PLEASE! CALL SOMEBODY! I NEED HELP! WHY ARE YOU JUST STANDING THERE? PLEASE SAY SOMETHING TO SOMEONE WHO CAN HELP! PLEASE!"

"It must be a scary, helpless, and frustrating experience when your life is in danger and help is right in front of you, but it never acts or speaks up, Miss Addison," Mother Madre suggested.

She walked over to Mr. Dyson, who was on the ground in a fetal position, crying, and saying, "I can't believe that I lost my virginity to some rock star that said they'd take me on the road, but then kicked me off the bus as it left for the next city. I feel so hurt, betrayed, and violated."

"Mr. Dyson, imagine there being one person feeling like you do now in the wake of every single show that a specific performer played

257

while on tours. A few lustful moments for the performer, and months or longer of heartache, embarrassment, and even self-guilt for the victim that allowed their innocence to be stripped away by a song and a tempting tongue."

Mr. Karcin's mouth seemed to be stretching abnormally wide and then he'd yell "OUCH!... and the cycle repeated over and over and over again. OUCH!...... OUCH!......... OUCH!

"Let me guess, Mr. Karcin," Mother Madre said without even looking down at her screen. "You're spending some time in the brook with the frogs near your old tree-house?"

"Un-Huh............ OUCH!"

"Everyone, please place that puzzle piece down on the table in front of you," Mother Madre instructed, and without giving any relief, said, "Now pick up another piece and hold it until I say so." She looked down at her screen and quickly ran to her satchel and pulled out a bucket larger than the satchel itself and rapidly placed it next to Mr. Karcin, who then began throwing up into it. "If less than a teaspoon of chemicals makes you feel like that, Mr. Karcin, imagine the impact on all of the water sources and wildlife that buckets upon buckets of toxins being added to them daily would have had. Keep that bucket close by."

Mr. Dyson stood on his chair, started dancing in place with his hands pumping into the air, and began singing along to something. "WAAAY-OH! WAAAY-OH-WAAAY! What a great time! What a great concert!"

"Music does spread joy to others, globally, universally, *and* Heavenly, Mr. Dyson. Nice work. Enjoy the moment," Mother Madre praised.

"Awww," Miss Addison expressed. "You are SO nice. Thanks for showing me how much you care about me. I drew you a picture of an angel because you are an angel to me, my teacher angel. Can I hold your hand on the way to reading time? I feel safe and loved near you."

"Love speaks louder than any words I could say right now, Miss Addison. What a warm, protective, and genuine feeling you are experiencing back. Your students were blessed to have you."

Mr. Connor paced helplessly back and forth, tugging at his hair and saying how worthless and inadequate he was. How, even though he was successful in a similar role under a different boss, he felt stupid under the new one. He kept saying that he was afraid to lose the house, but not to let the kids know that anything was wrong. He ran over to the bucket near Mr. Karcin and added to the growing deposit of vomit.

Mother Madre looked at her screen and said, "Ah, the feeling of being devoid of any self-worth, Mr. Connor. That can slip right from the ridicule one endures from a boardroom on into the bedroom, where one's lack of confidence may erode relationships, including the one that is found within the individual's soul."

"Ah-HA-ha-ha! AAHH-Ha-ha-ha!" Officer Williams was laughing hysterically. "HA! Stop! Let me catch my- AAAHH-HA-HA-HA-HA!

"So, it appears that you were the joke-teller at the badge company whenever one of your coworkers was feeling blue, of if you just wanted to raise the spirits in the room. I never saw the comedic side of you while playing the role of the officer. Laughter is always good, Officer Williams, as long as you are laughing with, and not at. Nice trait to have."

Jigsaw Afternoon continued on for quite a while, with each staff member's puzzle slowly growing over the course of the activity. Meanwhile, down in the boiler room, Sim searched through a large box of various scrap pieces of wood with hopes of finding the right diameter dowel to fix the arm of Miss Addison's broken wooden doll. Nothing came close to being the right size, so he figured he could venture out to the tree-house site and find a branch that might work. He grabbed the body of the doll, a jigsaw that hung on the wall of tools, and Mr. Karcin's woodcarving knife before heading to the door that he went in and out from when they built the tree-house floor. Sim was sad to find it locked, so he crossed the hallway to the opposite side of the building and tried the door there. He felt excitement when it opened easily. He couldn't wait to hand the fixed doll to Miss Ambry once he found the right piece of wood for the project.

That side of the building looked much different from the tree-house side. There weren't any trees at all. Without trees, there was no shade on that side and Sim had never felt the outside air feel as warm as it felt at that moment. He felt as if he was in an oven. The ground underneath his feet crunched as he began to walk in effort to reach the other side of St. Perpetua. It appeared that he was treading on broken pieces of greying seashells, or something. Could the ground cover be made of pieces of bone? The pieces sure looked like the same material as the bones that made up the skeleton in Dr. Nihil's science room. Looking up, he saw a figure ahead of him through the air of heat waves that distorted his vision. Was it Mr. Karcin? He ran up to him, but then stopped abruptly when he got closer to it. It appeared to be skeleton-like, with wrinkled skin and longer than normal arms, fingers, and legs. At first, Sim was scared, but then it began to speak with him in a kind voice, asking what he was doing. Sim explained how he was looking for the right tree branch to fix the arm of the wooden doll.

"But where would you find sticks out here?" it asked.

"On the other side, where the forest is."

"Forest?"

"Yeah, where Mr. Karcin and I started to build our tree-house."

"A tree-house? I love tree-houses!"

"We don't have walls on it yet, but would you like to see the floor we built?"

"You are inviting me? Then I can go on that side now. May I bring some friends to see it, too?"

"Of course! We still need to add more lag-bolts to it, so maybe just I should go up on the tree-house floor, but you can look at it."

"Perfect! What is your name?"

"Simeon, but my friends call me Sim."

"Sounds good. I will call you Simeon. I'll swing around to the other side once I gather some of my friends. Sound good?"

"Sure," Sim responded, and then continued to walk through the heat over the broken pieces of whatever it was below his feet.

The academy was much larger than he had realized. He felt like he had walked forever before finally reaching the other side of the immense building. With a parched throat, he scavenged the forest floor for just the right branch to fix the doll's arm with, but he was also hoping to find a brook from which to get a drink of water. Eventually, he found a branch that had a slight bend in it sticking out at shoulder-level to Sim from a tree's trunk, which looked to Sim a little like an arm with an elbow. "Perfect!" he said. "I can carve the rest of it to look like a real arm!" Trusting his sense of direction, he made his way through the thick forest, eventually locating the tree-house floor, suspended high up above his head. He placed the branch, doll, and knife in his back pockets and traded the jigsaw in his hand for the ladder, which he struggled to maneuver into place so he could climb up.

261

"Miss Addison is going to be so happy when she gets her doll back," Sim said, while dangling his feet off the edge of the wooden platform while sending shavings from the branch in his hand onto the forest floor below as he whittled away at it. He thought about how proud Mr. Karcin would be of him, taking on the project all by himself.

Soon, something whisked quickly by him. Then another, and another. Before he knew it, the trees were swaying back and forth because the movement of the beings was creating a strong wind. They were going so fast that Sim could only see a blur circling through the forest. A loud whistling and screeching sound kept getting louder and louder. Sim placed the branch, knife, and doll on top of the platform and held his hands over his ears. His fear began to grow, yet he felt too paralyzed by it to climb back down the ladder and run into St. Perpetua Academy. Every few seconds, a hand emerged from the loud blur, holding a clear glass of water. Sim felt so thirsty that he eventually took it.

Back inside the Activities Room, everyone's last puzzle piece was finally put into place. The staff members sat back in their seats, completely exhausted. Nobody said a word, but rather thought about the activity that they each engaged in. The silence lasted for several moments while each weighed the impact that they had on others, both good and bad. Each one of them was wishing that they had examined themselves earlier as they continued to reflect.

Eventually, Mother Madre broke the silence. "You may now look at the pictures that your puzzle has formed."

Everyone leaned toward the table to take a look at their personalized jigsaw puzzle.

"How beautiful. Mine is of an angel's wings," Miss Addison said.

"So is mine, but it has chrome exhaust pipes coming out of them. Cool!" Mr. Karcin added.

"Look at that! Mine has a police badge on it!" said Officer Williams, while standing up to get a better look.

Mister Connors looked at his and asked, "Mother Madre, I think that I speak on behalf of each one of us when I ask this question. Is it possible that we've already died?"

BWAAP! BWAAP! BWAAP! BWAAP! BWAAP!...

Everyone placed their hands over their ears as the St. Perpetua emergency alarm went off.

Mother Madre looked down at her screen, then shouted to the others in effort to be heard over the alarm, "EVERYONE TO THE EVACUATION ROOM! THIS IS NOT A DRILL!"

Each staff member got up and quickly left the Activities Room, except for Officer Williams.

"DID YOU NOT HEAR ME OFFICER WILLIAMS? TO THE EVACUATION ROOM!"

"PLEASE, MOTHER MADRE, I AM THE OFFICER HERE. HOW MAY I HELP?"

Mother Madre took Officer Williams' hand and scurried him down to her office and closed the door. The alarm was much less loud in there.

"Officer Williams," Mother Madre began, while shaking her head and looking at her screen, "it appears that young Sim has been snatched by a spirit from the Hollow of Lies."

"Where have they taken him?"

"It's not that they have taken him anywhere, yet. Sim must have invited them to the side of St. Perpetua that they have been banished from a long, long time ago."

"What do you think their motivation is, Mother Madre?"

263

"Sim is like gold to them. A young boy that left the world too young, in the eyes and hearts of his friends and relatives, which means the chances are good that voices from down in the valley will be eager to hear from him."

"I'm sorry, but I don't quite understand."

"This is like an open door for the evil spirits to give misinformation to those still in the world about their loved ones who already passed, which is always manipulated such that it attempts to throw them off from their Christian beliefs. Many souls are at stake. This is a very, very, very bad thing, Officer Williams."

"How may I help, Mother Madre?"

Mother Madre walked behind her desk and pulled a crucifix from the wall and handed it to Officer Williams. Here, place this into your holster. Your goal will be to reach Sim on the tree-house platform and press the cross against the spirit that has his arm around him. It will make the evil spirit disappear, instantly."

"I think that I can handle that, Mother Madre."

"This won't be an easy mission. Evil does not play nicely, Officer Williams."

As he walked out of St. Perpetua Academy, Officer Williams could hear the evil screeching of the demon spirits as they circled throughout the forest. He wondered how they could move so swiftly without hitting any trees. Having never been outside on the academy's grounds, he made his way through the woodland, trying to find where the tree-house floor might have been built. Noticing the pattern that the demons were flying around in, he guessed that Sim might be found in the center of their flight. All of a sudden, their pattern changed, and he found himself ensnared in vines of thorns.

The demon draped one of its long arms around Sim. "Go ahead and take a sip," it said. No longer did his voice sound soothing and inviting, but rather sounded like rocks clicking and banging together like a thick and heavy static. Like jagged stones, with a scraping mixed-in with the gravel & sandpaper-sounding words.

Afraid that the demon might push him off the platform, Sim did as he said and placed the glass to his lips, then quickly spit and threw the glass.

"What's the matter Simeon? You don't like vinegar?"

"I need to go back inside now."

"Awww, but I want to enjoy the tree-house with you first."

"But it isn't even done yet."

"Just say the word, Simeon, and I will snap my fingers and it will be all build for you. Would you like that?"

"I'm building it with Mr. Karcin."

"Karcin-smarcin. Wouldn't it be fun to see it all built, just like that?"

"I just want to go now."

"Wait! What is that I hear? Is that your Gandpa?" the demon alluringly said.

Sim listened intently. The sound of the flying demons changed their tone. Collectively, they sounded like a single loud whisper in the wind.

"Can you hear me, Sim?" the voice whispered.

"Grandpa, It's me! Sim!" the boy yelled out. The demon that was sitting with him repeated his words.

"I love you. More than you will ever know, and forever!" the voice whispered.

"I love YOU Grandpa!" Sim responded.

The demon repeated his words, and then spoke into his ear, "What is something fun that you did with your Grandpa? Can you think of something fun that only you and he would know?"

"I remember making a gerbil cage with Grandpa. I remember wanting to take it home right away, before it was done."

The demon reworded what he was told, and then said, "Grandpa, do you remember when we built that gerbil cage?"

The loud whisper blew strongly around the boy, "Oh yes, Sim. That was one of my favorite weeks ever."

"And remember how I wanted to take it home before it was done? Well you taught me about patience that week," the demon said.

"Yes, that's right! It sure is you, Sim! Oh, how I miss you," the whispered voice answered.

"I miss you, too, Grandpa!" Sim replied, but the demon answered very differently – "Don't worry about missing me, Grandpa. We'll see each other again, but forget about that stuff you learned in church. It's not real."

"That's not what I said," the boy insisted.

The voice whispered back, "What do you mean, Sim?"

The demon didn't wait for the boy's response before saying, "There is no God. Just love and light, Grandpa."

"No, I didn't say that!" Sim shouted.

"Relax young man," the demon said, while squeezing tighter the hold that it had on Sim. "The spirit readers can't receive *your* voice below."

Officer Williams' pant legs were shredded by the time that he finally made his way out of the briar patch. He knew not to trust the flight of the demons overhead to guide him toward Sim, so he prayed and asked God to provide him with a sign. Just then, a reflective flash hit his eyes through the trees so he decided to walk in that direction. All of a sudden, the flying demons began to mimic the flash so that they were hitting his eyes from all directions. It caused him to lose his sense of travel as it pertained to the original flash. Looking over to the St. Perpetua Academy building to get his bearings, he saw flashing coming from Miss Kylee's window, too. At that point, he realized that an evil mole had made it inside St. Perpetua. He froze in place and prayed again. The name Sim appeared, carved into a tree in front of him, then again a few trees beyond that one, and still into more trees beyond that. Soon, every tree in the forest had Sim's name carved into it. As he began to become disoriented again, there was an additional single flash that caught Officer Williams' eye. It came from the carving knife in Sim's hand, which he was nervously moving around while he sat on the edge of the platform and dangled and kicked his legs back and forth uncontrollably. Officer Williams made a beeline toward the tree-house floor.

"It will be Grandma's and my sixtieth wedding anniversary soon, Sim. We sure wish that you could have been there to celebrate with us. She misses you so much, especially bringing cookies and milk down to the woodshop while we worked on projects," the whispered voice said loudly.

"Well, you don't want to know what *I* know about Grandma. You aren't the only man that she's been kissing. I'd stop going to the church if I were you," the demon delivered.

"NO GRANDPA! THAT WASN'T ME!"

"Shh-Shh-Sh-Sh-Shhhhh," the demon insisted. "He can't hear you at all."

A few dozen yards away from the tree-house platform, a branch cracked under Officer Williams' feet.

267

"What is that noise?" the demon asked, and then looked down onto the forest floor. "Well, well, now. A gun won't do you any good here, Mr. Policeman Rescue Hero." He focused on Sim's face, and then asked, "Do you want to look down at your Gramps, Sim?"

"For real?"

"Look right down there."

"That's not my Grandpa. That's Officer Williams."

"Not anymore!" the demon declared, before waving his free arm down toward the ground.

Right in front of Sim's eyes, a large hole opened up in the ground just ahead of the tree-house platform. Two entire large trees slipped down through the hole and disappeared, along with the tall ladder that Sim climbed up onto the platform with. Officer Williams barely caught a grip onto a root from one of the platform's corner trees, which had become exposed through the side of the hole. He looked so tiny to Sim, as he dangled far, far, below him and struggled to climb up to the rim of the hole. Beyond him, the eyes of a human never saw a depth so deep.

"I'm dizzy," Sim said. "I think I might get sick."

"You'll be fine. See how far down you can see? Well your Grandpa's house is a million times past the point that you can actually see. That's a DEEP hole, don't you think?"

"Un Huh."

"Go ahead. Be a boy. Throw something into it."

"I don't want to hit Officer Williams, and I don't want to hit my Grandpa's house, or *any*one's house."

The demon squeezed Sim's arm harder and said, "Throw the knife."

"But it's Mr. Karcin's."

"Mr. *Kar*cin, Mr. *Kar*cin, Mr. *Kar*cin. THROW THE KNIFE SIMEON!"

"You'll need to let go of my arm first," the scared boy said.

Knowing that Simeon couldn't run very far away on the platform, the demon let go of his grip on the boy. Sim scooted away from the edge, stood up, and stared down at the knife in his hand.

"THROW IT!"

Sim threw it as far away from the hole's edge as he could so it wouldn't hit Officer Williams, who was still making his way up the root system to get out of it.

"Isn't that fun, Simeon? Throw something else. What do you have in your pocket?"

Simeon pulled out the branch that he wanted to carve the doll's arm from. He didn't wait to get screamed at again. The flying demons were swirling around more furiously and making loud evil sounds of their own by that point. The boy threw the branch like a boomerang, but it didn't return to the platform. He prayed in his mind that it didn't hit Officer Williams below.

"What else?" asked the demon. "Empty the pocket!"

The next thing that Simeon's fingers touched in his pocket was a small wooden cross that he had been whittling as a gift for Mother Madre. He had worked on it a long time, but decided that he should pull that out of his pocket next, instead of Miss Addision's broken doll.

When the demon saw it he gasped and froze in place, but because Simeon didn't know the power that it had over the evil being, he threw it high over his head, barely clearing the edge of the platform. It glanced off one of the flying demons, sending the demon careening into one of the trees of the forest, which instantly caught on fire.

Down below the platform, Officer Williams made it to the edge of the hole and crawled along the forest floor underneath the platform high above his head. His fear of heights tested his valor, but he understood the gravity of the situation and scrambled in his mind to figure out a way to climb up one of the four corner tree trunks. He noticed the jigsaw that Sim had left on the ground earlier, and began to cut notches into one of the tree-trunks at the far end of the platform, placing a foot or fingertips into them as he went along.

The smoke was getting more intense as the flying demons fanned the flames as they whisked the air around the burning tree until the one next to it also began to burn. Soon, half of the forest was on fire and the flames were quickly approaching the tree-house platform. Officer Williams could hear young Sim coughing several feet above his head. A burning ember hit his hand, and he dropped the saw. The officer clung to the side of the tree trunk, barely hanging on, and prayed for God to help him. A tree fell near him, leaning against the edge of the platform. If Officer Williams could make it to the trunk of that tree, he could easily make it to the top of the platform, but the closest branch was a few feet away and a second hole opened up in the ground just below it. He became paralyzed with fear until he heard the demon tell Simeon that if the fire reaches the platform, then he gets to keep the child. At that moment, without hesitation, Officer Williams leaped to the branch and traversed over to the tree's trunk, which he was able to quickly make his way to the top of. He raced across the platform, and just as the demon turned around to grab him, he pulled the crucifix from his holster and held it to the demon's chest. It let out a piercing scream before falling off the platform and into the hole. Sim looked over the edge and saw that the hole was filled with what appeared to be a lake of fire. All of the demons that were flying throughout the forest became silent, and then disappeared altogether.

"Come on, Sim, we don't have much time!" Officer Williams said, while grabbing the boy's hand and leading him to the tree that was leaning on the platform. "Ok, get on my back and don't let go!" Flames were raging around them, and the officer looked down to see that the base of the leaning tree was already engulfed in flames, too. "Lord, please!" Officer Williams shouted above the roar of the flames, "Take me, but please spare the boy!" Instantly, a soaking deluge of rain doused the entire forest, extinguishing the flames in no time. Sim's arms clung around the officer's neck as he made his way down to the forest floor. Finally feeling like a real hero, Officer Williams carried Sim on his back, all the way through the forest, until they were back inside St. Perpetua Academy.

Mother Madre and the relieved staff were there to greet Officer Williams and young Sim when they walked in.

"Mother Madre," Officer Williams began, "I think that evil has found it's way inside-"

"She's gone."

Everyone celebrated. Once hugs were exchanged, Mother Madre asked the staff to wait for her outside the Hall of Truths while she tended to Sim. She brought him back to the boiler room, where there was a brand new whittling knife waiting for him, along with a selection of choice woods for Sim to do what he would with them. Once he promised Mother Madre to never leave the academy again without an adult, she left the boiler room and headed to the Hall of Truths.

CHAPTER 15

Mr. Dyson, Mr. Connor, Miss Addison, Mr. Karcin, and Officer Williams were seated on chairs that were assembled in a line along the hallway wall outside the door of the Hall of Truths. Mother Madre carried five rolled-up mats under her arms, along with her satchel, as she approached. She said, "As you wrap up your curriculum here at St. Perpetua Academy, this next activity may be considered a gift for each one of you."

"But, didn't you say that I would make music teacher tenure, Mother Madre?" Mr. Dyson asked.

"Yes, Mr. Dyson, and you have done an excellent job in achieving that. The eternal tenure waiting for you is so much greater than anything that you may imagine, and the music that you will be part of includes sounds more beautiful than those made by any musical instrument you have ever heard."

Mother Madre paced in front of the five that were sitting there, handing out the mats and smiling at each of them in a loving way that none of them had seen on her face up until then.

"One by one, I will call you into the Hall of Truths, where you will lay down on your mat. Upon laying on it, you will be granted an interactive dream, within which you may interact with the subjects. Nothing, regarding you being here at St. Purgatory, will change as a result of the actions that you take in your dream, but some closure and/or comfort may happen during each of your dreams. Again, consider this activity a gift. I hope that you all use it well. We can begin with you, Mr. Dyson, and then we'll work our way down the line, in the order that you are all sitting in right now."

Mr. Dyson followed Mother Madre into the Hall of Truths and positioned his mat on the floor in front of the stage area. Mother Madre sat at the long table, at the end closest to the stage, and took her screen out from her satchel.

"You may lie down and close your eyes, Mr. Dyson."

"Time to wake up! Rise and shine D.D," record company executive Terrence said, while placing a cup of gourmet coffee near his mat.

Dyson Devlifar struggled to open his eyes. He had just landed the night before and his body-clock hadn't had any time to adjust to the new time zone that he found himself in. He exhaled a moan as he rolled onto his back and looked up at the thatched roof above his head. He could hear some djembe-drumming coming from outside. "Not bad," he said. "Maybe I could incorporate a beat like that into the next record."

"Now that's a great idea, D.D., and we could expand our charity to raise money for animals in this region, or at least let the contributors think that their money is helping that cause, Ha-Ha," Terrence responded. "Now get up or else we won't be celebrating any big-game kills today. The safari hunt jeep leaves in less than a half hour."

Dyson sat up, took a sip of his coffee, and then rubbed the back of his neck. "Well, at least the coffee is good. I can't say the same about the kink in my neck. This is the best bedding that a high-end safari company can provide?"

"This is the most authentic safari hunting company on the continent, serving the most elite of the elite. They just hosted a Royal Prince here last week. He bagged a cheetah and a giraffe within a few hours!"

"Wow, it sounds exciting to just even *see* those creatures in the wild. What if anyone learns about me going on a hunting safari, considering the animal charity?"

"D.D., why do you worry so much? You know that I'll be covering your tracks, so to speak, Ha-Ha. Besides, if you were to lose any money on record sales, imagine the amount of money *I'd* lose! Also, I wouldn't worry about 'The D.D. Foundation for Animals' losing any funding. Charity suckers are born every single minute."

Twenty minutes later, the two men were being driven in an open-air vehicle with various guns mounted to a rack, a cooler filled with food and several adult beverages, and a trunk loaded with ammunition, assorted tools, and binoculars. A driver named Desta pointed out interesting facts about the plains as they raced toward the acreage where he felt the trophy animals would most likely be spotted.

"I wonder how much the owner of the safari pays this guy to drive rich people around in the hot sun all day," Dyson said to Terrence, under his breath so the driver wouldn't hear.

"Ha-Ha! Get this, Desta. D.D. was just asking me how much I thought the driver was getting paid by the owner to drive us around all day!"

Desta joined in the laughter.

"Why would you do that, Terry?" D.D. asked, after being embarrassed and surprised by him repeating his words to the driver.

"Relax, D.D.," Terrence jibed. "Desta owns the company, along with the thousands of acres that we are hunting on today. He may even have as much money as you do!"

"I'm sorry, Desta," Dyson said. "It just seems like a lot of work in the hot sun when you could hire someone else to do the driving for you."

"No wahala. I like driving around on the land," Desta answered.

"Wahala?" Dyson questioned.

"Right, sorry man. Wahala means worries. No worries."

"But what about witnessing the killing of so many animals, week after week? That must get to you after a while"

"Quite the opposite, my friend. It bothered me a lot at first, but then I just got used to it. Mostly, I got used to the money. You understand, yes? But, to be honest, I have been doing it for twenty-five years, so if someone offered me the right price, I'd think about getting out of the business."

Terrence just smiled while D.D. spoke with Desta. They went back and forth on the topics of hunting for trophy versus food, ethics, and the balance of the regional economy of that part of his country. Abruptly, Desta pulled off of the dirt rode that they were driving on and raced down a bumpier path.

"Did you see some game, Desta?" Terrence asked.

"Hoof prints. There might be a migration happening up ahead. Get your guns ready."

About two miles down the path, Desta slowed the vehicle to a crawl. D.D. was in awe of what appeared in front of them, about a hundred yards away. Several giraffes grazed off some tall trees.

"Maura Pheme is going to be thrilled," said Terrence.

"Maybe Maura should've been here instead of me so she could kill her own soul. Wait, did I say soul? I meant hunted animal trophy. No, actually, I did mean soul."

"What gives, man?" Terrence asked. "Maura has given you new fame and fortune. Bringing a giraffe back for her new foyer as she requested from you is the least you could do for her."

"Well, what is it? You promote me to the world as some champion for all animals, yet behind the scenes you ask me to kill them."

"Relax, D.D., I'll take one down myself," Terrence said, before facing his rifle toward the giraffes and peering through the gun's scope.

"No, YOU relax, Terry. Pull that trigger and I'll expose the entire organization, and its multiple scams, to the entire planet. I'm sick and tired of being a puppet to line your greedy little pockets with money."

"Think about what you are saying, D.D., because if you-"

"If I what, Terry? No. You and Maura have no control over me anymore. Mr. Desta, I would like to buy your business and land. From this point forward, all of my music profits will go directly toward the preservation of this land and the animals that live upon it." D.D. took out a small pad from his safari vest and wrote a number on it. "Will this many dollars be acceptable to you, Desta?"

"Wow! More than acceptable, my friend."

"Put the gun down, Terrence. The hunt is over."

"The dream is over, Mr. Dyson. You've made an excellent choice, which will have a positive effect on animals for generations to come. The D.D. Divine Animal Preservation will be a model by which a thousand more preservations will follow. You truly had a positive impact on the world, Mr. Dyson. Nice job."

"Thank you, Mother Madre."

"You may roll up your mat. Please do me a favor and ask Mr. Connor to come in. After that, I'd like for you to take a seat behind the piano in the corner for a special song during his dream."

Mr. Connor walked into the Hall of Truths and placed his mat on the floor. Mother Madre put a special tie around his neck and instructed him to lift his head while she sprayed him with his favorite cologne.

"I agree that promises are meant to be kept, Mr. Connor. Enjoy the very special and tender moment that you are about to experience."

Mr. Connor reclined on top of the mat.

"Oh, I almost forgot. Let me give this teddy bear to you before you close your eyes," insisted Mother Madre.

Taking the teddy bear from her, Mr. Connor smiled when he noticed that the face on it looked a lot like his, and that there was a set of angel wings sewn onto the back of it. He tucked it under his arms, put his head back down, and closed his eyes.

Connor Dander made his way up the stairs that led to his son's bedroom. He looked at the walls and remembered painting the murals of animals that still adorned each one of them. The sound of his son making "brrrrr" sounds with his mouth and lips while he pushed his toy motorcycles from one end of the room to the other rushed back into his ears. He gazed over to the corner where his bed was located, and saw his son tucked-in under his covers, sleeping. Connor walked over to a small bookshelf along the wall where he had painted a jungle scene with a banana tree and monkeys. Skimming over the selection of books there, he couldn't find the one that his son always asked him to read before bedtime. Sitting on the edge of his bed, Connor noticed a photo of himself and his son, framed, with a funeral prayer card tucked into the corner of it. Even though he had an idea of his own passing, it really sunk in at that moment. He leaned over to kiss his son and felt a book under the covers. It was the book that he was looking for on the bookshelf.

"Hmm?" a sleepy voice came from the boy as he rolled over and opened his eyes. "DADDY!"

Connor's son hugged him harder than he ever felt hugged before, by anyone. "I love my man so-so-so-so-so-so much!" he said to his son. "Do you want me to read your favorite book to you?"

"Yes, please, Daddy!"

"Once upon a time…"

For the next several moments, Connor read the book to his son, while they laughed together and pointed out various pictures that were illustrated on the pages.

"This is the best dream ever, Daddy," the boy said, just before falling back to sleep while his father read the last page.

Connor read, "The End," and placed the book near the framed photo on his son's nightstand. He leaned over and whispered into his ear "But my love for you will never end." He kissed his son's cheek before tucking the teddy bear under one of his son's arms.

As he entered his daughter's room, he could smell the perfume that she wore to the last Father/Daughter dance that they had attended. Her dried-out bouquet of flowers hung just above the princess castle painted on her pink wall. Connor remembered that he planned on painting more, like a horse-drawn carriage and an elegant ballroom, but unexpectedly moved on from the world before he had the chance. The photo that they took together at the dance hung on the wall in a frame above her bed. The tie that Mother Madre had placed around his neck was the same as the one that he was wearing in the picture. He remembered how ill she felt that night, as he leaned over and kissed her forehead.

"Daddy?" she said, while rubbing her eyes.

"Hi, Honey-Bunch," Connor said, while holding her hands to help her sit up in bed.

"I missed you, Daddy."

"I know, because I missed you, too. You look so pretty. The nightgown that you are wearing looks just like a wedding dress."

The piano melody that had been echoing over and over in Connor's head began playing.

"Hey, Daddy! That's our song!"

Connor took his daughter's hands again and helped her get out of bed. "May I have this dance?" he asked.

"Yes, Daddy! Two times, remember?"

"Of course I do, Honey-Bunch."

He led her to the center of the room and elegantly swayed back and forth while her feet tried to mirror his footsteps.

"You're such a great dancer, honey!"

"Thank you, Daddy."

Eventually, the piano notes faded.

It was evident that Connor's daughter was getting tired. "Would you like me to hold you for the second dance?"

"Yes, please, Daddy."

As the piano notes began again, Connor inhaled the scent of his daughter's long hair while gliding her gently around the room in her arms.

"When I grow up, I'm gonna marry somebody just like you, Daddy."

"I love my girl SO much," he whispered into her ear, just before her head rested on his shoulder and she fell back to sleep. He wanted the music to go on forever, but knew that he had to place her back into her bed once the song ended. He kissed her forehead one more time, and then removed his tie and draped it over the framed photo above her.

Mother Madre was holding a tissue just above Mr. Connor's forehead as he woke up. He accepted it from her and wiped his eyes.

Mr. Dyson walked around from behind the piano and placed his arm around Mr. Connor as they walked out of the room together.

Next to enter the Hall of Truths was Miss Addison. She walked quickly, unrolled her mat, and immediately rested upon it.

"You appear to be on a mission, Miss Addison."

"I believe that I am, Mother Madre."

"Then, don't let me delay you. You may close your eyes."

Addison Ambry looked around her cottage. She couldn't believe how cluttered it felt to her. A painting of a man with a gun sat on her kitchen table. The paint was still wet. With a jogged memory, she went into another room and began clearing out boxes, carrying them one by one and stacking them just outside the tiny house until she reached her trove of paintings in the room. She flipped through them, one at a time, remembering moments of her life as she went along. When she got to the painting of the convenient store robbery-murder that she witnessed, she turned it over and began writing as many details as she could remember about it onto the back, and then placed it aside before sifting through more paintings.

Eventually, she dug deep enough to extract a painting of a police officer with his uniform pants around his ankles, standing behind a naked woman inside Smitty's bathroom. The officer's face in the painting was amazingly detailed. Addison walked into what was once her bedroom and pulled a plastic container from under her bed. Inside was a pair of panties with an obvious stain on it. She placed the panties into a plastic bag and secured it to the back of the drawing after she wrote a very detailed account of what happened during the double-rape. She placed that painting aside, too, and added details to a few other paintings, including several that she painted of her student, Angela, with bruises while wearing torn clothing.

When she had finished going through the several paintings, she took out a pair of scissors and began to cut the painting of the man pointing a gun at her. It was still drying on top of her table, but she cut it into tiny pieces and threw them all into the trash. She felt that there was something inaccurate about that particular painting. After doing so, she picked up the phone and called the local antiques dealer. She knew that they would drive through the town of Hope once every week on garbage day, searching for treasures that someone may have thrown out that they could sell. She explained to them that there would be several pieces of original artwork at the end of her driveway, and that they should arrive right away before someone else snags them from the side of the road. Addison did mention that they should read the details pertaining to each piece on the back, and that some would be of interest to the police.

Gazing around the tiny cottage one last time before picking up the artwork that she had detailed, Addison placed them into the back of her Jeep and drove to the end of her long dirt driveway, picking up a muddy shoe along the way. Once the paintings were carefully displayed against her mailbox, she felt a separation from her body as her Jeep headed toward the police station, with the ripped door and muddy shoe.

Instantly, Addison found herself back at her mother's grave. She kneeled down and said a prayer, asking for the opportunity to see her mother in Heaven, even if only for a moment. When she finished, she looked to the side and noticed that there was a fresh grave right next to her mother's that didn't have a headstone mounted yet. She looked back down and prayed again, for her own soul. A four-leaf clover caught her eye, just as she heard the roar of an engine starting up. A backhoe began digging near the minister's wife's grave. Addison plucked the four-leaf clover from the ground and headed over to speak with the backhoe operator.

"EXCUSE ME PLEASE!   EXCUSE ME PLEASE!"

The worker spotted Addison and turned off the machine's engine. "May I help you, ma'am?"

"I'm sorry to bother you, sir, but does this grave have anything to do with Minister Tricket?"

The man jumped down from the backhoe, and said, "Sadly, yes it does, ma'am."

"Yes, it is sad for the people left behind, but he's in a better place now," Addison responded.

"Well, not quite yet. The cemetery is proactively preparing. Minister Tricket is in hospice care at the church rectory. Unfortunately, he isn't expected to make the day."

"Thank you, sir."

Suddenly, Addison found herself at Minister Tricket's bedside. He was struggling to breath. The air inside the dark room was stagnant and stifling, so Addison walked over to the window, opened the blinds, and lifted the pane. Rays of light streamed into the room, along with the scent of lilacs. Minister Tricket took in a deep breath, held it in, and eventually exhaled.

"Minister Tricket, it's me, Addison Ambry. I just want to let you know that Mrs. Tricket *is* in a better place. You can be there soon, too, if you're ready, and I am here with you so you won't need to die alone."

Addison placed the four-leaf clover in one of his hands, and then held his other hand.

"Here, I found a four-leaf clover in the cemetery. Today, I think it stands for The Father, The Son, The Holy Spirit, and you, Minister Tricket."

The minister turned his head toward Addison, smiled, and then looked back up toward the ceiling. "It's so beautiful here," he said, feebly, and exhaled his last breath.

"Letting go can be like a breath of fresh air, isn't that right, Miss Addison?" Mother Madre asked, while helping her up from the mat.

"It sure does seem like that, Mother Madre. I feel so much lighter now."

"Ah, and exactly as you should feel. Angels always fly better when they aren't weighed down."

"I sure hope that getting rid of my paintings will made a positive difference."

"We shall soon see, Miss Addison. Please send Mr. Karcin in," Mother Madre said while looking at her screen. "Oh, and by the way, Minister Tricket and his wife are doing well. Your time with him during his last worldly moment was beautiful, just like your soul."

"Mother Madre, would it be ok if I brought some materials into my dream with me?" Mr. Karcin asked.

"You will find all of the materials that you need just inside the shed near the river."

"Thank you, Mother Madre."

"Don't thank me yet, Mr. Karcin. Your particular dream may prove to be a difficult one to experience. You will be witness to some very disturbing things."

Bane Karcin took one last lap around the Hope Metal Badge & Button Company on his motorcycle. The factory's first shift of employees hadn't arrived at work yet, so he revved the engine loudly so that he could feel the motor's final vibration underneath him before lowering the kickstand and turning the bike off. He walked into the boiler room and opened the top draw of the desk. His friend's obituary was no longer there. The dirty magazines that he kept in a different drawer were still there, and Bane wasted no time in cleaning them out and throwing them into a trash bag. He opened the phone book on his desk that the telephone sat on top of and looked up the number for the local drug rehab facility. He copied the name and phone number onto a large piece of cardboard and taped it to the outside door. There was more that he wanted to take care of inside the boiler room, but figured he should get the outside work done first before the factory workers arrived.

Inside the shed near the river, he found several blank metal signs, some paint, posts to mount the signs to, and a sledgehammer to drive the posts into the ground. Placing the signs on top of the shed's workbench, Bane began to paint words onto them – *No Dumping…* *Poison Water - No Fishing… Call Environmental Police…* He couldn't believe how badly the river smelled to him as he pounded the posts of each sign into the ground along the Black Bank River. As soon as the sledgehammer came down upon the last post, Bane Karcin heard 'BANG'! He turned around and saw his friend, Willy Brock, lying dead of a self-inflicted gunshot wound to the chest.

"Oh my! Willy! What have you done? WHY?"

Bane ran into the boiler room and called the Hope Police Department to anonymously report the incident. His hands were shaking and his soul was in shock and disbelief that his friend would have taken his own God-given life. Not knowing if he should be standing over his friend's body when the workers and cops would arrive, he decided to continue to clean up after his old self in the boiler room. He went through every nook and cranny of the factory's oldest space and began dumping his stashed drugs into the toilet. Eventually, he made his way into the shed, looked back out at his friend's bloody body lying on the ground through the shed's small window, in disbelief, and just waited.

Soon, he heard the voices of Hope's chief of police and the town's forensic detective.

"This is perfect," Chief Parker said to the detective, "and will define our narrative to the press."

"How so, Chief?" the detective asked.

"We can make it look like Willy was working closely with Smitty. Take notes, Detective," Chief ordered, while handing him a hundred dollar bill and waiting for the easily influenced detective to take out a small notebook from his pocket. "Okay, so even though the hit on Smitty's daughter's teacher was a called-in favor from a mafia friend of mine, because she knew too much, we will say that Willy shot the teacher at close range right inside her classroom, then drove himself here to take his own life."

"What about Smitty? How will he be protected from being prosecuted?"

"There will be no more protection for Smitty. He will most likely be locked-up for the rest of his life, and I will take over Smitty's Bar as of today. We signed final papers and put the deed in my name late last night. It's a done deal. The spoiled jerk has been protected for too long. It's bad enough that he got away with the murder of his wife. The show is over for him."

"The show is over for you, too, Chief!"

Chief Parker turned around and saw the State Police Commissioner pointing his pistol at him.

"What are you talking about, Commissioner?"

"Once you and your corrupt detective raced over here so you could spin the truth in attempt to pin the murder of school teacher Addison Ambry onto one of your own men that took his own life, an antiques dealer came into the station with some fresh evidence of past crimes," the Commissioner revealed.

"What evidence? What crimes?"

"Let's see. In addition to the unsolved convenient store robbery-murder, of which the perpetrator has already been identified, located, and taken into custody this morning, the previously unreported rape of the same Addison Ambry that you ordered today's murder of. We were handed full details of the rape, along with DNA evidence that matches your DNA, Parker." The commissioner took out two sets of handcuffs and began walking toward Chief and his detective. "You are both under arrest. You have the right to remain-"

BANG!

Chief Parker fell to the ground, dead. His eyes remained open as blood pooled onto the ground from the back of his head. The forensics detective voluntarily fell to the ground, face down, and placed his hands over his head to be cuffed.

The commissioner turned around to see an extremely intoxicated man drop a gun to the ground and light a cigar.

"So, you thought you'd get away with stealing my family's business, didn't ya, Chief?" Marshall Smith said in a loud slurred voice. "Well, not today, Chief. NOT TODAY!"

The commissioner focused his eyes back and forth between the detective on the ground and the drunken man that had just killed Chief. He quickly understood who the drunkard was and monitored his movement as the man drew on his cigar to get it well lit.

Inside the shed, Bane Karcin couldn't believe what he was seeing from the tiny shed window. Hope's Chief of Police was lying dead on the edge of the Black Bank River while his blood flowed like a trickling stream toward the detective who was face down, awaiting arrest for helping his boss. Drunk Smitty started to stagger toward the shed while blowing cigar smoke from his mouth.

"What is he doing?" Bane thought to himself. "Why would he walk to the shed?"

Bane Karcin ducked down below the window as Smitty seemingly walked right up to it from the outside murder scene. All at once, he could smell gasoline and hear gurgling sounds before hearing the empty gasoline can hit the pavement. He looked back out through the small window and saw that Smitty was drenched in gasoline.

"I'll see you in Hell, Chief!" Smitty yelled before placing the lit cigar against his leg. The drunk bar owner instantly became fully engulfed in flames. He didn't eventually run to jump into the river, nor did he fall to the ground and roll around to extinguish the flames. Smitty just stood there in one place as long as he could, as if he was used to that sort of heat, before falling to the ground, where the State Police Commissioner allowed him to burn fully.

"I'm glad he did that," the commissioner said, while handcuffing the forensics detective. "I didn't really want to deal with all of the paperwork and formalities that would have resulted from me blowing the head off a child-killer."

"I'm sure that wasn't the most pleasant dream that you've experienced, Mr. Karcin," Mother Madre said, just as he was waking up.

"Wow. I can't believe it. I just can't believe it," Mr. Karcin said, while shaking his head as he rolled up his mat.

"Please do me a favor and bring this paperwork to my office, and then ask the school nurse to come see me here. You may find her hanging around Dr. Nihil's science room. Then, take a seat back outside the Hall of Truths, Mr. Karcin."

Mother Madre then went out into the hallway, herself, and asked Officer Williams to follow her into the Hall of Truths. Once he set his mat on the ground like the others had done before him, Mother Madre asked him to first sit at the table with her.

"Officer Williams, you did a very brave and noble thing here at St. Perpetua Academy in rescuing Sim."

"Thank you, Mother Madre. I was just doing my job."

Mother Madre looked down at her screen, paused for a moment, and then continued, "Officer Williams, life is a God-given gift. I do need to mention that extinguishing one's own life is very much frowned upon in this realm. Do you understand that?"

"Yes, Mother Madre, I imagine that it is."

"Officer Williams. I can offer you one chance to fix that if you are willing to go through with it."

"Yes, Mother Madre, I would like a chance to change the bad decisions that I have made, which have resulted in me being here at St. Perpetua Academy."

"You must understand that it will not change you being here at St. Perpetua, but rather the means by which you got here. Are you still willing to go through with the dream, Officer Williams?"

"Yes. I must."

"Go ahead and lay down on your mat."

Officer Williams remained in his seat. His face showed deep concern.

"Take all the time you need, Officer Williams."

"I must admit that I am very nervous."

"Do you have faith, Officer Williams?"

"Of course, Mother Madre."

"But?"

"But, what if there is no 'ever-after' this time?"

"Let me ask again, Officer Williams, do you have faith?"

"I do believe, Mother Madre. Yes. Yes, I do."

"Very good. If you don't mind, I will have the school nurse nearby during your dream."

"Wait. School nurse? Should I *not* have faith, Mother Madre?"

"You absolutely *should* have faith, Officer Williams. I am inviting the nurse in so *she* may learn about faith, and witness a soul returning after what will happen in your dream."

Officer Williams walked over to his mat, brushed some dust off from his uniform with his fingers, and then put his head down.

Willy Brock brushed some powdered sugar off from his uniform and picked up the fried dough from the ground, and then turned to see where it might have come from.

"He made me do it, Mister," a young girl shouted, just before she ran away from him and blended into the crowd of carnival-goers that were gathering in front of a troupe of juggling clowns.

Willy threw the fried dough into one of the mesh metal trashcans that dotted the temporary fairground. As it hit the side of the can, an apparent weightlifter swung a wooden sledgehammer onto a ring-the-bell high-striker game – 'DING!'

"Interesting," he thought to himself, as he slowly continued along.

"COME ON... COME ON!" some kids were cheering from Willy's left side, as several metal water guns were spraying steady streams of water into the open clown mouths that were mounted inside of a carnival trailer, while balloons were being inflated above each clown's head. 'BOOM!' One of the balloons burst, some children cheered, and Willy jumped back. Someone looking on made a comment about the scaredy-cat cop.

Willy could see the House of Horrors up ahead. He decided to stop and have his caricature drawn. A woman sat down under the next canopy where folks were getting their hair braided.

"Might as well have my hair braided while my daughter is missing," the woman said. "Hey, shouldn't you be out there acting like a cop instead of having your face drawn?"

Wondering if the woman was speaking to him, Willy turned his head to look at the lady. She was.

"Seriously, the town pays you to be here and this is what you're doing?" she continued.

"Actually, ma'am, the carnival pays for the police detail, not the town."

"I should have known that. I work for the carnival. Now I *really* feel like we aren't getting the protection that *we* are paying for."

"I'm on my break right now, lady."

"Um-Hmmm," she responded, clearly not believing him.

"Did you say that your child is missing? Yet, you decided to get your hair braided instead of letting anyone know, or looking for her yourself?" Willy jabbed, just before getting up and handing some money to the artist. "No need to finish it," he said, and then glanced back at the drawing that was almost done. He gulped when he saw it, as it jolted a memory. At that point, he knew what needed to happen.

Passing the Ferris wheel, he looked up as riders scraped the sky and headed back toward the ground, if only for a quick moment before launching back up again. Willy thought about the irony of it as he entered the food-truck area just ahead of the House of Horrors. Inhaling deeply seemed to feed him while he slowly passed each one, even though he felt completely devoid of any appetite. He thought about how scents could trigger memories, and he wanted to give himself all of the chances that he could of remembering the world. His break was almost over and he wished he had enough time to ride the Ferris wheel himself, just once, to get an aerial view of Hope before he left. Instead, the woman with the new braided hair walked by him, holding the hand of the young girl that had taunted Willy with the fried dough. His heart began to beat louder while he waited for the pair to get several steps ahead of him.

Just as he expected, the woman headed toward the House of Horrors. While she began arguing with the carnival worker there, Willy ducked into one of the porta-potties. He emptied all but one of the bullets from his gun into the toilet, and waited.

BANG!

The carnival worker shot a gun into the air as he took possession of the woman's daughter. Willy took a deep breath and opened the door of the portable toilet. Relieved to see that most of the carnival goers had scattered in fear, Willy quickly tiptoed behind the House of Mirrors, entering it through the attraction's back door. He instructed the few kids that were in there to exit through the door that he had come through before making his way to the front of the maze of mirrors. From his vantage point, he could see the girl trying to wiggle out of her captor's arm in front of the House of Horrors, while her mother kept screaming to let her go. Willy positioned himself within the mirrors so that there were six images of him that would be visible from the kidnapper, and he pointed his gun toward the sky and pulled the trigger – BANG!

The startled man inadvertently let go of the girl's arm while turning to see where the shot came from. As the girl and her mother ran away from the scene, the armed carnival worker took a shot at Willy – BANG! A large mirror shattered to the ground. BANG! – BANG! - - BANG! Three more mirrors were blasted to pieces.

Two images of Willy were left standing at the House of Mirrors. Willy said a quick prayer and BANG! The mirror next to him exploded. Knowing that the gunman most likely had only one bullet left, Willy walked out from the House of Mirrors, got seven steps toward the House of Horrors, and BANG!

"Welcome back, Officer Williams. Very well done," Mother Madre said.

"That was pretty intense, Mother Madre. Thank you for allowing me to make things right."

"Oh, you sure did. As a matter of fact, the Hope Police Academy just changed its name to The William Brock Police Academy. It sure appears that you left a reputation as a great role model. There are more future police officers enrolling in the school than ever before, and the new Smitty's Family Tavern sponsors the annual Willy Brock Memorial Softball Tournament, which raises funds for the youth of Hope through anti-bullying initiatives, and the new Youth Cadet program."

"That's amazing."

"Not as amazing as what awaits you and your peers, Officer Williams. You may invite everyone back into the Halls of Truth while

I walk the school nurse back to her office," she said, before pausing to study something on her screen with concern. "I may be a little while, so consider it social time until I return."

The school nurse was speechless as Mother Madre walked her back to her office. "Take all the time you need, and then consider spreading the good news to Dr. Nihil," Mother Madre suggested, before closing her door and heading toward the boiler room to check on Sim.

"What are you working on?" Mother Madre asked, as she ducked under a beam at the bottom of the stairs.

Sim jumped up and hid something behind his back.

"I don't want to disturb your work, Sim, but I think that there is someone that you might want to visit in a dream soon. Go ahead and find a spot to hide what you have while I set up a mat for you to rest on."

Sim did as Mother Madre said, then took his place upon the mat, and closed his eyes.

"He hasn't opened his eyes in three days, and it's been even longer since he's eaten anything," the doctor explained to Sim's grandmother, while his grandfather lay still on top of a hospital bed that was setup in his living room. "I'm afraid that he only has a day or two, three at the most."

Sim watched from a loveseat in the corner of the room. He could tell that his grandmother was unaware of his presence as she spoke to the doctor while holding her husband's hand. Eventually, she got up to make some tea and Sim walked over to the dying man.

"Grandpa, it's me, Sim," the boy said, as a tear fell while he surveyed his sheet-covered body in front of him. Holding his hand and getting close to his ear, Sim whispered, "I need you to have just a little more patience and live a few more days, okay Grandpa?"

Sim felt his grandfather squeeze his hand.

Mother Madre was holding Sim's hand when he woke up. "I was holding your hand because you were crying. Is your dream over already, Sim?"

"No, Mother Madre, but I need to ask for some extra time there, if I could."

"Yes, Sim. Take your time."

"Thank you," the boy responded. "Oh, and Mother Madre, if it's ok, even if I start to cry, I will need to use both my hands, so-"

"I'll make sure that I refrain from holding your hand, Sim," Mother Madre said, with a loving smile on her face.

The boy closed his eyes again.

The scent of his grandfather's woodshop in the basement was Sim's favorite of all smells, and he took a deep breath while he looked around at all of the tools before heading toward his Grandpa's pile of wood. For some reason, he knew that he'd find some long enough planks of burled maple and cedar, his grandfather's favorite wood species, to complete his most important project yet.

Over the equivalent of two and a half days on earth, Sim measured, cut, nailed, glued, planed, sanded, and varnished, the most beautiful casket for his grandfather to be buried in. The cedar-lined elegant box was to house the body of one of the most important men that ever lived, at least to Sim, and because Jesus Christ was the other most important man in his life, he knew that his Grandpa's soul would continue on elsewhere. Once he returned the chisel and hammer to their place on the wall, Sim purposely knocked over a large jar of metal washers, which created a loud crashing sound.

His grandmother and the doctor rushed down the stairs, and Sim climbed up the stairs to be near his grandfather's side for one last time on earth. As he stood by his body, he said, "Grandpa, it took a little while but I made something for you. I just want you to know that God is real, grandma loves you very much, and you were my best friend on earth." Taking both of his grandfather's hands in his, Sim continued, "You have done so many amazing things with these hands on earth, Grandpa, and now you get to use them in Heaven."

His grandfather regained consciousness for a brief moment and whispered, "You did an amazing job. It is beautiful, Sim," and then breathed his last breath.

In the basement workshop, Sim's grandmother and the doctor marveled at the beautiful coffin that somehow appeared there. His grandmother rubbed her frail fingers over the carved letters that she discovered on its lid, 'I love you, Grandpa. More than you will ever know, and forever.'

Mother Madre gave Sim a hug as he woke up. "You have a beautiful soul, and your handiwork is amazing, young man," she said.

"Thank you," Sim said, wiping his eyes one last time.

"Sim, I'd like for you to join us in the Hall of Truths."

"Is it okay if I finish what I was working on first?"

Mother Madre briskly rubbed the boy's hair. "Absolutely, but come on up right afterward, Sim."

"I will, Mother Madre. Thank you."

Smiling at the young boy, Mother Madre grabbed her satchel and left the boiler room.

CHAPTER 16

The staff was hugging, talking, and laughing, when Mother Madre arrived back at the Hall of Truths. She paused just inside the doorway to take in the moment. She was pleased with the impact that St. Perpetua Academy had on each of the special souls in the room.

"Okay, everyone. Please take a seat," Mother Madre asked.

Conversations wrapped up, and soon all members of the staff were seated at the long table, facing Mother Madre, who sat at the end of the table, opposite the stage.

"Before I continue, I'd just like to announce that there are some open classes if anyone wants to make some extra money by teaching them."

Everyone looked around at each other strangely. Finally, Mr. Connor said, "I'm sorry, Mother Madre, but I'm not sure what the word 'money' means."

Mother Madre placed her elbows on top of the table, folded her hands, rested her chin on them, and said, "Thank you, Mr. Connor."

"Excuse me, Mother Madre, but I don't quite understand the word, either," Mr. Karcin admitted.

"Thank you, Mr. Karcin," she replied with a smile.

"Nor do I, I'm afraid," Miss Addison added.

Mother Madre nodded and smiled, then whispered "Thank You," and continued to nod her head in approval as Officer Williams and Mr. Dyson showed signs of confusion over the word. She mouthed the words 'thank you' one more time, as she took a silent moment to obviously reflect, while looking at the faces, one by one, of those seated around her.

"I couldn't have asked for a better selection of students."

"You mean teachers, Mother Madre?" Mr. Connor attempted to correct.

"No. I mean students. We all are."

"Meaning, like, we are learning all the time, right?" Mr. Karcin asked.

"Of course, Mr. Karcin, we learn, perpetually. Truly, though, we were taught through the children at St. Perpetua, along with the many lessons that we reviewed together during our time here."

"Are we being transferred, or something?" Officer Williams asked.

"Yes, or something," Mother Madre answered, adding, "All that are in this room will be moving on, except for me."

"Because you are the principal here, I imagine that you must stay?" Miss Addison inquired.

"I was the principal at St. Perpetua for your 'class', if you will, but will be moving up once you graduate."

"Into a superintendent role?" Mr. Connor asked.

"No, Mr. Connor, moving up at St. Perpetua is actually moving down."

"I'm confused," Mr. Connor said.

"The more humble a person, the better, especially where you are all going. During worldly life, everyone looks up to the person that sits on the highest seat, when in fact they should be giving credit to the lowly that make it possible for there to even be a seat. Who would you contact when the heat goes out, or a burst pipe causes a flood? My goal is to eventually be assigned to the boiler room where Mr. Karcin did a superb job. I have a lot of work to do on myself before I choose to move on."

"You can *choose* to move on?" Mr. Dyson asked.

"Each of you could have moved directly past the program here at St. Perpetua, but somewhere along the path of your existence, each of you made a choice to go through a soul-enhancement program before continuing on to eternity. You've all professed Jesus Christ as your Lord and Savior, which gave you entrance into God's Kingdom. Nothing that you worked on here added to your chances of eternal life. There isn't a single soul that has lived without sin, so any acts that you could have performed would have still left you short, so nobody should ever boast about their works. We are all here because of God's grace."

"Mother Madre, please excuse me for saying so, but you aren't stuttering anymore."

"In life, I sat on a high seat, and would often stutter whenever I said something that wasn't the truth, or could hurt another. Part of my personal soul-enhancement curriculum included conscientiously stuttering whenever I was speaking an important truth, with hopes that you would lean into those words a bit more. Once your wings were formed during our Jigsaw Afternoon together, the stuttering stopped. By the way, some of the brightest people I've ever known and admire stutter. I found them to be wise because of the way they carefully chose their words."

"If you aren't going to be the principal after we leave, who will be taking on your role?"

"Oh, he should arrive here any moment," Mother Madre answered.

From down the hall came shouts of exaltation. "I DID IT! I DID IT! WOO-HOO! Well, THE LORD DID IT!"

Mother Madre stood up to see what was going on in the hallway, but hadn't even taken a step in that direction before Dr. Nihil came springing into the Hall of Truths, professing his faith in The Lord.

"Dr. Nihil is going to be the new principal?" someone asked.

"No," Mother Madre said, while trying to quickly figure out where Dr. Nihil's invigorated spirit was coming from.

"I finally did it! Seventy-Seven sticks perfectly distanced from each other, after I asked God to help me! I believe! I BELIEVE! What an amazing feeling!" Dr. Nihil exclaimed, as he leaped around the Hall of Truths.

"Excellent, Dr. Nihil. Please take a seat," Mother Madre said, before continuing on. "Before I say goodbye to all of you, I'd like to commend each and every one of you for being willing to take an honest look at yourself. It is upon truth that anything lasting is built. Anything erected on top of deceit will eventually come crashing down, and I do mean anything and everything. I hope that while you were reflecting on yourselves, you each saw the beauty inside of you, and in each other."

At that moment, everyone around the table looked at each other with a genuinely caring and loving look.

"I honestly can't tell you what awaits you once you leave St. Perpetua, but from what I have been told, you will be entering into an eternal paradise. There is no promise that you will recognize each other once the transition happens, so feel free to give one last hug to your fellow St. Perpetua Academy graduates."

"What about young Sim, Mother Madre?" Mr. Karcin asked.

"Sim is just finishing up a personal project that he was working on, but he'll be joining us very soon."

While everyone was engaged with each other for a few final moments, a man walked into the Hall of Truths wearing a Chief of Police uniform. Mother Madre remained seated and said, "Welcome to St. Perpetua, Padre Parker. Please wait for me in the Principal's Office." As the new principal began to exit the Hall of Truths, Mother Madre added, "Oh, Padre Parker, please hand your badge to Officer Williams."

Eventually, everyone settled back into their seats. There was a knock at the majestic Hall of Truths door, and upon Mother Madre's welcome, young Sim entered the room. He walked over to Mr. Karcin and handed him a perfectly carved and impeccably sanded heart made of wood. Carved into it were the words, 'Thanks for being my best friend at school. Love, Sim.' Mr. Karcin gave the boy a hug, and explained how he was his best friend, too, and that he learned so much as a result of their friendship. Sim then walked to the head of the table and handed Mother Madre a beautiful hand-carved wooden cross that hung from a string weaved of jute fibers. Mother Madre hung it around her neck and the entire wall behind her transformed into a beautiful large gate with inviting beams of light radiating from it. Everyone at the table gasped in awe.

Mr. Karcin's trumpet students walked into the Hall of Truths, dressed in glowing white gowns, and stood on each side of the gate.

Mother Madre gazed down at her screen, and then back up at the faces of those around the grand table.

"Dr. Nihil, please rise," Mother Madre instructed. "I'm glad that you finally came around. Enjoy your eternal reward," she said, while signaling him to pass through the gate.

The trumpets sounded and he skipped and jumped in excitement as he passed through the gate and disappeared.

"Mr. Connor, please rise. Thank you for your work here at St. Perpetua Academy. I think we've all learned everything there is to know about S.W.O.T. analysis and business management, and I believe that you may have learned a lot about fairness and patience."

"I sure have, Mother Madre. Thank you."

The trumpets sounded and Connor Dander disappeared beyond the gate.

"Mr. Karcin, please rise. Thank you for keeping St. Perpetua's building running smooth and clean. You have certainly cleaned up nicely, yourself. And as for your work with Sim, you have had an impact that will last beyond this realm. Enjoy your Heavenly reward."

"Thank you, Mother Madre," he responded, and then told Sim that he loved him. The trumpets sounded and Karcin Bane disappeared beyond the gate.

"Mr. Dyson, please rise. Your music filled St. Perpetua and our ears with a musical beauty that will live on at the academy for generations of souls to come. Several of your musical compositions have been added to the eternal hymnal here, and your personal song, Mr. Dyson, will play on forever. Enjoy an eternity filled with the sweetest of melodies."

"Thank you Mother Madre," Dyson Devlifar said before nodding to the trumpeters, who sounded their instruments as he passed through the gate and disappeared.

"Simeon, would you come here, please?" Mother Madre requested.

The boy stood up, and wrestled the heavy chair to push it in before leaving his place at the table. When he stood in front of Mother Madre, she held both of his hands.

"May I call you Sim?"

"Yes. You're my friend, Mother Madre."

"And you are mine, Sim, as well as an amazing soul who will do remarkable things in Heaven. Now, there is another very special soul just on the other side of that gate. Listen carefully."

At that moment, Sim heard his grandfather's voice calling him.

"GRANDPA!" Sim shouted.

Mother Madre let go of the boy's hands, the trumpets sounded, and the boy ran through the gate.

"Officer Williams, please rise. From what I understand, there has never been a soul at St. Perpetua that has reached the level of bravery that you have achieved here. Thank you for your service here at the academy. I'm sure the assignment that God has planned for you will be more rewarding than anything you could ever imagination."

Willy Brock walked over to Mother Madre, shook her hand, thanked her, and then handed the police badge to her that he had been given. Mother Madre smiled, nodded approvingly, and watched Willy pass through the gate and disappear as the trumpets sounded.

Turning back around slowly to face the table, Mother Madre kept her head down while she began to fold her screen back up. She seemed to be taking her time with the process while Miss Addison sat silently, wondering if maybe it wasn't yet her time to pass on. A teardrop fell onto the table in front of Mother Madre, and then another one, and another one, reminding Miss Addison of falling rain. She walked over and took the seat next to Mother Madre, rubbing her arm while the principal searched for a wad of napkins that were tucked way down inside her satchel.

"Miss Addison, I just want to tell you that of all the souls that I have ever met, whether on this side, or on the world side, you are the purest of them all. There is much about myself that I must work on here at the academy, and you have set the standard for which I will strive, along with that of The Lord's, of course."

"Thank you, Mother Madre."

There was a long silence while Mother Madre finished folding her screen before placing it back inside the satchel one last time. She looked nervous and scared.

"Mother Madre?"

Miss Addison and Mother Madre turned around and saw a young girl emerge from the light beyond the gate. Together, they said "Angela" at the same time.

"This is for you," the young angel said as she handed Mother Madre the most beautiful flower that she ever saw. "It's a forgiveness flower from my mother and me."

Mother Madre accepted the flower with a smile, and then watered it with a tear of joy.

Angela took Addison Ambry's hand and they walked through the gate as the trumpets sounded.

They all lived happily after, forever.

No End

Amen

For God so loved the world that he gave his one and only Son, that whoever believes in him shall not perish but have eternal life.

John 3:16

Please read THE BIBLE next.

Made in the USA
Middletown, DE
24 July 2018